"All right," he said, "let's hear you play."

She started "Lover Man," laying down the intro-duction until she rolled up to the opening eight, letting the first words slide out.

The sound of her own voice coming from the speakers thrilled her. It was as if her most private, secret thoughts were being magnified into a public statement. And she was awed, listening to the low dreaminess of herself spreading out like open fingers. Hands of sound—she made them—wrapping themselves around the heads of those listening like the touch of a comforting mother, bringing her sweet babies safely close to the nourishment and sustenance of her ample self, holding them with tenderness as they took strength from her . . .

"Sixteen years old," Nick said. "Perfect pitch. True as pure gold. D'you **believe** that left hand?" Nick knew, hearing her sing, that Lisa Hamilton was a natural. With problems. Listening to her, captivated by the husky, intimate yearning of her voice and the wild urgency of the chords and changes she played, he had an intimation of the interior, hunched-up, private person behind the sounds. A living instru-ment. But hung-up.

"You call me," he told her, "when you're inter-ested in some part-time bread maybe for openers, like weekends, give me a call. I'll take care of you."

And Lisa would call him soon—when the longing and the loneliness got to be too much, and music was the only answer.

*Further Titles by Charlotte Vale Allen
from Severn House*

CHASING RAINBOWS
DREAMING IN COLOUR
INTIMATE FRIENDS
LEFTOVER DREAMS
MEET ME IN TIME
MIXED EMOTIONS
MOMENTS OF MEANING
NIGHT MAGIC
TIMES OF TRIUMPH

Non-fiction

DADDY'S GIRL

SWEETER MUSIC

Charlotte Vale Allen

This title first published in Great Britain 1994 by
SEVERN HOUSE PUBLISHERS LTD of
9–15 High Street, Sutton, Surrey SM1 1DF.
First published in hardcover format in the USA 1994 by
SEVERN HOUSE PUBLISHERS INC., of
425 Park Avenue, New York, NY 10022.

British Library Cataloguing in Publication Data
Allen, Charlotte Vale
  Sweeter Music. – New ed
  I. Title
  813.54 [F]

  ISBN 0-7278-4595-0

Typeset by Hewer Text Composition Services, Edinburgh.
Printed and bound in Great Britain by
Redwood Books Trowbridge, Wiltshire.

God respects me
When I work,
But he loves
Me
When I
Sing.

Tagore

PART ONE

Chapter 1

Instead of going straight home, as she usually did after classes, she began walking, heading downtown. She walked along River Street toward the city center, crossing to the far side of Old Street, heading north. As she was passing the old Colony Club she stopped, hearing a music unlike anything she'd heard before. Sounds that roared against each other, subsided briefly, then flared again; tauntingly, daringly meeting.

As she drew toward the doors to look in the windows, the tendrils of music wrapped themselves around her, holding her attention. It was dark inside and she couldn't see. She pushed open the door and stood, hypnotized by the circle of red light centered on the elevated bandstand. In the circle three black men were playing with flying fingers, their foreheads creased and damp with sweat as they smiled, making little approving grunts to each other.

"Hey! We're closed!" a thin blond man called to her from behind the bar.

She stood unhearing, lost in the music.

"Hey, kid!" he said again. "Split! We're not open!"

She moved several steps, needing to be closer to the music, not noticing the figure that stepped out of the shadows beside her.

"Go polish some glasses, Harry," he said, sounding confident. Harry wouldn't argue, as he took Lisa's arm under the elbow. "You like the sound?" he asked, and watched her nod. "Come on. We'll sit down over here."

He led her to table in front of the stand, propelling her gently into a chair.

"How old are you?" he asked, examining her face.

"Sixteen," she lied, not looking at him. "How old are you?"

He laughed. "Too old to answer that." He tilted back in his chair. "What's your name, dear?"

"Lisa," she replied, unable to break away from the sounds. "Lisa Hamilton. What's yours?" She turned to look at him for the first time.

"Nick Montefiore." He held out his hand to her, palm upward.

She laid her hand across his. "Why did you make him let me stay?" she asked, already turning back to the music.

"I like the way you listen," he said, knowing she'd stopped hearing him.

When the trio closed the final eight, Lisa let out her breath and swivelled round to look at Nick.

"I feel that way," she said.

"You feel that way. You play?"

"I can."

"You want to play now?"

"All right." She looked up at the piano.

"Come on then," he said. "I'll get you set up."

He switched on the mike, turned the spot back on, then returned to the table, curious to see what she'd do. The boys in the trio were standing at the bar drinking brews, making signals at Nick with uplifted shoulders, asking what the hell he was doing. Nick held up his hand. "Wait!" he said, smiling.

She started "Lover Man," laying down the introduction in a nice, easy four-four, letting her left hand pump a steady, insistent bass. She rolled up to the opening eight, letting the first words slide out.

The sound of her own voice coming from the speakers thrilled her. It was as if her most private, secret thoughts were being magnified into a public statement. And she was awed, listening to the low dreaminess of herself spreading out like open fingers, touching at the vacant chairs and tables, moving up and out, down to the bar. Hands of sound—she made them— wrapping themselves around the heads of those listening like the touch of a comforting

12

mother, bringing her sweet babies safely close to the nourishment and sustenance of her ample self, holding them with tenderness as they took strength from her.

Everyone fell silent as Lisa sang, even Harry the barman, looking at one another almost sheepishly, grinning. Nick listened, not so much surprised as satisfied with his instinctive judgment. Lou came over and slid into the vacant seat, setting his beer down on the table.

"What you got there, Nick?" he asked, his drummer's fingers beating out Lisa's tempo on the tabletop.

"Sixteen years old," Nick said. "Perfect pitch. True as pure gold. D'you *believe* that left hand?"

"She's got great time," Lou said. "Shit, man! Gotta go play with the girl."

Lisa approached the chorus, laying down harder with her left hand, heightening the tempo, letting her right hand plow into the changes, building. She felt reckless, totally freed from herself. The brushes came at her like insinuating little thrusts, adding punctuation to all she had to say.

Daniel set his glass down on the bar, climbed over the rail and picked up the bass, coming in on the second bar of the last eight before the repeat.

They went back to the top, playing eights with Lisa doing the first chorus, then hanging out while Daniel filled eight bars full of his message; telling her he knew about all of it, thrumming and stroking the bass as if it was his lovely, brown lover; all the way down to the last note where Lisa picked up to sing the bridge. With her back cushioned by the wall of Lou's brushing and Daniel's deep, plucking probes, she restated the dream coming down, easing off, sliding in to the final eight. Her fingertips rested on the frontpiece; she half-closed her eyes as Lou picked up the sticks to thrash through eight bars. She took a deep breath as they played out together. Silence.

"Do another," Daniel said, leaning toward her, his voice very close to her ear. "Go on, sweetheart. It's *fine!*"

Fine was sweet and round. Fine was beautiful and had no need of words.

"Yes, okay," she said. "We'll do 'By Myself,' in the original key."

Nick knew, hearing her sing, that Lisa Hamilton was a natural. With problems. Listening to her, captivated by the husky, intimate yearning of her voice and the wild urgency of the chords and changes she played, he had an intimation of the interior, hunched-up, private person behind the sounds. A living instrument. But hung-up.

At the end of the second number Daniel set down his bass with extravagant caution, then kissed Lisa's cheek, letting his hand fall lightly on her shoulder.

"You're beautiful, child," he said. "You make me dream." He walked off the stand, pausing at Nick's table to say, "I think I just had a vision. It was rare!"

Lisa came back to the table and sat down.

"Where are you going with that music?" Nick asked.

"I'm studying at the conservatory. What do you do?"

"I'm an agent."

"You get jobs for people?"

"I do. You want me to be your agent?"

"What would I have to do?"

"Play and sing. Like you just did. How much material do you have?"

"Songs?"

"That's right."

"A lot," she said thoughtfully. "Dozens."

"You'd have to join the union."

"I see."

"I can't think of anybody who sings the way you do," he said. "Of course, now that I know about your background, the changes you play make sense to me. That took a little figuring."

"Oh?" He'd instantly captured her attention.

"They're not typical, your changes. Very innovative, with the classical trim. You play very . . . neatly. None of those sloppy arpeggios amateurs think are jazzy." He questioned her eyes. "Ever performed publicly?"

"No."

"Pretty girl," he said offhandedly. "Taking voice?"

"No."

"How'd you pick up the bel canto?"

It was her turn to question his face. He knew the words, the right things to say.

14

"From my mother's old records, I suppose. That's where I get almost all my material. I liked the way Jo Stafford sustained her breathing. Sinatra does the same thing. I'd listen, waiting to hear them breathe. But if you hear the records, you notice right away they don't breathe in the natural breaks. They hold and carry through."

"Any brothers or sisters?" he asked.

"An older brother, Jimmy."

"Jimmy. What does he do?"

"He goes to university."

"Do I make you nervous? You seem kind of uptight."

"No, I'm fine."

"Okay. So, listen! What're you going to do with it?"

"Oh, I don't know. I'm tired of school. If I thought I could, I'd probably quit and . . . do something. I don't know."

"That turned you on, eh?"

"I liked it," she admitted, glancing up at the darkened stand.

"Yeah," he laughed softly. "It shows. You look good singing. Another maverick."

"What?"

"It's what somebody called me once. A maverick. One of the ones who run around outside the herd. Not intentionally. But like being permanently out of stride. You know?"

"I think so."

"What do you think about?" he asked.

"Music. I hear my own voice singing inside my head. It's always music. And songs I hear that make me stop, make me listen. Sometimes I catch the first four bars of something I've never heard before and I have to stop what I'm doing and just listen."

"For example?"

"Lots of them. Lots of the Beatles' songs. 'Yesterday,' and 'In My Life.' Do you know that one? It's very beautiful. I take the songs and put them inside my head and I can hear my voice way off, up there somewhere floating, singing the words, over and over, all the time."

"And that makes you happy," he asked incisively.

"Some. What d'you do when you're not an agent?"

"I used to try composing. But I couldn't go anywhere with it. I'm not innovative, like you for example. I couldn't seem to get past all the other music I'd ever heard."

"I don't understand," she said. No one had ever talked music with her before. It was as though she had suddenly discovered she could speak in another, very familiar, language.

"It's pretty simple. Like wanting to be a writer, say, but having read so many books that influenced you, they've managed to interfere with your own style—whatever it is. You're so hooked on remembering this and that about other people's books you can't seem to cut through their stuff to get down to your own. Like the stuff I wrote. A bit of Tchaikovsky, a bit of Rochmaninoff, a bit of Mahler, a bit of Vivaldi, a bit of Dvorak, a bit of this, a bit of that. But no little bits of Nick Montefiore. I couldn't work through the bits to find my own style. So I cooled it and started with something I do well."

"I see," she said, looking as if she did.

"Tell me about your family. What does your father do? What's your mom like?"

"My father's semi-retired. He's chairman of the board of Hamilton's. You know, the store downtown."

"Right," he said, thinking *Je-sus Christ!* "Old, young, what type?"

"Forty-five. Good-looking. Athletic. He swims twice a week at his club. He just . . ."

He waited for more, sensing something.

"My mother . . . See, I'm adopted. So, she wasn't my real mother. Anyway, she died a few years ago. And now I think he's going to get married to Jeanette. She's the one who's always taken care of my brother and me." She stopped, unsure of where to go with it.

"You like her?"

"She's . . . I like her. A lot."

"Well good!" he said, wondering about it. "Here's my card. Telephone me if you decide you'd like to work."

"Listen to me, Lisa," he put his hand over hers. "One thing for sure, you've got nothing to worry about. No one's going to come on to you. That's what I'm around for. So,

16

if you decide you're interested in some part-time bread maybe for openers, like weekends, give me a call. I'll take care of you."

"I liked it," she said, smiling. "I might do it. What do you mean 'come on to me?'"

He grinned and shook his head. "I won't let anyone make any advances. Okay?"

"I see."

"You call me," he said.

She sat for a moment longer, liking the look of his face; liking the fact that he looked scrubbed-clean and young, with eyes that didn't shift around at all but looked straight at her; liking the fact that he didn't mind explaining things she didn't understand; liking his ability to talk a music language. Then she got up, said good-bye, and went home.

She wasn't altogether sure what had happened. She thought about the sensations she'd experienced hearing her own voice amplified for the first time; about the odd privacy established by being in the center of a circle of bright light that seemed to illuminate herself to no one but herself. It had been twenty minutes of extraordinary revelation. Seeing herself, hearing herself, feeling out new, unthought-of boundaries for herself. She wanted to go back and do it all again. But with more people, an audience; people to see and hear. But only see and hear, not touch or explain or try to convince. They'd have to accept what she was willing to give. And she didn't know yet what or how much she was actually willing to give, but she wanted to think about it.

Each morning, music case in hand, she set out for the conservatory. She spent the day going from one class to another, scarcely aware of the goings-on around her; automatically performing; automatically absorbing information; occasionally coming alert when something interested her. But once the classes ended, there was nothing she wanted to do. She began staying after-hours to play and sing in one of the practice rooms. She felt inhibited about experimenting with her songs at home. So she spent an hour or two in a drafty practice room in the after-class silence of the building and sang, remembering how she'd sounded that afternoon in the old Colony Club. She played and sang and got through each day and finally the school year ended.

And her routine all at once gone, an itchiness inched its way through her brain until she took to sitting in the park afternoons, idly considering her home and the people inside it.

They'd never been where they were needed, she thought. Nobody was ever there. Except Jeanette. And sometimes Jimmy. But as a small child, those times when she said to herself, "Now they'll see and be sorry," as she brought a scraped knee or bruised elbow—gingerly, like rare gifts—home to be repaired, it was always Jeanette who shook her head sympathetically and went for the iodine and bandage. Not Letty or her father. They didn't know, weren't ever there to see and be sorry.

She remembered family friends contriving to say how much she looked like Letty. She used to try to see what they meant by that since there seemed to be whole worlds of difference between the woman upstairs and the child downstairs with Jeanette.

Their hair was a similar color. Her mother's hair, Lisa thought, looked like sunlight breaking through the study windows on a cloudy day. Her own hair was always long. It was trussed into painful pigtails Jeanette laced up every morning. Neatly, with ribbons. And at midday when she came home, the ribbons were trailing or lost. Her mother's hair was hidden behind her head, between the back of her neck and the pillow and Lisa couldn't ever imagine how it would look all spread out, loose around Letty's face.

Those same people too often said Letty had been, "so beautiful." And the way they said it, quietly, reverently, with sober-looking faces gave Lisa an uncomfortable, tight-stomach sensation. It was as if what they were really saying was, "She was a beauty. Too bad she . . ." She couldn't ever finish the statements in her mind because the word "dead" or "died" inevitably figured in and she didn't want to think about that or believe it could happen. She had never, she realized, wanted to believe that.

Though her mother and father rarely appeared where

or when they were needed, Lisa never came through the door without hoping—it was a perennial surprise party in her brain—that her mother would be there, smiling at her, saying, "Well, it's about time you got here." And her face would be soft and rounded and secretly amused and Lisa would know her mother was happy to have her home, finally.

Papa was semi-retired, he said, but he went every day to his office. In a pin-stripe suit and camel-hair overcoat, with a hat and a black umbrella, he went out. And when he returned, after shedding the coat, hat and umbrella, he went straight upstairs. Lisa would listen, hearing the particular way his feet sounded on the stairs, then the half-dozen steps down the hall followed by the opening of the door, an exchange of words, then the careful closing of the door. She wondered what it was they said to each other day after day, for so many years.

She held whispered, imaginary conversations with herself, pretending they said this and this, or that and so. But the words rang hollowly and she knew that whatever they did say, it had nothing to do with the weather and how things went today at the office. She knew that what they talked about had to do with the reasons why Letty no longer left her room or her bed.

She and Jimmy were adopted. And that was why, she decided at age six or seven, the two of *them* had so little to do with her and Jimmy. Jimmy had come from somebody else too, wasn't her real brother. He'd been four years old and she'd been six weeks when they'd been brought to the house in the park. And she wondered endlessly why *they* had brought her and Jimmy to live there in the house if all *they* had ever wanted was to be upstairs together in that room.

They said they loved her. Every night before bed, she went down the hallway to say goodnight. She'd sit on the side of the bed while Letty asked about all the things Lisa had done during the day, and Hugh stood, arms folded over his chest in an attitude of listening as Lisa responded. Lisa looked into the faces that smiled at her, her mother's especially. Letty's eyes sometimes seemed not to see. Her mouth gave Lisa quick, dry kisses. And she'd get the strangest feeling, sitting there making up stories for these two people, her mother and father, as if, if she could only say the right combination of words, think the proper pattern of thoughts, Letty would get up out of bed, brush her hair and dress herself and, at last and forever, be downstairs waiting when Lisa came home from school or play. But she could never think of the right words, although she knew they were all up there, hidden away inside her head, and all she had to do was pry them loose and set them out in the air to be heard, to work their miracle. It never happened.

So, at the end of her spiderweb of fabricated schoolday adventures she'd stop, gazing into the sometimes green, sometimes gray-blue of Letty's deep-set eyes, waiting. And Letty—who had invariably been studying Hugh during Lisa's entire recital—would touch Lisa's face with her cool hands and say, "I love you. Kiss me goodnight, now." And Lisa would. And Hugh, too. And go to bed. They said they loved her.

They gave her a piano when she told Jeanette she'd like to have one. It was there on a Thursday when she came home from the park. She hung the park key on its hook beside the back door, noticing that Jeanette had an unusual look about her, a flush of color and a hot look in her dark eyes. She could read Jeanette, understand the meanings of her gestures and inflections, because Jeanette had always been with her, as far back as her memory could go.

"Someone put a surprise for you in the study," Jeanette said that day. "Viens, chérie!"

Jeanette's hand, too, was hot as it closed over hers, leading Lisa through the dining room to the front of the house and into the study. When Lisa pushed open the door and saw it, the breath leaked out of her lungs like air out of gashed bicycle tires.

"Mine?" she asked, feeling Jeanette's hand tight around hers.

She'd been unable to take her eyes from the polished gleam of the upright Baldwin, the inviting expanse of perfect black and white—like a photograph. She wriggled her hand free to move several steps closer, forgetting to breathe, lost in astonishment.

"I can have lessons?" she asked, whirling to look at Jeanette who was leaning against the doorframe, smiling.

"But of course!" she said. "Mais certainement!"

"How did they know?" Lisa asked unnecessarily. For Jeanette was the bearer of all messages and the guardian of all secrets and injuries.

Lisa stared at her piano, feeling air returning to her lungs in big, painful pushes that made her throat hurt and her eyes sting so that she ran to hide her face against Jeanette's breasts and cry.

Jeanette stroked Lisa's head, making small sounds at the back of her throat, murmuring, "Such a strange little girl, Lisa. You are pleased, chérie?"

She wanted to ask all the "why's" again: Why didn't they come down to surprise me? Why isn't Letty here to say this is mine, for me? Why? Why? Instead, she nodded her head into the comforting abundance of Jeanette's breasts, clinging.

"Alors!" Jeanette eased her away, reaching into her pocket for a tissue. "Blow! Then upstairs to thank mama and papa, hnnh?"

At that time, when she was eight, Lisa had been convinced Jeanette was her real mother and had somehow contrived to lend her to Letty. She couldn't supply any logical reasons behind this munificent gesture of Jeanette's, but she was quite certain that this was the case. Jeanette, for one thing, seemed so much younger than the woman upstairs, more likely to have an eight-year-old daughter. And she did all the things mothers were known to do: the running of the house, making up menus for the cook, ordering the wines and groceries, buying clothes for the children, telling the cleaning lady what needed doing. Everything. Lessons in French until she and Jimmy could converse without groping for appropriate words or tenses. It was Jeanette who, often and spontaneously, went for her sweater or coat, then took down the park key and, her hand enclosing Lisa's, led her to the park for fresh air and an appreciative tour of the flowerbeds. It was she who took Lisa to see *Fantasia* and each newly arrived

Disney film. Jeanette took her to museums, to art galleries, to afternoon concerts, to the fair every September. And when they went on these outings people assumed Jeanette was Lisa's mother. After all, she dressed very well, not like a servant or an employee of the household; she was very pretty and young and good to be with. So people assumed Jeanette was the mother. Lisa did too. Except that she wasn't. Jeanette told her so. Regularly.

"Go thank mama!" Jeanette told her.

She blew into the tissue, mopped her eyes, took another incredulous look at her piano and went slowly upstairs to express her gratitude to Letty.

Letty said, "Your color is very high, Lisa. Are you happy?"

Lisa nodded, her eyes fixed on Letty's long, graceful neck.

"You say so little," Letty said softly, cupping Lisa's chin to raise her head. "What are you thinking?"

"I don't know. Just things."

"Your father and I want you to be happy, you know, Lisa."

"I know that," Lisa said quietly.

"I hope so. Could I have a kiss?" Letty held out her arms and Lisa leaned into them, pressing her lips against the cool smoothness of Letty's cheek. She longed to remain there, gently held, breathing in the scent of Letty's cologne, her hair softly stroked by the long, always-cool hand. But Letty said, "I should be resting now. It was just that I wanted to see you. Jeanette has cake for you. I will see you later, to say goodnight."

Jimmy came home and admired the piano, standing pounding his fist into the palm of his catcher's mitt, saying, "Gee, Lee! You're going to have to practice all the time. Maybe you shouldn't have said you wanted it."

"I *do* want it. I'm going to have lessons."

"Well, that's great." He pulled her pigtails. "I'll come hear when you can play something."

It was a landmark time. Hugh changed his pattern. Instead of proceeding directly upstairs upon arrival home, he stopped first at the study door to watch and listen to Lisa practicing. No words were exchanged. He'd stand for perhaps two or three minutes, then turn away and continue on upstairs. And, even while her fingers moved on the keyboard, Lisa listened for the sound of those six steps down the hallway, the door opening, the lift of voices, the closing of the door. And then she returned to her music.

It was always "her" music. She thought of the scales, the Hannon exercises, the short pieces in the first books as hers, no one else's. She went through them, one after another, eating up the music with avid eyes and fingers, treasuring every newly learned chord and interval until little else seemed to matter but her music and the increasing access to it within her ability. Miss Comstock, her teacher, was cautious but consistent in her praise, privately confiding to Jeanette that she'd never before had a student of Lisa's caliber and talent. Jeanette beamed with pride.

Upstairs the door to the master suite now stood open between four and seven, during Lisa's practice hours. Letty lay with her eyes focused on the ceiling, letting the vibrations from below penetrate her, entirely open to the sounds.

"She has talent," Jeanette said, bringing up the afternoon tea. "She will perhaps do well with this."

"Perhaps," Letty said. "Perhaps."

Letty closed her eyes and listened to the quiet clinking and liquid melody of tea being poured, everything falling within the bubble of music that enclosed the house.

"Does she talk to you, Jeanette?" she asked from behind her closed eyes.

"Un peu," Jeanette admitted. "She is a silent child. It is not her way to talk."

"Do you think she understands?" Letty opened her eyes. "Do you think so?"

"No," Jeanette said truthfully. "I do not think that she does. But in time. In time."

Letty's hand rose. Jeanette held it.

"You do so much for all of us," Letty said. "Where do you find it? Is it from your religion?"

"No longer," Jeanette said obliquely, concealing the full truth. "Some, perhaps."

23

"I fear for both of them, Jeanette. I think, sometimes, we've done the wrong things. I get so confused. If I could believe the way you do . . ."

"It is not everything," Jeanette said.

"Jeanette," Letty cried out, tears pushing from her eyes, "I get so frightened sometimes, about so many things. I hate to think of Lisa being . . . harmed . . . by all of this. How can she be expected to understand?"

Jeanette held her, calming her.

"She will be fine. She is a good child, très ombrageuse. Understanding will come to her. You should not make yourself to feel so very unhappy. All things will come, in time."

She talked on, cradling the younger woman in her arms as she prayed silently Letty would go. In her sleep. Peacefully. Soon.

Jimmy was four years older, red-cheeked and black-eyed with lustrous blue-black hair. "An Irish buccaneer," he once called himself fancifully, fielding imagined line-drives with his mitt. He was bright, openly uncomplicated and immensely popular. He had many friends. They populated the basement game room and, upon occasion, were requested to lower their voices or refrain from telephoning after nine o'clock. It was Jimmy who, through a sense of filial obligation he felt but couldn't comprehend, ushered Lisa into her kindergarten class on her first day of school. It was he who explained, "He thinks private schools'll wreck us, so we have to mingle with the regular kids. Whatever that means." Hugh's reasoning made little sense to them. Neither of them wanted to go to the private schools that had been a topic of discussion upstairs and down for many months before the matter was settled.

Midmornings and midafternoons, during recess, Lisa stood in the schoolyard waiting out the half-hours. With time, her thoughts turned to her music and she stood alone, her head filled with sound, her mind emptied of everything but the melodies she played to accompany the overhead flight of a bird or the wind whipping the leaves on the trees. The music gave her a certain positive insulation, relieving her of the need for anyone or anything else. School was never anything more than waiting time, time to get through until she could go to her lesson and then home to practice.

The summer Lisa was twelve she spent most of her afternoons—when not practicing—alone in the park, reading or listening to the sounds inside her head, wondering about the combinations of this note and that, making that sound. It was a preoccupying mental exercise she enjoyed enormously.

The last Friday in July she was sitting in the park, smiling to herself as she ran up little melodies in her mind, when slowly her attention shifted directions. She thought she must have sat on a wet bench without noticing. She stood up and looked down at it. Nothing. No wet slats. Nothing but cracking layers of paint, well dried by the sun. She peered over her shoulder at the back of her dress, twisting around, catching sight of a blur of red. Her breath caught in her throat. Glancing around to confirm she was alone, she lifted her dress to see that her underpants were wet with blood.

She dropped her dress and stood staring sightlessly in panic, low whimpering sounds coming from her mouth. Something terrible was going to happen to her—was already happening. Her lips quivered and her eyes flooded with tears. In terror, consumed by thoughts of her imminent death, she ran home to hide in the downstairs closet.

Jimmy, arriving home about twenty minutes later, opened the closet to find her huddled under the coats, wracked by convulsive sobs.

"What's wrong, Lee?" He dropped down on his knees. "What're you doing in here?"

"I'm dying," she sobbed, her face chalky.

"You're *what*?"

"I'm bleeding to death. I know I'll die."

He stared at her for several seconds, then reached to cup his hand over the back of her head.

"You're not dying, Lee," he said softly. "Hasn't anybody talked to you?"

25

"What about?" She stared back at him with enormous, fearful eyes.

"Wipe your face." He gave her his handkerchief. "We'll go upstairs."

She got up and came out, feeling miserable and uncomfortable, letting Jimmy take her hand and lead her upstairs. He didn't knock at the bedroom door the way they were supposed to but just opened it and took Lisa inside. Letty looked at the two of them, letting the book she'd been reading drop onto the blanket, prepared to smile. The smile got lost as she took in the look on Jimmy's face and the red-eyed misery on Lisa's.

"It's time for you to have a little talk with Lisa," he said meaningfully.

Letty looked confused. Lisa looked down at the dusty tips of her shoes.

"*You* know," Jimmy said, his hand in the middle of Lisa's back, gently urging her to move toward Letty.

Letty didn't know what he was talking about. She looked at him and then at Lisa and then back to Jimmy, who inclined his head to one side, trying to visually transmit his message. Lisa heard the front door open and Hugh's footsteps on the stairs and felt her stomach muscles clenching up like a fist. She wanted to go to her own room. She didn't want to stay there.

"What've we got here?" Hugh asked, coming around behind the two of them to stand beside Letty at the bed.

"You . . . She has to talk to Lisa," Jimmy said, feeling anger slowly building inside. Why the hell were they being so thick?

"Oh!" Letty said suddenly, a faint wash of color painting her cheeks. "Oh, I *see!*" she said, holding her hand out. "Come here, Lisa," she said.

Jimmy turned to go, then looked back at the door, noticing the back of Lisa's dress for the first time.

"Oh, holy hell!" he whispered to himself, running downstairs to get Jeanette.

Lisa stood staring at Letty's hands which were fastened whitely to the flowered border of the blanket. Hugh couldn't make sense of what was happening. The silence in the room was fraught with unstated opening sentences

26

and Lisa was about to start crying again. Then she heard Jeanette's footsteps on the stairs and held her breath and her tears.

Jeanette appeared in the doorway and Letty looked at her hopefully. Jeanette understood at once and said, "Lisa, Viens, chérie. You will talk to mama in a few minutes."

Gratefully, Lisa hurried across the room.

Hugh caught sight of the back of Lisa's dress and felt faintly nauseated as he sank down into the chair beside the bed, slowly letting out his pent-up breath.

"You will have a bath, chérie," Jeanette said. "Then your mama wishes to speak with you."

Lisa took her bath, all the while listening to Jeanette who stood in the doorway staring at the far wall, explaining.

"I had thought mama had already spoken of this to you," she said, sounding a little angry. "Or long ago, I would have made certain you knew what it is to be a woman." She bent to pick up Lisa's dress and stood for several moments examining it. "This is ruined," she said, at last. "It is too bad."

"Why don't they love me?" Lisa asked, her voice sounding very small in the big bathroom.

"Ah, they love you. You must comprehend, chérie. Illness turns the eyes inward. Your mama is good, very gentle. She would hurt no one, not ever. But she has great fear and it fills up the mind. Understand this, chérie, and be forgiving of her. Someday, a time will come when you will wish you could fly backward to make changes."

"You all treat her as though she's the child in the house and not me."

"Don't be jealous, Lisa!" Jeanette said sharply, folding the dress into a small parcel. "To be jealous of a sick woman is to be a foolish, foolish child."

"I'm not jealous," Lisa lied.

Jeanette said nothing.

"Is she going to die?" Lisa asked.

Jeanette's eyes grew very dark, her mouth tightening.

"What is it you ask?" she said in a voice that held all kinds of danger signals.

"Is she?"

"Not yet," Jeanette said slowly. "But do not ever think death will bring attention to you, Lisa! You must love her without thought of the things she does not do for you. Think of all that she does do. Remember what I tell you, because a time will come. I promise you. It will come. And then you will wish you had never thought the things that you do."

"I don't want her to die. I never said I did. I want her to get up and do things."

"I think," Jeanette said, holding out a towel, "no one would wish this more than your mama. Now hurry. She waits to talk with you."

"Is she very old, Jeanette?"

"Old?" Jeanette folded her into the thick towel and turned her so they were facing, "Old, chérie? You think she is old?"

"I don't know. Is she?"

"Come," Jeanette said, going into the bedroom.

Lisa followed, watching as Jeanette selected underwear from Lisa's bureau. "Put these on," Jeanette said, moving to the closet to select a dress. "I am older than your mama," she said. "She is thirty-four. It seems very old to you, chérie?"

"No, but . . ."

"Thirty-four is *young*, chérie, understand? It is very young to be always in bed, already for four years. Think of it! Do you know she cannot stand without someone to help her? And the medicine. Pain." She shook her head. "Do not have jealousy of your mama, Lisa. She is not this way because it is her wish, I promise you. Put this on. But you have something more in your mind? True?" She sat down on the bed. "Dis-moi, chérie. Qu'est-ce que tu as?"

"I want to go to the conservatory," she said at last, studying Jeanette's face. She enjoyed looking at Jeanette, enjoyed speculating on the reasons why she seemed so content to shape her life around the Hamilton family.

"I see," Jeanette said at length. "You wish me to speak of this to mama and papa."

"Please?"

"I will find a time," she said, "We shall see."

"Jeanette?"

"Yes?"

"Why didn't you ever get married?"

Her eyes opened wide and she smiled.

"I have never wished to be married," she said.

"But wouldn't you like to have your own house and children?"

"I have enough," she said, "I am not unhappy with my life."

"What did you do before you came to live with us?"

"I worked in the store, with your papa."

"You did?"

"I was his assistant. When you children came here, he invited me to work in the home. It was a satisfactory arrangement. I enjoy doing for your family many things I would not enjoy to do for myself," she laughed softly.

"I don't understand."

"To be paid for certain duties makes them pleasurable in many ways. And I have much freedom and privacy. This is very good."

"But . . ." Lisa stopped, unable to find words to fit to the question.

"I have no need for more," Jeanette said, straightening Lisa's pigtails. "We each have need of different things, chérie. Mine are fulfilled here. I work and I am able to sleep each night. Now, no more of this. I will speak to them about the conservatory. One thing more."

"What?" Lisa stopped in the doorway.

"I have six years more than your mama, chérie. I am forty."

Lisa stared at her, then turned and went down the hall to Letty.

Lisa did not question Jeanette's ability to make whispered wishes come true. Perhaps it was because neither she nor Jimmy had too many requests to make. So, when a few weeks later, Hugh sent for her, Lisa went to him, knowing it had to do with the music school.

"It is my understanding," he said, "that you no longer wish to attend the public school."

"No, papa."

29

"You wish to attend the conservatory?"

"Yes, papa."

"Why?"

For some reason, she hadn't been prepared for that question. It stopped her cold. She sat gazing at him with a feeling similar to the one she'd had when summoned to the school principal's office at the start of grade five. It had been, she later learned, a purely routine visit. But at the time she'd been filled with doubts, trying to imagine what she could have done wrong to warrant the summons. For the better part of fifteen minutes she'd sat opposite the man, her head bent, replying to his questions in monosyllabic undertones until, finally, he'd said, "Do I frighten you, Miss Hamilton?" And, looking up, she'd seen that he was a smiling, sympathetic man who couldn't ever frighten anyone. "No, sir," she'd answered, wondering what she had been frightened of if it hadn't been him.

Looking at her father, noticing the clean side parting of his blond hair and the faint gloss of his manicured fingernails, she wondered now why she was so tongue-tied and heart-thumpingly scared. All kinds of words knocked against each other inside her head, like the kids at school all hurrying to get through the doors at recess.

"It would make me happy," she said uncertainly, studying his gold tie bar and cufflinks, the brilliant sharp-looking whiteness of his shirtfront and cuffs. She could smell his Lilac Végétal. She knew the scent so well. Once, she'd gone into her parents' bathroom and stood for a long time holding his bottle of Pinaud's Lilac Végétal, the top in one hand, the bottle in the other, eyes closed, breathing in the crisp, satisfying fragrance.

"Certainly your mother and I wish you to be happy," he said, steepling his fingertips precisely, tip to tip to tip all in a row. "But 'happiness' is hardly sufficient reason to enroll you in such an intensive course of musical studies. I've been in touch with the registrar and investigated the requirements and curriculum. Both are stringent. And while I have no doubt whatsoever that you're sufficiently gifted to meet the entrance requirements, I do wonder about your intentions, Lisa." He let the steeple collapse and his hands folded one over the other. "What will you do—if you manage it—after you complete the eight years?"

"I don't know. Play the piano. Something."

"That's not good enough." His voice was patient, indulgent. "There has to be something more substantial."

"Can't I decide later what I'll do when I finish, papa?"

"Please understand me." His voice softened, his eyes looked darker green, warmer. "I wouldn't interfere with your progress, Lisa, if I could see a productive end in view. But you can't simply leap headlong into eight years of training and study on feeling alone. How would you feel if I said you'd have to continue on at your present school?"

"Oh, *please*!" she begged. "Please don't make me go back! I can't talk to anyone there. I don't understand arithmetic or why I have to study history and geography. Why do I have to study those things if I don't understand them? I understand my music. I . . . I love it. I feel . . . right . . . when I play. *Please*, papa!"

His eyes directed themselves to the window, then turned back

"It's a fine day. Would you care to go for a ride? We'll talk more. You look pale. It might do you good."

"I'd like to."

"Good."

She sat beside her father as he steered the car effortlessly, his eyes moving this way and that, attempting to anticipate the unanticipated from other drivers on the road.

"I don't understand your craving for music," he said after a while. "I can see you have talent. There's no question of that." He glanced over at her. "But eight years seems an awfully long time to spend strictly on music, with some sort of musical career in view and an indefinite one at that. What makes you so positive this will satisfy you, Lisa?"

She watched his mouth moving and his hands on the wheel, thinking, *He talks to me as if I'm old, grown-up.* It made her head ache slightly, trying to match, within her own thoughts, the tenor of his words.

"It's how I feel." She was close to tears, hating having

31

to try to explain to him things she couldn't explain to herself. "It's what I know I want to do."

"Is it so awfully difficult to talk to me?" he asked, looking over again. "Is it?"

She couldn't answer.

"I see," he said. Stopped for a light, he extracted a cigarette from his monogrammed case, lit it and returned the case to his pocket, exhaling an aromatic stream of smoke.

She hadn't been keeping track of where they were going and looked around in surprise when he pulled into the public parking lot at Indian Hill Park.

"I think it's mild enough for a stroll through the zoo," he said. "Do you like the zoo?"

She didn't. She didn't like the smells or the sounds of the animals but said, "Yes, papa," and got out of the car, nervously smoothing down the flaps of her coat pockets.

She walked along beside him, glancing sidelong at him every few steps, thinking he looked and smelled so good.

"You're twelve years old," he said, staring into an enclosure containing a dirty white polar bear. "You'll be twenty if and when you graduate from the conservatory. My primary concern is that you don't misdirect your talent and energies to find, after eight years, you've done something you'd have been wiser not to. Why do you look at me that way?"

"What way?" she said guiltily.

"Suspiciously," he said softly, tossing his cigarette away, his eyes searching hers.

"I . . . I'm not . . ."

He put his hand on her shoulder and she felt emotions lumping up in her throat, making her blink several times.

"We do care about you, you know." He smiled a gentle, encouraging smile. "Things would be very different if your mother weren't ill. You have to understand, Lisa. None of this is what we had in mind when you and Jimmy came to us. I know we leave much too much to Jeanette. But without her, we simply couldn't manage, none of us. It's important to me, very important, that you have what makes you happy. I know you have certain . . . needs that aren't being fully met. I know that. And it worries me. I'm guilty of not spending nearly enough time with you children. But there are other things . . . priorities. It's difficult to explain."

"Mother?"

"That's right." He brightened, pleased by what he believed was her intuitive understanding. She was tall for her age but she seemed very, very young—somehow unformed—to him. He wished, for a moment, he could put his arms around her and hold her. But the expression on her face, the mix there of confusion and suspicion, acted as a barrier between them. "It all has to seem very bewildering to you now," he said. "I suppose we expect a great deal—too much, probably—from you and Jimmy in terms of understanding. I can't honestly say I understand all of it myself. But we are here if you need us and you shouldn't be afraid of approaching us. But you . . . never do. What is it, Lisa? You say so little, seem so hidden away behind your twelve years. Can't you talk to me?"

"I want to," she admitted, feeling the heavy weight of his hand slowly driving her down into the earth. "I don't know what you want me to say."

His hand came away from her shoulder and she breathed deeply, as if she'd been swimming underwater for a long time.

"Would you like something?" he asked, spotting a vendor across the walkway.

"No, thank you, papa."

"I think some peanuts," he smiled, taking her hand, leading her across the walk to wait while he bought a red and white striped bag of peanuts.

"You don't want any?" he asked, holding the bag out to her.

"No, thank you, papa."

They started walking again and she looked at the unopened bag in his hand, its top neatly folded over and she wanted the peanuts now, after saying she didn't.

"We've made arrangements for you to take the entrance examinations," he said, opening the bag, looking inside then closing it again. "Next month."

"Examinations? What will I have to do?"

33

"Play a selection, sight-read. All things you can do easily. Transposition, harmony, theory. Miss Comstock has more than adequately prepared you. I don't think you'll have any problem passing."

"Oh." Her mind raced through the pages of the books she'd gone through with Miss Comstock, afraid she wasn't prepared.

"We'd better start getting back," he said, sensing the outing had failed. It gave him a heavy feeling, a certain guilty sadness. "You're sure you don't want these?" He held up the bag of peanuts.

"No, papa. Thank you."

She watched him drop them in a wire trash basket, wondering why she'd said no. Now that they were gone, her mouth was wet for the taste of them.

Chapter 2

That same afternoon, Lisa sat sideways on the edge of Letty's bed, watching and listening to Letty as she fumbled for words and glanced hopefully every few moments over at Hugh for reassurance, attempting to reiterate the same things Hugh had said earlier. As she listened, Lisa suddenly began to see Letty for the first time as a person. Not just her adopted mother but a person, separate and distinct, someone she hardly knew. She saw a pallid, terribly thin, frail woman with large liquid eyes and a mouth that seemed almost to tremble when she paused between words. The bones of her shoulders jutted forward against the baby-soft wool of her crocheted bedjacket and Lisa realized she loved this person; loved recognizing that this person found it as difficult to express herself in front of Hugh as Lisa herself had. And she was quite positive,

all at once, that Letty, too, would have refused the peanuts. She didn't know why, or what it was she was really
discovering but she wanted to say, "I love you," Her
mouth moved awkwardly around the shape of the words
but they wouldn't emerge. She sat in silence until Letty
struggled to the end of what sounded like a speech she'd
prepared like homework.

"I know how you feel, really," Letty said. "It'd be
wickedly wrong of us to stand in your way. We won't, you
know."

Lisa nodded, choked by the knot of lovewords that
refused to come out of her throat.

"You make me happy," Letty went on, her hand on
Lisa's arm. "I lie up here with the door open and listen
to you play and it's like . . . a glimpse of heaven." She
stopped and looked over at Hugh. "Hugh, leave us to
talk," she said quietly. "Please."

It was something that had never happened before. Lisa
felt excited and hot, dizzy with expectation.

She watched as Hugh bent to kiss Letty's forehead,
watched the way their eyes met for a moment before he
straightened and went out. Then Letty extended her arms
and gathered Lisa close against her, her hand cool, almost
cold, on Lisa's face.

"We've forgotten so many things," Letty said, resting
her cheek against the top of Lisa's head. "Too many
things. Try not to judge us too harshly. It isn't from lack
of love for you. Not that at all. You know, I used to take
you out in your carriage and Jimmy would trot alongside
and I felt so happy, so . . . complete. People would stop and
look into the carriage and I'd stand back, accepting all the
compliments on what a lovely baby you were. feeling
so proud and happy, as if I'd made you myself. I felt I
had. You were such a good baby. Always laughing. All
you ever did was laugh and eat, then go to sleep and wake
up laughing. God! It was such fun having you. It was all
I'd ever wanted, the two of you and Hugh. And then,
suddenly, all the things I'd been warned about all my life
caught up with me and I was ill, and it seemed as if someone had decided to take all the color out of the world so
that all of it, everything, was gray and bleak and pointless.

35

Nothing existed but my fear. I was so horribly afraid. It's hard to imagine how enormous that kind of fear can be, how consuming. It wipes out everything else so that nothing exists but the fear, making more fear. I let so much time go by, lost in that. How can I tell you, Lisa?" Her hand moved on Lisa's arm, tightening. "I don't know how. There doesn't seem to be a way to tell you. The days were routine. You and Jimmy were routine. I'd see you and try to listen and say that I loved you. And that was true. But all the time I was listening, I couldn't think of anything but how afraid I was because . . . I finally could see what was happening. But then, seeing it, I didn't know how to stop it. There's no stopping any of the rest of it. Don't hate me . . . us. Please. None of it was meant to be this way." Her voice cracked and broke and Lisa felt the jerky rhythm of Letty's breathing and lifted herself away to see tears running down her face.

"Oh, don't!" Lisa whispered, shattered. "It doesn't matter. Honestly, it doesn't! Please don't cry. Please don't"

It came over her so swiftly, so totally, the room seemed to tilt as she felt love surging upward through her. "I love you," she said, secure within the circle of Letty's thin arms, her heart tumbling. "I love you. Everything will be fine."

"You're a good child," Letty said. "You've always been good."

"I love you," Lisa said again, giddy with the headiness of this new state of being, of loving. "I *love* you."

She lay quietly against Letty feeling happier than she'd ever dreamed possible, believing absolutely that loving and having at last spoken out, all things would change. They would. She was utterly convinced of it. She stared at her own hand lying curled on Letty's shoulder and dreamily relished the life beneath her fingers; the satisfying wealth of feeling protected and being so close, this close, touching this person she loved who loved her back; this person who could say the things she had.

Someone was touching her shoulder and she opened her eyes to see that the room was dark and Hugh was whispering to her to come away. She saw that Letty was asleep, her lashes lying darkly against the rise of her cheeks, her mouth slightly open. Letty slept soundlessly, her breathing almost undetectable.

"Shh," Hugh whispered, taking Lisa's hand, leading her out of the room. In the hallway he said, "It's time for dinner. Go tidy yourself up, then come down."

"Is she all right?"

"She's all right," he said gently. "Go along now."

She went toward her own room and, at the door, turned back to see him quietly easing the door closed behind him as he returned to the darkened bedroom and Letty.

In the weeks that followed, the whole world and everyone in it seemed endowed with brilliance and clarity. Lisa went about smiling, unable not to, hurrying upstairs whenever allowed to sit with her mother, holding her hand, spilling out her plans for the conservatory, her preparations for the entrance examinations, anything and everything.

Letty listened, smiling back, holding fast to Lisa's hands as her eyes seemed to drink in Lisa's words and smiles.

Sometimes, when she knew Letty would be asleep, she crept into the room to sit in the chair beside the bed to watch Letty sleep, positive she saw daily more flesh to the bones, more color to her face. It was all changing, just as she'd known it would.

She sailed through the entrance examinations, never doubting for an instant that she'd pass easily and be accepted into the school. Afterward she hurried home, intending to go straight upstairs to tell her mother and father how well she'd done. But Dr. McKenzie was in the foyer with Jeanette, and Lisa knew from their faces that she wouldn't be allowed to go up to her mother that afternoon.

While she was standing there looking at them, she heard Jimmy come in through the back of the house and felt his hand close around hers.

She construed the expressions she saw on Jeanette's face and the doctor's to mean what she wanted them to mean, telling herself they were discussing the improvements, how much better Letty was. And Jimmy's hand around hers was further confirmation of the miracle. It was, she

37

thought, his way of acknowledging his faith in the new directions their lives would take as soon as Letty was up and around again.

She'd made her declaration of love and seen it begin to work its effect on Letty. Any time now, she'd be getting out of bed afternoons to sit in the chair for a time or perhaps even take a little sun in the park. Lisa knew exactly which bench they'd sit on and what they'd talk about, how they'd both look. So Dr. MacKenzie's increasingly frequent visits, his penetrating Scottish voice speaking in the study with Hugh or out in her sitting room with Jeanette meant only more changes for the good, signified nothing else.

The acceptance letter came, and the family celebrated with wine upstairs in the master bedroom, although Letty drank nothing. And midway through the celebration drink, Lisa noticed Letty's hand inching up over the bedclothes to disappear under the left side of her bed jacket and stay there. Her eyes looked dull and distant, and Hugh cut the celebration short, telling Lisa and Jimmy that it would be continued later over dinner.

Out in the hall, after Jimmy and Jeanette had gone down the stairs, Lisa tiptoed back to stand with her ear against the door, listening. Hugh was talking in undertones and there was another sound, a rasping series of sobs that sent a chill of alarm down Lisa's spine. She flew away down the stairs and into the study where the sounds of the music she made erased what she told herself she couldn't possibly have heard.

Hugh did not come down to dinner that night and Jeanette apologized. "He will take a tray upstairs with mama," she said. "He is sorry, he asks me to tell you." Jimmy nodded gravely, staring down into his untouched dinner. And Lisa simply continued eating, refusing to take heed of the ominous clouds darkening the atmosphere of the house.

At the end of October, she was awakened in the night by heavy footsteps and Dr. MacKenzie's voice speaking quickly in response to something Hugh was saying. Then there was silence in the hallway as the bedroom door closed. Lisa sat up in the dark, instantly fully awake, straining to hear. There were distant sounds she couldn't identify and then Jeanette's footsteps running up the stairs and down the hallway, followed by the opening of the door to the master suite and its subsequent closing.

Pulling on her robe, she opened her door and stepped out. Jimmy was sitting on the top step with his head in his hands, his hair sticking up every which way. And she knew then what had happened but refused to believe what all the signs were telling her. She was about to speak to Jimmy when the bedroom door opened and Dr. Mac-Kenzie appeared, his tie askew, his jacket over his arm. And, beyond him she could see Hugh, his back to the room, at the windows; and Jeanette was standing at the foot of the bed in her blue silk dressing gown, staring straight ahead, crying.

Dr. McKenzie said something that Lisa didn't hear because she was pushing past him into the room to stop dead on the threshold, her eyes trapped by the sight of Letty's gray, lifeless face on the pillow and her upturned, loosely dangling hand.

Lisa screamed. All the faces turned slowly, white faces turning at the sounds she was making and couldn't stop making as she ran to the bed to take hold of the hand that beckoned her. She felt the warmth that was still there as she buried her face against the bony hardness of Letty's shoulder, but there was no softness left, no movement, no sound except a high-pitched wailing she heard coming from somewhere. She wondered who was making those strange noises as she fought away all the hands that touched and pulled at her, fighting them away until Hugh picked her up and the strange animal cries stopped as she stared at his wet face, hearing him saying words she didn't understand as he carried her to her own room where he held her while Dr. MacKenzie put a sharp stinger in her arm and she fell and fell and fell and kept falling until there was nothing.

The pain of loss seemed like a permanent ache in her stomach. There were things that happened afterward, but she wasn't sure if they took place inside her head or in reality. Time seemed to pass either very slowly, in agonizing inches, or very quickly, in miles, so that there were events in her memory that lasted and lasted. A funeral in bright sunshine on a very cold day, with dozens and dozens of people lining the streets outside and, later, the area around a hole in the ground. Over it all lay a blurry glaze, like the thick finish of a pottery jug, something that dulled and smoothed the edges somewhat, leaving all remembrances and feelings with a heavy, almost impenetrable aura of sadness and grief.

She returned to school numbed, only to be struck, as she walked home alone, by that never-distant pain. She sat down on a bench at a bus stop and cried for her mother. Her mother was dead, and love hadn't been able to save her. She cried, seeing cars and buses going by in a glare of moving color. I want my mother, she thought, wiping her eyes and nose on her sleeve. I want her back. But Letty was in a hole in the ground and wasn't ever coming back. Not ever. She felt emptied, deprived, bleached of all coherent thought and feeling, and dug deep into her studies at the conservatory in a state of distracted depression. No matter what anyone, everyone told her about how much better it was this way for Letty, Lisa didn't believe. Because it wasn't better for Lisa this way. And she wanted Letty back.

Hugh seemed unchanged by time or loss. Each day he left the house in one of his meticulously tailored, pin-stripe suits, camel hair overcoat and black hat. And each evening, he returned. But now instead of hurrying up the stairs and taking those six steps down the corridor, he settled himself in the living room with the evening paper.

Something else was happening too. Lisa could feel it. Between her father and Jeanette. Occasionally, she came upon them in some attitude of 'intimacy. It was never anything more significant than a near-touching of hands or a slight inward inclination of two heads close together in conversation. But it all made Lisa feel outside their lives, outside what was going on within the house.

She was spoken to. Hugh asked about her studies, if she required anything, and she responded without thought, saying she was fine, needed nothing. She was aware of something—disappointment?—on her father's face, the hope there for communication. She was aware, too, of that hope diminishing as more months passed and she found herself no longer able to discuss her thoughts and feelings, unable to do anything about the blackness she frequently experienced.

This blackness came often, settling over her like gummy tar, adhering to her mind and body with dominating insistence, leaving her, when it went, with the feeling that her eyes had shrunk, and the inside of her head turned hard and dry and dead. She went through days and weeks staring out at the world with her shrunken eyes, blinking in a vague effort to moisten them. They seemed to have become so dusty she couldn't close them.

Jeanette was always there, offering things to eat and drink, letting it be known her arms and her comfort were also available. And sometimes, watching herself from a great distance, Lisa accepted Jeanette's arms, standing within them, wondering why she no longer felt anything. Jeanette's fragrant proximity had no effect on her. Lisa couldn't talk, couldn't think and wished to do neither. She wanted only her music, wanted her head filled with nothing else. No memories, no explanations, no coaxing echoes of Jeanette's melodious voice. She played her piano, prepared her schoolwork and sat for long hours either in the park or in her room noticing, occasionally, that it was spring, or winter, that time was going away from her.

Yet after a time her mind seemed to want to work. It clicked back on against her will and she began, over and over, to examine the things she'd said and done, the feelings she'd had—how she'd believed so totally that her love would keep Letty alive. Because without Letty, there was no longer even the illusion of a mother. I am no one, she thought. Who am I? You went away without telling me. Now I have no one.

She'd been a fool to have believed such fairytales. So stupid. A baby to think the things she'd thought. I love you, so you'll live forever. Embarrassing, crazy. She felt shamed to think she'd believed that stuff.

Finally, forced to think because her brain wouldn't stop when she wanted it to, she put that crazy part of herself aside, shoving it far back in her mind to a place that

41

seemed like the darkest part of a hidden closet—a place where it was unlikely those stupid, little-girl ideas would ever be discovered to shame her again.

When she'd succeeded in accomplishing this self-hiding, she began to feel less dried-out. Her eyes seemed able to move more easily, as if they'd been oiled. And her awareness began to expand even more, taking in the reality of what was happening around her.

She studied her father and Jeanette across the width of the dining table each evening, slowly coming to realize a number of things. It seemed as if she'd never really seen Jeanette before. She was beautiful, and Lisa hadn't noticed. Her thick, black hair flowed from a high, rounded forehead. Her brown eyes were almost black with a sort of shine to them, the whites almost blue. And her skin was very white, flawless, like a child's. Her mouth was full, the upper lip deeply bowed, the corners of her mouth uptilting as if she were constantly on the verge of smiling. Lisa couldn't stop looking at her, at the length of her neck and the lifted prominence of her breasts, the slow curve of her hips, her rounded knees and narrow ankles. Lisa was astonished by Jeanette's beauty.

Looking at her father now, she could see that he, too, saw Jeanette differently. It happened so slowly—it always seemed that way to her, even later—that there wasn't any reason to be angry or to let them know that she was aware of what was taking place. She couldn't be altogether certain that *they* knew what was taking place, since they made no remarks either to her or to each other that held any clues. But Lisa's suspicions flourished, causing her to pay extraordinarily close attention to whatever was said and done within her viewing range. She'd know how she really felt about it, she thought, when she had some more substantial idea of what *they* knew. For the present, she simply felt confused. And left out.

Jimmy said nothing to help enlighten her but went his own way, stopping now and then to ask how she was enjoying the conservatory, how she was feeling. She responded truthfully, admitting that she enjoyed the new studies, vastly preferring the new kids to the ones at the old school.

Time kept moving. She still spent hours at a stretch recalling those few months of loving shared with Letty; longing for that time, for the return of the feelings she'd had then—of loving, being loved. With her death, Letty had taken all the loving Lisa thought she had to give. To anyone.

Hugh was becoming impatient. He could no longer see any reason for delay. Jeanette insisted on waiting until Lisa showed herself completely recovered from the shock of her mother's death.

"You are too impatient," she told him. "If she is expected to be respectful of those things you wish to do, she has the right to expect your respect for her feelings."

"Lisa always does what she wants to do. It's beside the point."

"Only in attending the conservatory. And that was something she had great need to do. It was not so very much a choice as a personal necessity. It is difficult for her to give of herself. Life comes slowly to Lisa. She requires much time to make sense of things, to fit all the pieces into one."

"The real issue here," he said, "aside from the fact of her exotic talent, is my having to sneak around my own home for the sake of a child's sensitivities. I have my own also, Jeanette. And it isn't fair to you, either. I don't see the point to waiting for Lisa to adjust. I don't *want* to upset her, but I certainly don't intend spending much longer in limbo because of Lisa."

"Was your papa this way with you?" she asked incisively. "Did he give you so little time and opportunity to know and express yourself?"

"I don't see that that matters. I mean, what . . . Oh, Jeanette," he smiled, "now you're going to say I'm preconditioned, that I'm visiting the sins of the fathers. Except that this time it's the daughter and not the son."

"Jimmy will go to California in August," she said. "It will then be only the three of us here. And I wish to have Lisa happy with the arrangements we make. For me, her feelings are very important. To be 'settled' in your proper sense makes no difference to me. That is your conditioning, chéri. Vraiment. Because you sleep with me, you feel guilty. It is not how you should be. Because you have guilt, it changes me to something I am not. I have no guilt because I make love with you without marriage. It does not matter. But Lisa matters very much."

"Are you trying to tell me you don't want to get married?"

"We are not children, Hugh. For now, being married will have to wait. If we do this now, it will upset Lisa. She and I must be on peaceful terms, sharing a confidence. If we marry without her understanding, she will hate both of us. She wishes only to be included in the family. But this you never do. Always you keep her outside."

"That's not true!" He sat up and reached for a cigarette. "It isn't true and certainly not fair. What the hell was I supposed to do, with Letty dying by inches for all those years? I . . . there was no time."

"Exactly. That is why you should make the time to be with her now. I think she is very brave. It is not so very easy to pick up the pieces and go on, as she has done. I wish you would see her, know her for what she is. She is special."

"We've never disagreed before," he said, looking lost.

"There was no reason."

"And now there's Lisa."

"Why have you so little feeling for her? I do not understand this in you. To her, you are papa and she loves you. But she knows you do not care for her."

"I just can't feel close to her," His mouth turned down slightly.

"What is the reason?" she persisted. "There is something. I can feel it in you each time I try to speak of Lisa."

"Could we change the subject?"

"Sometimes," her voice was very quiet, "I do not know you, Hugh. You brought her here to make her your child, but you have given her so little. Really, so little. I could see this perhaps if she was bad or ugly even. But she is not bad and very wonderful to look at. She says many things she has not meant to say but it is not hard to understand this. Growing up is difficult for each of us. I think you have responsibilities you do not honor, Hugh."

"You're asking me to change what I am."

44

"Oui. That is what I do."

For several seconds she studied him carefully, taking in the regularity of his features, his clear, untroubled-looking green eyes, the straight, narrow lines of his nose, the always-surprising sensual curve of his mouth, the firm, clean line of his jaw. He was a young-looking man with a firm, well-tended body and a firm, well-tended stubbornness.

"I love you," she said, after a time. "When I look at you, I think to myself I would like to make a child with you. It is true. You are so very good to me, so thoughtful, so gentle. You make me think and feel I am young again. I have loved no one as I love you. But I love Lisa, too. And because you do not make an effort to be loving—you are not even yourself with her—this comes before the feelings I have for you. I do not ask you to become altered into someone different. I ask you only to try to understand her, to care for her. You could show her only a small amount of the kindness you show to me and she would be so very happy. Could you not try to do this?"

"I loved Letty," he said, drawing her close. "But it was different, not like this. I'm not making comparisons," he added quickly. "But you know she wanted the children. I've always tried to be a good father to both of them. With Jimmy, it's easy. Lisa is another matter altogether. I knew her mother."

"Whose mother?"

"Lisa's."

"What?" She eased away from him. "You knew Lisa's mother?"

"I didn't actually know her. Letty and I had a meeting with the adoption people. We saw the girl there. She was . . . " He stopped, shaking his head.

"What was she?"

"Young and dirty. Literally filthy. I didn't want anything that came from someone so filthy. I know it's ridiculous. But I can still see her so clearly. That long, stringy hair, the grime in rings on her neck. Bitten fingernails."

"Oh, Hugh," she whispered. "Do you think this is what Lisa will become? She is not like this. She is very pretty, very careful of herself. You can't punish Lisa because the girl who made her was dirty. That is . . . démence!"

"Insane? Haven't you any irrationalities? Have you got everything all perfectly ironed out inside your head?"

"Of course I do not. But Hugh, this is a dreadful thing, to hold yourself away from Lisa all of her life because one time you saw this poor girl. What happened to her?"

"I have no idea. We only saw her that once."

"Lisa looks like her?"

"Not in the least," he stated firmly.

"You must forget this girl then," she said. "That is the answer, eh?"

"Maybe so," he murmured, touching her ear. "I'll try."

"Please!" she said. "Try very hard. Lisa could so easily be a fine woman, someone you would be proud to have as yours. But she needs much love, much understanding, much patience. Please, do this."

"If you want it, I will."

"Not for me, Hugh! Really! See her as she is, not as the baby of a sad, dirty little girl. See her for your own self. It may give you pleasure."

"I promise I will try. For all our sakes. Now, can we change the subject?" He kissed her shoulder, his hand gliding down to cover her breast.

"I am too old," she sighed, responding.

"For what?"

"To have your child."

He leaned on his elbow and looked at her. "Is that true? Or are you just guessing?"

"I am not certain. But I think it must surely be too late."

"Find out," he smiled. "Make certain. If it isn't too late, I want it very much. I love you, Jeanette. And I *will* try with Lisa, you know that."

"I know, chéri. That is some of why I love you. I know you always keep your mind open and that is very rare. Viens, chéri. Ah," she sighed. "Comme ça. Oui, comme ça."

Chapter 3

Jimmy said, "Maybe you're spending a little too much time behind that piano, Lee." He said it kindly, with a look of concern, as though he was a little frightened she'd start screaming at any minute. The comment came from nowhere, seemed apropos of nothing. And his expression made her terribly self-conscious because she suddenly wanted to try to explain to him where she'd been for so long and what she'd been doing while she'd been there. But if she did that, he might realize how crazy she'd actually been and lose whatever feeling for her he had. And she didn't want that to happen. She couldn't stand the thought of losing another familiar person. No one *really* belonged to her. But at least these people were familiar. They had the appearance of belonging all together—a family. She thought that if she said any of the dangerous things in her head, she'd risk losing even the appearances.

Having seen that expression on Jimmy's face, she was less surprised than she might have been to see it appear on Jeanette's features when she went one afternoon to Jeanette's rooms seeking company, hoping somehow to make contact again. With the return of her mind and the flow of fluids in her body, she felt deeply lonely.

Jeanette was sitting at the small desk in her sitting room, writing a letter. She looked up with a vague smile as Lisa knocked and came in. She waited and Lisa groped for words, for something to say. But looking at Jeanette's expectant face, she suddenly hadn't any idea whatsoever what she'd hoped to prove by this visit.

"What is it, Lisa?" Jeanette asked, setting down her pen, indicating Lisa should sit in the other chair.

Lisa remained standing, disoriented, like someone who'd set out for a swim from a beach she'd known well and arrived back to find it all changed. She'd been away— where? she wondered—for years now.

"I just thought I'd see . . . what you were doing." She glanced around the room, noticing things she didn't think she'd ever seen before. A rosary on a small table beside the loveseat. And, next to it, a photograph of herself and Jimmy, small children, in a shining, silver frame.

Jeanette sat watching her.

"You have come to talk?" she asked.

"I don't remember this picture," Lisa said, lifting the photograph, gazing at herself and Jimmy, her heart racing. "When was this taken?"

"You wish to talk, Lisa?"

"No . . ." She lifted her eyes to Jeanette's face, shakily setting down the photograph.

"What are you thinking? Are you feeling unwell?"

"I . . . no. I . . . You're beautiful, Jeanette. I didn't know that. I have to go now." She turned to go but Jeanette got up to stop her.

"Come to me again. We will talk."

"I don't know," Lisa said, threatened by tears. "I don't know." She escaped and made her way to the front of the house, to the safety of the piano and her music.

In the night, she lay in bed, feeling Jeanette's presence downstairs drawing at her like a poultice. She could feel herself steadily filling with words, with the return of the desire to give voice to her words. She lay, listening to the night sounds of the house, the creak and shift of the old house as it settled more solidly into the earth; the distant murmur of a radio being played in Jimmy's room; the occasional hum of a passing car, the arc of its lights swinging across the ceiling as the car moved past the house.

She wanted to break the isolation of her long silence, wanted to ask Jeanette . . . what? Who am I? Do you know who I am? Why do I feel so ugly, so black sometimes? She switched on the bedside light, glancing at the clock. It was early, only ten-thirty. Jeanette would still be up. She rarely went to bed before midnight. Lisa pulled on her robe and went downstairs, through to the west side of the house where Jeanette had her rooms.

She knocked softly and opened the door. The sitting room was dark and the bedroom door was ajar, a dull light spilling out into the sitting room.

Jeanette was standing naked beside the closet. Looking at her, Lisa wanted to cry. Jeanette's hair was loose and fell in long, lazy coils down her back. Lisa stared, watching Jeanette close the closet door, watched her move through the room toward the chest of drawers, her breasts swaying as she went. The sight of Jeanette made Lisa feel lonelier than she ever had in her life. And the loneliness made her want to cry out, shout at Jeanette. But she could do no more than simply stand there, staring, unable now even to move as Jeanette's head turned and her eyes connected with Lisa's.

"Come, Lisa," she said, opening a drawer, removing a nightgown.

Lisa was immobilized. It wasn't as if she'd never seen Jeanette without clothes before. She had. Dozens of times. When she'd been very small, Lisa often would climb into Jeanette's bathtub with her. Why? she wondered. What's happening?

She turned and walked away, into the kitchen. She stood by the kitchen window feeling so weighted-down she might sink right through the kitchen floor, down into the cellar. She was so lost in her blackness, she wasn't aware of Jeanette until she felt the woman's arms come around her, turning her.

"Talk with me, Lisa." Jeanette held her hand over the back of Lisa's head and Lisa felt Jeanette's strength bending her; knew Jeanette could melt her down, dissolve her.

"You must talk, Lisa."

Jeanette's body was a deception, she felt, another lure toward eventual foolishness, a return to that shameful, crazy childishness.

"Tell me," Jeanette insisted, maintaining her hold.

Lisa was the taller, but Jeanette was much the stronger. Her physical strength, the force of her arms, her body, amazed Lisa.

49

"Lisa, it is three years since your mama died. So many months, you speak to no one, do not cry or show any feelings. Only the silence. And dreams you make for yourself. This is not good, Lisa. Not good."

"I don't!" Lisa protested.

"I see things you do. I know you. I know you all of your fifteen years, Lisa. The things you do not understand, you take them away with you to change, to make them different in your mind so you will be able to hold these things inside of your head in the way you wish them to be. But not as they are. Tell me what is in your mind. If I cannot know what is there, I can do nothing to help you."

She felt drained, weakened and tired and somehow defenseless in Jeanette's grip. She sighed, her resistance ebbing, letting her head drop on Jeanette's shoulder as she began to cry. Hopelessly, wordlessly, crying.

"Speak," Jeanette urged.

"Why does everybody expect me to understand so much? Always. Everything that happens. I don't. I don't understand. I get the feeling you're just very clever . . . I don't know."

"What does this mean? What do you wish to say?"

"I *don't know*! I don't know! I forget things. I don't know."

"Let me help you," Jeanette said softly. "I would help you. But how can I do it, if I cannot make you say what is in your head?"

"Nothing fits," Lisa said distractedly. "I can't make anything fit."

"What things?"

"I don't know! Let me go."

"Always you have a desire to make all things fit together," Jeanette observed. "Like the scales you play. What does not fit, chérie? Can you tell me?"

"I used to pretend you were my mother . . ." Lisa stopped abruptly, not knowing where she'd been about to go, thrown into total confusion by the things her voice could say without her permission.

"We all pretend. What more?"

"I'm no one!" Lisa whispered. "I . . . I don't know who

50

I am." She sounded like a fool and tried to pull herself away from Jeanette, embarrassed. "It doesn't matter," she said. "Nothing matters."

"Everything matters," Jeanette corrected. "I like you, Lisa. Oh, I love you. But in special ways, I like you. When you sing, when you think no one hears and you sing. Then, I like you so very much. Ah," she smiled gently, "you think no one knows. But I hear you sing the music from the records belonging to your mama. How do you come to sing this way?"

"It makes me feel good. Christ! Does everyone sneak around spying on me?"

"No one spies! I listen. That is different. If you will not speak to anyone, someone must look to see you are well. So angry, Lisa. You have such anger with all of us?"

"I don't know," she said miserably. "I shouldn't have come down here . . ."

"But you came. Now you are here, *talk*! Tell me!"

"There's nothing to tell. Let me go, Jeanette. I want to go."

Jeanette released her. Lisa continued to stand where she was, feeling suddenly cold, removed from Jeanette's body. She felt the blackness sucking her down like quicksand, tears forcing themselves upwards into her eyes. She tried to hold them down, keep them away but they kept rising. And now that Jeanette had let go of her, she wanted to seek comfort once more inside the circle of Jeanette's arms. But something kept holding her back, kept her silent despite a steadily painful yearning to give voice to all the thoughts and feelings welling up inside.

"You are someone," Jeanette said, at last. "You are you. But you feel you do not know who you are?"

"How can I know?" Lisa erupted angrily. "How can I? My mother's dead, but she wasn't my mother. No, that's not . . . I'm no one, nothing. Give up on me, Jeanette. I'm hopeless."

"Lisa, I tell you only one thing. You are listening?"

"What?" Lisa asked despondently.

"No one knows, chérie. Even with a mother and father, it is not enough. It takes much of a lifetime to know who it is you are. For each of us, it takes time. You must be patient with yourself, Lisa. It will come. But you are someone."

"Who?"

"You are you, Lisa."

"Lisa. But how do I know what *she* called me? How do I know what *she*. . . . I don't know."

"Who is this 'she?' "

"My *mother*! The *real* one."

"Real is an illusion," Jeanette said quietly. "Letty was real. The rest you may never know. Concentrate for now on becoming you, Lisa. All of us must live with questions that have no answers."

"That's not enough."

"It will have to be enough. No one can give you more."

"I already knew that."

"Lisa, you must be kinder to yourself. In time you will come to know all that is important for you to know, who you are. All."

"D'you really believe that?"

"I *know*," Jeanette stated. "We all must travel through time in order to know who it is we are, chérie. Be patient. I promise you, it will come."

"You promise me?"

Jeanette looked into Lisa's large, hopeful eyes and smiled reassuringly. "I promise you," she repeated. "It *will* come."

True to his word, and with his insights somewhat clarified by airing that old memory, Hugh made a tremendous effort to be accessible to Lisa, beginning by taking her out to dinner. He found it hard to know where to begin, seeing the expectancy on Lisa's face. He lit a cigarette and with his fingers wrapped around his martini glass—an illusion of support—he cleared his throat and attempted, in roundabout fashion, to introduce the subject of his marriage to Jeanette.

"Letty has been dead three years," he said, looking somewhat surprised by this realization. He stopped, wondering if this was a good beginning.

"I know that, papa," Lisa said, watching him closely.

"It was such a long time," he said, suddenly quite

anxious to hear himself talk openly about it to her. She seemed so receptive. "It wasn't something that was planned . . . I mean, I wasn't looking for anything. Oh look," he said, facing her squarely, "you and I haven't ever been able, for some reason or other, to talk easily together. It's not the way I've wanted it. I don't know why it's been that way. But I'd like to try to change it. You're fifteen years old. You seem . . . intelligent. All that time Letty was ill, it was a terrible strain, Lisa. Any number of things we couldn't say or . . . do. In time, it seemed too much of a strain. I needed someone to talk to, someone who'd understand what was happening."

"Jeanette," she said quietly.

"Yes." He felt relieved. Her face held no animosity. "I've grown to love her. I want to marry her. But I felt . . . I feel it's important that you understand, that you feel a part of what's happening. I know it's been very hard on you these past few years. It's been hard on all of us. I don't know why we . . . you and I have never spent much time together. But now that we've made a start, I'd like us to continue. I want you to be happy. It's . . . We've never been awfully good with our children, the Hamiltons. Maybe it's about time we changed all that." He searched her face hopefully.

"Yes, papa," she said, unsmiling, waiting to hear more.

"Tell me how you feel," he urged. "What you want. I don't know what to make of you when you look at me that way."

"I don't want anything, papa," she lied.

"How would you feel about Jeanette and I marrying?"

She saw something in his eyes that seemed to be telling her it really mattered how she felt about this and she couldn't understand what had happened to put that expression there.

"I don't know," she answered truthfully.

"It would upset you?"

"Don't you care anymore now that she's dead?" Her heart was fluttering. She felt she was on the edge of potentially dangerous truths.

"You can't keep on caring—not in the same way, Lisa

—for someone who's no longer here to reciprocate. I loved her. Very much. But she's dead."

"And Jeanette's alive."

"Yes."

"I see," she said, thinking they'd close her out. It would happen. They'd have each other and she'd have to find something all her own. But she found she didn't mind. Maybe she'd be able to do her practicing at home. They might let her do that. Jeanette liked her music. She was always saying that. "I don't mind," she said, finally. "She's very beautiful."

"That's not why I want to marry her, Lisa."

She lifted her head and regarded him with genuine interest. "Why then?" she asked.

"Because she's sensitive and intelligent. Any number of things. She loves you very much."

"And?" She wondered if he'd declare himself.

"And we love each other," he said, flushing.

"That's good." She smiled for the first time.

He studied her smile, thinking her smiles were so rare that when she gave them it was like finding your home still standing after a tornado. He smiled back.

"You wouldn't be upset, then?"

"No, papa, I don't think so." She wanted to tell him about her suspicions, her guesswork, but said nothing.

"I got tickets for a concert next week. I hoped we'd go, the two of us."

"That would be very nice. Thank you."

"Lisa," he said softly, tentatively touching her hand, "don't you like me?"

"I love you, papa."

"That isn't what I asked you."

"Sometimes," she said slowly, her heart fluttering again, "I think you're mean. You don't think about how I feel. You only care what I think of you."

He stared, the words penetrating far past layers of protective insulation. His immediate reaction was to deny what she'd said but he knew, taking a rapid retrospective glance at the past three years, that she was right. He hadn't thought she possessed such insight.

"I care very much how you feel," he said. "If it's appeared differently to you in the past, I'll try to change that in the future."

Hearing him say that, she felt as if—she'd seen some workmen do it once on one of the skylights at the conservatory—she'd been dipped in solvent and come up all clean, freed of tar. He spoke with sincerity; his eyes boring into hers, wanting her to believe. And she, too, wanted to believe.

"Would it be all right if I practiced my singing at home, then?" she asked cautiously, forgetting he knew nothing about that.

"Singing?" His eyebrows lifted.

"Sometimes I like to."

"By all means." His fingers tightened over her hand. "If it gives you pleasure, if it makes you happy. We enjoy your music."

"Okay," she said, wishing he'd let go of her hand. He was pressing too hard. "I guess I don't mind."

"Good." He squeezed her fingers and removed his hand. "Let's order now. If you're ready."

Jimmy, who'd long been talking and planning his move, left for California the second week of August. The following week, with Lisa in attendance, Hugh and Jeanette were married in judge's chambers.

Lisa witnessed the brief ceremony with a return of her feeling of apartness; hearing the exchange of words, watching her father and Jeanette gazing at each other with matching expressions of adoration Lisa found incomprehensible. None of it made any sense. When the ceremony was completed and the couple embraced, she saw their mouths meet and felt a sudden inflow of understanding and longed to feel their kisses on her own mouth, to taste their love, experience it for herself.

Their faces shone with happiness and she stared at them feeling a huge bubble of painful proportions interfering with her breathing. She stood woodenly, watching her father's and Jeanette's friends offering kisses and congratulations, wondering how all the words that had been spoken in those few brief moments could so change everything.

Then Hugh appeared in front of her, taking hold of her hand. She looked at him, thinking he was very handsome, very dignified. Feeling suddenly helpless, she put her arms around his neck and kissed the softness of his cheeks, holding on hard. She breathed in the familiar Lilac Végétal and kissed him again before stepping away. He kept hold of her hand.

"I'm happy for you," she said, finding words as elusive as ever as his eyes searched hers.

"Lisa," he said softly, "Be happy, my dear. We . . . I . . ."

"I know," she said. She did, she realized. She knew exactly what he was trying to say to her. He embraced her again before being towed away by his friends.

Jeanette, who had been watching, moving quickly across the room.

"We will get papa and leave for home now," she told Lisa, "To arrive before the others."

Lisa turned slowly. There were so many questions she wanted to ask. It seemed too much, the noisy people. And her father. And Jeanette. Jeanette looked unreal, like a picture of Jeanette in a beige peau de soie dress with her hair knotted loosely at the nape of her neck, the color high in her cheeks. And a ring Hugh had put on her finger. Lisa lifted Jeanette's hand, staring at the ring. She looked at the gold band and then at Jeanette, feeling Jeanette's fingers close firmly around her own hand. She hadn't expected to cry. But it was, finally, too much and she couldn't say any of the things she wanted to say.

Jeanette, with her free hand, blotted Lisa's face.

"Now," she whispered, drawing Lisa close to her, "we are family, as it should be. I have a secret to share with you. I am so very happy, chérie. You will be happy with me?"

"Yes."

"Come. I will tell when I find papa."

The three of them went out to the car while the others, in twos and threes, headed for cars parked nearby. Jeanette began a sort of ceremony, putting Lisa's hand in Hugh's.

"I wish to make an announcement," she said, smiling

radiantly. "To my family. Zut! I feel so silly now," she laughed.

"What?" Lisa asked, sharing her laughter.

"What is it?" Hugh said, equally amused.

"It is so silly. Now I cannot make myself speak the words. I don't know how to say it," she told Lisa, then looked at Hugh.

"*No!*" Hugh exclaimed, guessing. He remained perfectly still for a moment, then laughed in a way neither of them had ever before heard him laugh: exultantly, jubilantly, throwing his arms around the two of them.

"Tell me!" Lisa laughed, caught up in their excitement.

"You tell her!" Jeanette said. "She will laugh with us."

"Jeanette . . . we . . . she's pregnant." He looked so delighted that for several seconds Lisa couldn't make sense of what he'd said. She looked at him, then at Jeanette, her eyes automatically going to Jeanette's middle.

"You are?" Lisa asked, incredulous, seeing no external evidence.

"C'est vrai;" Jeanette laughed, drawing Lisa back into the small circle. "A miracle!" she declared. "For an old woman. It is a dream."

"How . . . I mean when?" Lisa asked.

"March," Jeanette beamed. "In the middle of March."

In the next instant, Lisa saw what seemed to her to be the proof she'd been seeking of the feelings these two people claimed to have for each other. Very gently, Hugh disengaged himself, his entire focus on Jeanette. He placed his hands on her face and gazed deep into her eyes.

"I *love* you," he told her.

Jeanette's eyes grew large and shiny as her arms came around him. She made a small, half-questioning gesture, asking, "Yes?" without words and Hugh kissed her mouth in answer. Lisa felt her apartness dropping down over her but before it had a chance to take hold, Hugh reached out and brought her close to the two of them before his mouth had left Jeanette's.

"I love this woman," he said to Lisa. "And you," he kissed her forehead, "are beautiful and very very dear to me. Please, be happy with us."

"Papa," she said, overcome, "Jeanette . . . Do I . . .? Will you . . ."

"Go on, chérie," Jeanette urged. "Say how you feel."

"I *am* happy for you. You're sharing something so important with me. It's . . . I love you. Both of you. I really do."

"Eh, bien!" Jeanette said sunnily. "Enough drama! We will be the last to arrive for the celebration. We are all happy, hnnh?"

The atmosphere in the house was so different. It seemed strange to Lisa to wander downstairs through the rooms Jeanette had occupied for so many years to find them empty of all trace of her. Yet, in some ways, it seemed as if Jeanette had always lived upstairs with Hugh; had always emerged from their bedroom in the mornings looking so gay and contented. She did the things she'd always done: ran the house, prepared the menus for the cook, told the cleaning lady what needed doing that particular Monday or Thursday, cooked elaborate meals on the cook's day off. All of it. But it was different.

Their two voices filled the house with words and laughter, always open to include Lisa if she wished to join them. And, experimentally, Lisa involved herself in their plans and excitement, all the while thinking, *This is how a family feels. This is how it is.*

In the afternoons she rehearsed at home. And instead of Letty upstairs listening, Jeanette was there taking her afternoon rest. The fact that Jeanette had been put under strict doctor's orders to rest each afternoon brought home to Lisa just how much of a risk Jeanette was taking with the pregnancy. But Jeanette said, "It is a lucky accident to be having a child at my age. Dr. MacKenzie," she laughed, "he says I am complètement folle. But he is too much concerned with age."

"Maybe he's right," Lisa said. "Maybe it is dangerous."

"Nonsense! I am very healthy, very strong. What do men know of such things? Even doctors. They do not know everything. He is foolish, fussing over me."

Nevertheless, she followed the orders, lying on the big

58

bed every afternoon with the curtains drawn and the door opened wide to receive Lisa's music. She lay with her eyes closed and her mind at peace, listening.

Chapter 4

In September, back in school, back in the school routine Lisa began to feel quietly desperate. She was tired of moving around the drafty building, going from one class to another, learning when she no longer felt like learning. The family life was settled, peaceful. But there was something in her head and in her hands that kept wanting to come out somehow—through her music, through her voice—somehow. She couldn't put it all together. She remained unable to accomplish it.

Depression inched its way through her brain until she began sitting in the park afternoons after classes, idly considering the relative effectiveness of various means of committing suicide. At first, she wasn't really aware of what she was doing. She held her face up toward the sun, eyes closed, and pictured herself going out to the kitchen to get the cook's favorite serrated breadknife, then locking herself into her bathroom and, with her head over the sink, cutting her throat.

She rejected that and next considered her single-edged razor blades. She always carried a package in her music case for cutting manuscript paper. The blades were slightly oily, exceedingly sharp. So simple to cut her wrists. She read often in the newspapers of people doing that. But with both the knife and the blades, there'd be a lot of blood and she hated the idea of making such a mess.

Sleeping pills were a possibility but she didn't have any. And risking a secret trip to the master bathroom seemed more dangerous than suicide. She found no humor whatsoever in her thinking, but went at each possibility with a kind of objective overall view, trying to see both her own part in the deed and the projected reactions of the family. She wanted it all to be quickly and neatly accomplished, with as little mess as possible. She found the idea of anyone having to clean up her blood repellent.

It was at the point where, having rejected the trip upstairs for her father's sleeping pills, that the full impact of what she was idly planning struck her. What am I doing? she asked herself, shocked, opening her eyes to take in the trees and shrubberies of the small park. That's not what I want to do, she told herself, shivering at the madness of her imaginings.

But she had to do something. And she didn't know what. Something. Then she remembered Nick Montefiore and ran back to the house to call him.

"Lisa!" he sounded very happy. "I thought maybe you'd decided it was no go after all."

"I'd like to sing."

"Great! I've got a dozen rooms that'd snap you right up."

"What about the Colony?" she asked hesitantly. "Could I play there?"

"You don't want to work that dive," he said. "I've got nice rooms, class rooms."

"No, that's where I want to work."

There was a long pause before he said, "What's your number? Give it to me. I'll have to get back to you."

She gave it to him.

"You want to work weekends or full weeks?" he asked. "And can you come up with a hundred and a half union bread?"

"I don't know. I mean, I've got the money. I hadn't thought about when I'd work. I haven't thought . . ."

"Let me see what I can line up and I'll get back to you in a while."

He made arrangements for her to play breaks at the Colony on Friday and Saturday nights. She accepted his terms without once stopping to think that Jeanette or her father might ask where she was going. She somehow didn't think they'd notice she wasn't at home.

The following Friday night she arrived at the Colony not at all sure she was doing the right thing. When she pushed through the doors and saw the tightly-packed mass of bodies beneath the pink-tinted smoke haze, panic rushed into her throat and she backed up several steps. Nick had been standing by the bar keeping an eye on the door and hurried over to take her by the arm and lead her through the tables and out to the back where there were several dressing rooms.

"Listen," he said, giving her a big smile. "For tonight, this'll have to do. But you're going to have to do something about your hair. And don't you have any *clothes*?"

"What's wrong with this?" she asked, looking down at the black pinafore and white silk shirt she'd thought very sophisticated.

"There's nothing wrong with it, dear. It's just that you look like a schoolgirl. This is a club for grownups. And grownups don't pay good bread for cheap draft and watered booze to listen to schoolgirls. I've got an idea. Come on in here for a minute." He opened one of the dressing room doors and showed her inside. "What've you got underneath that?"

"Underneath?"

"Take off the blouse and let's have a look."

She looked around the room and then at Nick.

He smiled and said, "I'll wait outside."

She removed the blouse, then went to the door to let him in.

"Your straps show," he said. "Better take off the bra, dear. And let your hair down." He stood back and looked her up and down. "Okay," he said. "You do that. Give me a shout when you're finished. It's about ten minutes till they break, so step on it. You got your numbers lined up?"

"How much do I have to do?" she asked, thinking she'd do this one night and not come back Saturday.

"Four numbers should do it. Open with an up tune, then a couple of ballads and close with another up number."

"Up?"

"Something with time, okay? Go on," he smiled. "Everything'll be just fine."

She unzipped the pinafore and removed her bra then stood back to look at herself in the speckled mirror on the back of the door. I look naked, she thought, trying to raise the neckline of the pinafore. It was a low scoop that only just covered her nipples. Oh God! she thought, her hands cold and her face and neck very hot. I can't do this! She removed the band and shook her hair down. I can't do this! she told herself as the door opened and Nick stood on the threshold staring at her.

"That's much better." he held out his hand. "You can leave your things with me. Nervous, huh?"

"I can't!" she said, her jaw feeling stiff, locked. "I can't!"

"You'll be great. Just get up behind that mike and sing. Forget about the people. Don't think about anything but the music. Okay?"

"I can't!" she said again as he took her arm and they went out of the dressing room.

"Listen, dear," he said softly, pulling her to a stop before the entrance to the main room. "You look lovely. Don't think about the yakkers and the boozers. And stop worrying about your neckline. You've got a very nice set there and, believe me, the only person who's going to mind one bit about your equipment is you. Just sing!"

The trio came down and there was a scattering of applause followed by an increase in the noise level in the room as Nick took her along the side of the room and up onto the stand.

"The switch on the mike is here," he told her, taking her hand and showing her where. "Light switch for the spot is there on the floor. Just step on the switch when you're ready to start. That's all there is to it." He squeezed her shoulder, smiled and left the stage.

She looked down to notice several people at the closer tables watching her, waiting. Their faces looked closed and shuttered. Her hands were sweating. She closed her eyes, counted to five, then reached to switch on the mike. She forgot everything Nick had told her and laid out the intro to her first number, "A Sunday Kind of Love."

The first few words of the lyrics came as a surprise to her. She'd forgotten the amplification, the enlargement of her voice. She threw more force behind her voice, projecting and then lost track of the people so close by and the beery-smoke smell of the room because she was caught in the lyrics and the changes and the sound of her voice bouncing back at her from the walls, the floor, the ceiling, and nothing else mattered. As she started the repeat, she was aware of Nick onstage and the sudden light and a bursting noise and looked up, finding herself in the spotlight and the nearest faces illuminated by the spill. And that *sound*! People were applauding and she hadn't even finished the number. But Nick said, "It's for you, dear." as he ducked off the stage. And she couldn't believe it or think about it because she was into the bridge and then going down to the closing eight, forgetting them all again because the sounds were important, getting them just so was important. And Nick was right. Nothing else mattered.

The wave of applause at the end shocked her back into reality and she looked at the people, hearing odd banging noises and saw that men were thumping their beer bottles on the tabletops. Nick appeared beside the stand, smiling up at her saying, "Beautiful. Go into your next number. Go on."

She looked back once more into the beaming faces and felt herself smiling, felt satisfaction crowding into her and went with the feeling, throwing all of it into the number she should have started out with, letting her throat open full to sing about going to "Kansas City."

Applause was the happiest sound she'd ever heard. It filled her top to bottom, front to back, side to side with elation; gave her a new kind of dizziness, one of total unity. She was, through her music, at one with every set of ears that listened. She'd gladly have stayed to play all night but allowed Nick to lead her to a small table at the back, her ears still hearing the sounds of all those hands clapping.

"What'd I tell you?" he said, ordering a Coke for her and a Canadian Club and water for himself. "Easy as pie, isn't it?"

"It really is," she smiled at him. "Really. I . . . it's . . ."

"Well, just relax now for a while. You'll get two more shots at the bright light and magic tonight. Do me a favor?"

"What?"

"Go shopping tomorrow and get yourself a couple of decent-looking dresses. If you need money, I'll advance you some."

"I have money."

"Okay, And no more ponytails."

"Yes, all right."

She could hardly concentrate on what he was saying, she was so anxious to hurry back to the stage and do it all over again.

Nick took a swallow of his drink, then looked at her over the rim of his glass.

"Your folks don't mind you doing this gig?" he asked, already knowing.

He was curious to hear what she'd say.

"Playing here?" she asked.

"Right."

"They don't mind that I do."

She studied him, liking the way he was dressed and his clean looks. He had a rounded face with dark brown hair neatly parted, dark olive skin, brown eyes, small white teeth that seemed to glow when he smiled. He wasn't very tall—not as tall as she—but managed to give the impression of size, of being far taller, bigger than he was.

"You don't look," he said carefully, "as though you come from a family that doesn't care about what you do. You're trying to get back at them for something?"

"When do I play again?" she asked, holding the glass of Coke between her hands.

"Ten-thirty. You didn't answer my question."

"I'm doing what I want to do. Stop asking questions."

"Understand something," he said firmly. "It's my job to ask questions. You're under age. I can't afford to put myself in a position to be the target for a lot of parental flak because Lisa didn't tell mommy and daddy what she was going to be doing Friday and Saturday nights. We work together, dear. I get you the gigs and make sure

64

nobody puts the make on you. You tell me the truth and pay me my ten percent."

"I'm not lying," she said. "My mother's dead. My father has a hard time understanding the things I want to do."

"I see." He drank some more of his scotch, never taking his eyes from her face. "Okay, I'll hang in here tonight and tomorrow night. No problems, you'll be on your own after that. Show up on time, do your gig and go straight home when you're finished. You can sit, have a Coke or ginger ale if you're invited. But no messing with the customers.. You mess around and that's it. None of my acts make it on their back. Either you cut it onstage or you don't cut it. Fuck around and I'll bounce you back to wherever it is you come from. Understand?"

"I wouldn't do that," she began, stunned by that word he'd used.

"Listen, dear. I don't think you *know* what you'd do. Keep your mind on what you're doing. Keep your hands on the keyboard, your mind on your music and your pants on. Then everything'll be beautiful."

"Don't talk to me that way," she said, blushing.

"I don't make a habit of it," he said seriously. "But you're the only kid act I've got. And kids like you are pure walking dynamite. So pay attention to what I tell you and keep to yourself. That's all."

For some reason, up until Nick spoke to her in that awful way, she'd never given much thought to her own sexuality. She returned home that night to look at her image in the mirror on the back of her bedroom door, wondering about the suitability of the size of her breasts and the long, squarish lines of her hips and thighs. She struck several poses, turning this way and that, finally making a face at herself and walking away. He was just trying to scare her, she thought. What he'd said was terrible. The words he used—not just that one, but the other ones—were strange, from another country. But she liked him. He likes me, she decided, preparing for bed. And it was possible he was warning her to behave for some other reason. Maybe what he really wanted was to do *that* with her himself.

But at their next meeting, the following evening, he made it very plain that the "hands-off" policy applied not only to members of the audience but to him as well.

"You don't have to worry about me, dear," he told her. "Virgins make me nervous. And I've got my own action going. I told you before, I don't think you know where your head's at."

"How do you know what I am?" she asked angrily. "You don't know what I am."

"Stay cool, Lisa," he said kindly. "I *know* what you are. You'll find all kinds of action when you're ready. I'm simply not the one for you to try your wings on. Don't go all huffy and uptight. We're friends, dear. It makes for good business."

The following Friday night, she looked up between numbers of her second set to see Jeanette sitting alone at one of the side tables, dipping a swizzle stick up and down in a tall glass.

Seeing Jeanette in that place was a colossal shock. It meant that she knew not only what Lisa was doing, but where, and how she looked doing it. Lisa watched her, forgetting herself in her fear of an impending confrontation, so it was a jolt when Jeanette's eyes lifted and met hers and Jeanette smiled. Her smile gave Lisa the shameful sensation that what she was doing behind the piano, in full spotlighted view of that roomful of men, was naked and shabby. But Jeanette applauded, still smiling, when Lisa finished the last number of her set and made her way nervously over to the table.

"How did you find out I was here?" she asked in a low voice, her hands sweaty.

"Sit with me, chérie," Jeanette smiled, compounding Lisa's nervousness.

She pulled out the chair and sat down, wanting to shout out at the men all around them; wanting to scream at them to stop staring, ogling Jeanette the way they were. They didn't even know she was pregnant, never mind being Lisa's stepmother.

"Your papa would not accompany me," she said, lighting a cigarette, offering one to Lisa. Lisa took a cigarette and held it shakily to the flame of Jeanette's lighter.

"You look very chic, Lisa. Very sophisticated. It is difficult to know you."

"Are you going to make me come home?" Lisa asked, feeling like an eight-year-old dressed in clothes found in an old trunk in the attic.

"We will discuss that later. I like very much your singing, chérie. All the people like it." She took the swizzle stick from the glass, laid it down on the table, then took a long swallow of her drink. Lisa was terrified now, positive Jeanette was going to tell her she'd have to stop; that she was neglecting her schoolwork. Something. She was sure of it.

"I can see you are happy up there," Jeanette said. "Where did you get this dress?"

"What's wrong with it?"

"I have not said there is something wrong with it." She put her hand over Lisa's. "Don't be nervous with me, chérie. I will stay until you finish and then we go somewhere together to eat, to talk."

"All right," Lisa said, somewhat less defensive now.

She couldn't sing with her usual freedom with Jeanette there. She'd start to lose herself to the lyrics and her eyes would drift over the faces to fix on Jeanette and she'd be dragged out of the dreams, out of the soaring high and back into reality. All she could think was: *If they make me stop here, I'll leave home. I'll run away. Play somewhere else. They can't make me stop.*

They went in Jeanette's car to an all-night restaurant. Once seated in a booth, their orders having been taken, Jeanette leaned her head to one side and said, "It is amazing. You were quite wonderful. It is too bad your papa is so stubborn. I know he would have enjoyed you."

"You think so?"

"You are so alike, you and papa," she laughed. "I would like sometimes to take your two heads in my hands and do this!" She illustrated a head-slamming gesture. "Such stubborn people! He would *adore* this music. And you would be happy to have him see you do this so well."

67

"Are you going to make me stop?"

"No, I would not do that."

"You wouldn't?" Lisa felt so relieved she was momentarily dizzy.

"I have had a telephone call from a very nice young man—Nick?—who wished to speak to me about what you wanted to do. This is a very sensible young man, I think. It would be irresponsible for such a man to make commitments for you without having the good sense to make certain that your family knows what it is you do. I have given him the permission to get you this job."

"You did?" Lisa was staggered. "Why?"

"Because this is something—I feel it very deeply— you must do. This singing, it is everything, eh? I feel in you how much importance it has. I know you. I see how you search about for something that is yours, only yours. And when you have the piano and the music. I begin to see that this is what you will have. It does not make me so very happy to see that you play in such a place."

Her *voice* was like music, Lisa thought, succumbing for a moment to the pleasurable cadence and lure of it.

"I would *never* make you stop your music. I know what it has for you."

"I can't believe it," Lisa said, studying Jeanette's brown-black eyes. "You *know*!"

"I think anyone would know, Lisa. To hear you is to know."

"It is?" The words dried the palms of her hands, restored her appetite.

"You are bored with school?" Jeanette asked, stubbing her cigarette before picking up her knife and fork.

"I hate it," she said, the edges of depression adhering to her like sticky flypaper at the thought of school.

"For a time," Jeanette said sagely, aware of something dark and destructive appearing in Lisa's eyes, "it will be best to continue. We will see what comes next."

"What does that mean?"

"Just that we shall see. One step at a time. For now, you sing in this place. There is no need to make decisions. That will come in time."

68

Suspicion wouldn't leave her. It narrowed her eyes and clenched like a fist in her chest.

"Why do you always try so hard with me?" she asked, closely watching Jeanette's face. "Always saying the right thing, so long-suffering." How can I say these things to her? she thought, appalled. How can I talk to her this way?

"What do you wish from me?" Jeanette asked quietly, unsmiling.

"I think you are a hypocrite!" Lisa exploded, all the tension finding sudden release. "All this time . . . supposed to be a damned Catholic with your rosary and your big crucifix and all these years . . . all this time you were fucking my father!"

Jeanette paled, horrified by this sudden change of mood, this attack.

Lisa, quivering with confusion and fear, watched as Jeanette lit a cigarette and drew hard on it before attempting to speak.

"The rosary and crucifix belonged to my mother," she said, controlling her voice. "I gave up my religion when your mama became ill." She paused, knowing by the bleak look in Lisa's eyes that Lisa could no more believe she'd spoken the way she had than Jeanette could. "I could not," she went on, "believe in a God who would give such pain to one who did not deserve it. So, I did not go against my religion by 'fucking' your father. And this 'fucking,'" she grimaced slightly, as if someone had hit her between the shoulder blades, "as you wish to call it, is something for animals. I am not an animal. Nor is your papa. You shock me. I think I am stupid, Lisa. I am never expecting the dreadful things you sometimes say. Never."

"So why do you keep telling me how much you love me?"

"Because it is the truth. I have great feeling for you."

"Your 'great feeling.' Spying on me, checking up on me."

Jeanette's hand closed hard on Lisa's wrist.

"Stop it!" she said sharply. "I do none of these things and you know it!" She opened her fingers, staring at Lisa's wrist for a moment before sitting back against the

69

booth. "I have never interfered with you," she said, deeply upset. "I have tried only to help you. You hate me, Lisa?"

"I don't hate you."

"Then you hate yourself?"

"I'm sick of talking about it."

"And me! I will not stop you, whatever you wish to do. It is not my place to stop you."

"I'm tired," Lisa said, in a choked voice.

"I know this."

'You're not going to stop me working here?"

"No."

"I don't understand you."

"I know that, Lisa."

"All right," she said exhaustedly. "I didn't mean to say that . . . what I did . . . about you . . . I don't *know* why I said it. All of a sudden, I *had* to! I couldn't help it. I lo . . . I care about you. I don't want to hurt anybody. Something inside of me says things I never meant to say."

"You cannot say 'love' Lisa?"

"I love you."

"Your love does not make people live or die, Lisa."

Lisa's head shot up.

"Your mama did not die because of your love. Your love had no part of it. You thought she would live if you gave her your words of love. It made you both happy that you could do this. She could go with a peaceful soul because you gave this to her. But love does not make people live or die, Lisa. Your love makes me happy but it could not make me live one day more than I should live. Nor would I die. Here," she passed over her handkerchief. "Cry. It is good. Perhaps now you might begin to stop doing and saying things from such terrible anger. I will not interfere with you, Lisa. But I will help you, if you will let me."

70

Chapter 5

Midway through the fall term, Mr. McElroy in Theory was replaced by a very tall, thin young man with long, flowing blond hair. He had a bushy red moustache under which his mouth looked very red and ripe like something secret that should also have been covered by the moustache.

"Welcome to the thrilling world of Theory," he laughed, greeting the class. "I'm Mike Fenton, your new guru. Call me Fennie." All the kids laughed. Lisa did too.

Until Fennie came, it seemed tacitly compulsory to walk quickly and quietly through the corridors from one class to the next. Noise, laughter, conversation were misplaced in that old building with its creaky wood floors and vaulted classrooms. But even the stiffest, most dedicatedly long-haired of his students warmed under Fennie's good-humored aegis. His classes were fun, full of excitement and laughter. The laughter spilled out into the corridors, echoed through the old building.

Lisa's mind wandered during his classes, speculating idly on his hands and the length of his fingers, noticing the freckles on his wrists and the fine golden hairs visible beneath his cuffs. She wondered if his hair was as soft as it looked and if his moustache felt stiff and bristly, or soft, too.

He drove a battered red MG sports car, and she sometimes saw him racing off down the street after classes. She longed to ride in that little car, sharing his laughter, free to study the shape of his ripe, red mouth.

From time to time, he gave her a puzzled look as if he was trying to remember something. She always looked away, feeling hot and uncomfortable. Then, one afternoon at the beginning of December, he called to her as she was leaving the classroom.

"Hold on a minute!" he said. "It's finally come to me."

"What?"

"It's been driving me crazy," he smiled. "But now I've got it. Take down the hair, take away most of the clothes, put you behind the piano at the Old Colony and you're the one!"

"That's right," she admitted, wondering if he'd report her to the school board.

"Well, that's the damnedest!" He laughed. "You're terrific! I've seen you about a dozen times, at least. I thought you were maybe twenty-two or three. That's what threw me off. The lights and the rest of it. You're how old? Seventeen, eighteen?"

"I'll be seventeen in a few weeks."

"Too much! Listen, I've got one more class and you've got what, two?"

"Yes."

"You want to meet me for coffee later? We'll talk."

"All right. Where?" She couldn't believe this was happening.

"Um." He looked at the ceiling. "Parking lot, right? Red MG."

"I know which one."

"Okay!" He laughed. "Later, then."

She telephoned Jeanette to say she'd be late, not to wait dinner.

"Better put this over your head," he said, handing her his scarf when she arrived in the parking lot. "The top's broken, won't go up."

He drove so fast she couldn't think or breathe. It was terrifying. His hand moved the gear-stick up and down as he wheeled the car around corners, up and down streets, in and out of traffic until he pulled up in front of a converted mansion out on Indian Hill near the park.

"I'll make some sandwiches," he said, climbing out of the car. "We can relax, talk."

She looked up at the facade of the old, red-brick house, still unable to breathe properly. Something was going to happen. She knew it. She was terrified but excited, too. She wanted to see what would happen.

He took her coat and hung it along with his own in a closet by the front door as she wandered into the big, bare living room, looking at the upright Steinway in front of the french doors and the stacks of music piled on top of it. There was an old sprung sofa strewn with pillows and a big, sagging armchair. The bare floorboards looked very clean. Everything did.

"Hungry?" he asked, leading her out to the kitchen.

"A little." She looked at the scrubbed refectory table and mismated chairs either side of it, the pots of plants atop the refrigerator and radiator. The kitchen window was so clean it seemed to have no glass.

"Hey, sit down! Make yourself comfortable. I'll get the stuff, then we can eat, talk."

He put bread, butter, plates of ham and cheese on the table, along with two bottles of beer. Then he got a knife and sat down opposite her and started preparing two sandwiches.

"I just can't get over it," he laughed, shaking his head. "Finding you in one of my classes. Too much! I've been to the club to hear you so many times, I know the names of all the waitresses, the barmen, Sue, Yvonne, Ginny and Fay, Lucy. Good old warped Harry, tender of the bar. And his comrade, Ralph."

She'd never seen blue eyes like his before, pale, pale blue like a bleached robin's egg. And the way he smiled made everything inside her race around like a mouse in a cage.

"You talk too much!" he quipped, biting into his sandwich. "I'm a jazz buff from way back," he said between mouthfuls. "Love the Billie Holliday stuff you do. And those old thirties things. 'Lush Life,' for God's sake! And 'Moanin' Low.' You just don't hear that stuff anymore. Don't you like beer?"

"No."

"I'll drink it." He picked up her glass and set it down beside his own, all the while staring at her. "You're so pretty. Really pretty." He shook his head again. "The difference between you downtown and you in school! It's mind-blowing. You're not taking voice, are you?"

"No."

"Didn't think so. How the hell did you get started down there?"

"I just did."

She was so quiet, he found it difficult to talk to her.

"Listen," he said, "what're you going to do?"

"I don't know. I'm tired of school. If I thought I could, I'd probably quit and just sing."

"Big turn-on, huh?"

"I like it."

He reached over and took hold of her hand, startling her.

"D'you have a regular boyfriend or like that?"

"I don't have any."

"You're kidding!"

"Nobody ever asked me. Except sometimes at the club and Nick said I'm not to."

"I'm not sure you're real," he said. "C'mon, let's go in the other room. Maybe you'll play a couple of tunes for me."

"If you like."

She sat down in front of the piano and started to play, forcing herself deep into the music, trying to lose herself to sound. And for a few minutes, she succeeded; forgetting about Fennie and being in his apartment and what was going to happen.

He sat cross-legged on the floor watching her, listening, captured by her tremendous facility and emotional technique. Her hands were so strong, he felt he could actually see the strength in her wrists and forearms. He got up and moved to stand in back of her. Then, on impulse, he began unfastening her hair, smoothing it down. She stopped playing and held her breath, waiting. It was coming now. Going to happen.

"Don't stop," he said, his hands moving through her hair. "Keep playing."

She began again, finding it impossible to concentrate. His hands on her head felt so nice. She closed her eyes, relaxing under the soothing stroking. Finally, she had to

74

stop, lifting her hands from the keyboard. When he took her hand, she got up and went with him to the sofa.

"Do you like me?" he asked, his hand moving up under her hair to stroke her neck, sending shivers down her spine.

She nodded.

"Want to?" He nuzzled the side of her neck.

"Don't make me talk," she whispered. "Please don't. I can't talk."

"Okay," he said, drawing her closer. "I won't make you talk."

He kissed her. She felt as if she was suffocating but didn't move away. When he kissed her again, the tip of his tongue moved on her lips, and she opened her mouth, her heart pounding, her whole body hot.

"Put your arms around me," he said, kissing her cheek, then her ear, his tongue investigating the depths of her ear, making her head buzz.

Her arms felt leaden as she lifted them, feeling the solid breadth of his back and shoulders, the muscles in his arms. She liked the way he smelled.

He kissed her again, harder, surprising her. Then he got up, easily pulling her up with him. This was it. It was happening for real. She didn't know why. Or who he was. But she couldn't stop it from happening.

He left the bedroom dark and stood with her beside the bed. She kept swallowing, watching him as he lifted her sweater; raised her arms obediently as he pulled it up over her head. He unzipped her skirt and it fell down past her hips, dropped to the floor. She didn't want to look, didn't want to see what was happening, but couldn't look away. He unfastened her brassiere and looked at her breasts before covering them with his hands.

"You're so pretty," he said, brushing his mouth against hers.

He still thought she was pretty, so it was better. She looked up at him expectantly as his hands moved down to her waist and slid down under the elastic rims of her slip and pants, down inside over her buttocks as he made a soft, satisfied sound and brought her against him, kissing her slowly. His mouth was so sweet. He tasted so good, made her feel less and less heavy, more and more eager. She could feel a hardness between them, and something funny happened inside her head when she realized what it was.

She didn't know what else to do, so stood there while he took off his clothes, watching his white skin emerge, thinking he looked better, nicer without the clothes than he did with them. But when his trousers were off and he removed his shorts, she looked, then quickly looked away. Big and curving up. Real. It was going to get put into her. For the first time she felt frightened. But he got her to lie down on the bed, lay down on top of her and she pressed herself close to him liking the feeling of his body on top of hers. The closeness was wonderful, better than anything she'd ever known.

He kissed her ear again. A giggly, laughy sensation. Then he kissed her breasts, opening his mouth, sucking on her nipple and something in the very middle of her body twisted pleasurably. And she felt a little crazy as the twisting continued when he moved to the other breast. She was aware of his hand on her thigh, moving up, and stiffened, anticipating being hurt. But she couldn't pay attention because he was kissing her mouth again, then her breast, so when his fingers moved against her, she quivered at the unexpected pleasure of the sensation, opening herself, wanting more.

"Beautiful, wet," he murmured. "Feel good?"

"Oh yes," she whispered. "Yes."

His fingers rubbed at her rhythmically so that she wanted to move somehow, wanted to touch him all over, made quite dizzy by the motion of his hands. And then, his fingers had stopped rubbing and were sliding down, moving into her and she wanted to stop, to know what he was doing but his tongue was painting spirals in her mouth and she couldn't speak or ask him what or why. But all at once, the air left her lungs and she cried out in pain, everything good gone. His fingers went away but she could still feel them inside as he held her, saying, "It's all right, babe. Just checking to see."

"What?" she asked, feeling the hurt, a throbbing pain.

76

"Ssshh." He kissed her, starting to stroke her all over again.

She wanted to ask him what he'd done but there was no time, no room. He was turning her over onto her stomach, kissing her shoulders, her back, moving down. She liked this, losing sight of that pain he'd given her.

Her mouth opened in surprise when she felt his tongue between her legs and hands lifting her, one hand making its way under her, rubbing again so that she gasped for air, falling completely open to him. He kept touching her with his hand while his tongue came and went, probing; going on until she was panting, her hands clutching at the bedclothes as her body, of its own accord, moved wildly up and down, against his mouth, his hand. She felt so hot. She was damp with perspiration as he turned her on her back once more, his fingers still rubbing against her and she watched him put himself slowly inside her. Her mouth opened to form a surprised O as he filled her, then he took his hand away and lifted her legs. She closed her mouth, then opened it again and he kissed her, his tongue moving in her mouth. "Beautiful," he said, his mouth wet, pausing a moment to raise her from below so that he felt so far inside of her she'd be split apart by him. But then he brought his mouth back, moving inside her, each movement reaching an apex of incredible pleasure. She moved up against him, unaware of what she was doing, aware only that he was going on and on, plunging so deeply into her body, making every movement more thrilling so that she spread herself until her thighs ached and she clung to him frantically, her eyes wide, staring, wondering what was happening to her as she heard the wet sounds their bodies made moving this way. But it didn't matter what they looked like or how they sounded because suddenly she could hear nothing, see nothing because she was all of her humming like the plucked string of a harp, flying away out of her mind and body in a blinding, deafening pleasure so intense, so piercing that cries came from her mouth but failed to reach her ears and her body was jerking, jolted, writhing madly to get to the end of something that was better than anything else, the best. He moved faster and faster and the feeling came closer and closer until she groaned, her eyes snapping shut as the feeling tossed her into the center of a whirlpool and sucked her down, down, down, taking her away so she was not aware of his continued movements, his final, completing thrusts. She was aware only of *feeling*. Something reaching all the way through into her, penetrating everything.

He lay on her for a long time, his mouth open on her shoulder. Then he sighed and looked at her. "First times usually stink. But you're dynamite, babe. All right?"

"Do it again," she said giddily. "Do it again."

Later, feeling very wobbly in the knees and sore now, inside, she dressed and he drove her back to the park. They couldn't talk because of the noise of the car until he pulled up in front of her house.

During the ride, she imagined the two of them doing this all the time; imagined feeling that fantastic feeling over and over again. But when Fennie turned off the car, he said, "Don't go rushing off for a minute, okay?"

"Okay,"

"It's like this," he said, looking all at once discomfited. "I've got to keep it cool with the conservatory people. You understand? It's like I need the job and taking me on, they've made a policy change. Every time they see me, the hair and the clothes, it makes them go pale. So, I really can't let it get around that I'm seeing one of the students. You know?"

She despised him. Suddenly, she was filled from head to toe with hatred for him, revulsion at what they'd just done together. She wrenched open the door of the car and ran away, into the house.

When they asked her what was wrong, she lied, said she didn't feel well, not well enough to be at school. Her father and Jeanette accepted that, shrugged their shoulders and left her alone. She stayed in her room trying not to think about Fennie, but thinking about him, hating him. You used me, she thought again and again. Used me. I hate you. And I was stupid for letting you do it. I hate me, too.

The week before Christmas, she was upstairs in her

78

room, lethargically wrapping gifts when Nick telephoned.

"I wanted to let you know," he said. "I'm moving to New York to join up with Amalgamated Booking."

"You're *leaving?*"

"First of the year. The thing is, I'd like to keep you on my books. So, if and when you want to, if you ever want to, call me in New York, and I'll take care of you. We could do some good things for you there."

"But *why* are you going?"

"Rising in the world, dear," he laughed. "It's a good gig. Amalgamated's a big-time outfit."

He gave her the new address and phone number, wished her a good Christmas and hung up.

The news that he was leaving, that she wouldn't have him to fall back on if she wanted to work, brought her down into the depths of the worst depression she'd ever experienced. She'd been keeping Nick in reserve. Just in case. Certainly, there were other agents in town. But Nick knew, understood the way she worked and felt. He was very patient with her, taking time to explain the things she needed to know. Other agents just wouldn't.

She put the gifts away unwrapped and sat down on the bedroom floor, trying to figure out why she felt so shattered. She knew why. And she didn't feel she'd be able to live with it. She got up and went in search of Jeanette.

With the pregnancy, Jeanette seemed to look younger and younger each day. Lisa found her in the kitchen with the cook, making paté. Her hair was plaited into two thick braids, and her face was pink from the heat of the kitchen. She was wearing an embroidered, smocked dress of a sunny yellow that gave her a very fresh, youthful look.

"Come help, chérie!" Jeanette smiled over at her. "We have need of more hands." She picked up a towel and wiped her hands, then reached for a cigarette that was burning in the ashtray. Lisa watched Jeanette inhale, feeling herself toppling helplessly into a mood so black it dimmed the sunshine in the kitchen and filled her mouth with a sharp, metallic taste.

"I need you," Lisa said faintly, holding on to the doorframe, pleading with her eyes. "I need to talk to you."

79

Jeanette put out the cigarette and they went through to Jeanette's old suite which had been converted to guest rooms.

"What has happened?" Jeanette asked, sitting with Lisa on the loveseat.

"Nick's leaving. He's going to New York. Jeanette, I know it shouldn't . . . I don't know why but I feel so terrible. I wish he hadn't called. What's wrong with me? Why do I feel this way?"

"Have a cigarette." Jeanette gave her one. "How is it you feel?"

"I thought he'd be here so I could keep on working. As soon as I heard his voice on the telephone I knew everything would go wrong. Jeanette," she whispered, "I'm so depressed. When I close my eyes, everything's black. I feel as if I want to die. I know I shouldn't feel this way but I can't help it. I can't stop. When he told me, all I could think was, I want to die. I know I don't really want to die. I just can't stop feeling this way."

"When Letty died, it was this way?" Jeanette asked.

"It was terrible. I couldn't explain it then. I can talk to you about it now but even while I'm sitting here telling you all about it, I'm thinking about going somewhere to die. I'm so scared. I don't care about anything. I keep telling myself I do. But when I feel this way, I don't care. I'm nobody and nothing matters. I'm not doing the things I want to do. But I don't *know* what I want to do."

"I do not know what to tell you, Lisa. You frighten me with all of this. What is it you wish me to say? Tell me."

Visibly shaking, Lisa crushed out her cigarette. There were so many things shouting inside her head she thought the noise would crack her eardrums. All she could do was cry. Jeanette watched, feeling utterly helpless, able to do no more than put an arm around Lisa's shoulders.

"I . . . Jeanette," Lisa held on, feeling a great aching pain in her chest. "I don't know . . . who I *am*. Nothing means anything. I went . . . I went home with one of the teachers from school . . . we did . . . I did everything. Then I hated him because he just wanted to use me. It's all because I'm no one. I don't know. I can never say the things people want to hear me say . . . about love. Caring. Am I sick, Jeanette? Do I have to go to a doctor? I *hate* my life. The horrible things I've said to you. I hate myself for that. I want to go away. I have to. I can't *know* here. I can't find out."

"You think to go away will change how you feel?"

"I don't know," she cried, hiding her face against Jeanette's shoulder. "I just have to *do* something. I have to be somewhere, do something so I can stop feeling this way."

"Where would you go?"

"Maybe I could go to New York."

"You have an attachment for Nick?"

"Not that way. He understands, Jeanette. He knows what I can do and he doesn't make me do anything more than that. *Please!* Please, I've *got* to go!"

"Oh, Lisa," Jeanette said uncertainly. "You are very young to make so serious a move. Your father . . ."

"I can't stay here forever. I can't. Sometimes I feel as if I want to crash down the walls, explode out of this house. I can't find out anything here. You've got to make him understand I have to go!"

"That is not so easy, Lisa. I am not sure I understand what you feel."

"I don't know either. I'm not sure what I want to do. I just know I have to keep working. It's all I have. If I quit now, I'll have nothing left. I'll die."

"So you will go to New York whatever your father says."

"I *have* to. School's finished for me. I told you that ages ago. And don't say I'm too young or any of that. Nick always looks out for me. I can take care of myself. I have to go, Jeanette. I just can't stay here for the rest of my life. There's nowhere for me to go here."

"And where will you 'go' in New York?"

"I don't know. I'll be working. That's all I care about right now. I don't want to go without . . . with bad feelings. I'd like it to be something we all agreed on."

"When would you go?"

"I haven't thought that far."

Jeanette sighed, knowing there was no way they would be able to prevent Lisa from making this move. "Think of it now, Lisa," she said seriously. "You must have plans formed in your mind before you fly away. It is no good to do this."

"Maybe after the baby's born?"

"What then?"

"I'm working it out. I want to take driving lessons and then get a car. I'll need a car. I could use my own money for whatever I need. I won't expect Papa to do anything. But you've *got* to make him let me go! Please, please, Jeanette! Nothing else matters to me. Only this."

"You will have to speak to him," Jeanette said firmly. "You must explain yourself to him."

"He'll never let me do it!" Lisa wailed.

"Perhaps. Perhaps not. *I* understand a little what it is you want, chérie. It is fair, eh, to make him understand too? You are not yet seventeen. It is very very young to go away from your home to do the things you wish to do. I know if we do not agree to permit this you will run from us. And I . . . this would grieve me. Papa and I will talk. But you must speak with him. You cannot go through life simply doing what you feel you must do. There are proper ways to accomplish these things. Not just for other people but for yourself, too. Would you not feel better going away from here knowing you still had a home to return to? You would not wish to burn all the bridges?"

"No." The idea of having to explain herself to Hugh—regardless of their increased abilities to communicate—gave her a feeling of futility. She knew absolutely he'd never understand.

"He might surprise you, chérie," Jeanette said. "Many times, the people we think we know can surprise us. For me, it was expected somehow that you would want to go. Now you will have to discover for yourself your father's expectations."

"He'll say no. I know it."

"Zut!" Jeanette sighed impatiently. "Again so stubborn! Wait and you will see what he says and doesn't say."

Hugh heard her out—Jeanette introduced the subject over dinner—then set down his knife and fork and looked across at her. Jeanette quietly excused herself and went out to the kitchen.

"I thought," he began. "I mean, I had hoped . . . Things seem to have been going so well. Are you so unhappy at home, Lisa?"

"I'm not unhappy. That hasn't anything to do with it. That doesn't even matter, papa. I just have to *go*. I have to."

"I see," he said, pushing away his plate, lighting a cigarette. "Jeanette will be very lonely for you. She's deeply attached to you, Lisa."

"What about you?" she asked angrily, surprising herself. "Don't you ever talk about how *you* feel? It's always *we* love you, *we* feel this way or that. We. *We*. Don't *you* give a damn?"

His eyes widened as he studied her pale features and he reached across to hold her hand.

"I care very much," he said, shaken. "We're very much alike, you and I. I seem to have as much difficulty as you stating my feelings."

"Please!" She closed her eyes, clinging to his hand. "I didn't mean it that way. The words came out wrong." She opened her eyes and looked at him. "Maybe it doesn't make any sense to you," she said. "I don't know if it does to me. All I know is that playing, singing, I feel alive, real. The rest of it, my life is just time to get through until I can get up there and sing. It's all I ever *think* about. I can't stay here and pretend to be a good little schoolgirl. It's not what I am, papa. I don't know what I am yet. But I know I want to get out and find out."

"I suppose that's your right," he said quietly.

"I won't change my mind."

"You don't have to. I won't keep you here, Lee. Not if you don't want to stay."

He'd never before called her anything but Lisa and his use of Jimmy's nickname for her reduced her to tears.

"Everything'll work out," he said. "I'll help you any way I can. Look at me." He touched her chin, urging her to open her eyes. "*I* love you. Your happiness is important to me. It's true. Sometimes, one has to go on instinct. I have to go with mine now. Because I don't understand why, at your age, you're so fired-up to do all this. But you can always come home, Lee. It's not a sin to want to come home."

"Part of me doesn't even want to go, not really. I'm *not* unhappy here, papa. Honestly. But inside, inside I know I have to get away. I feel as if I stay, I'll come apart in this house and blow the walls open. I'd like to go after the baby's born."

"Go when you're ready. I can see it's what you have to do. You're a complicated girl. So much of what you say and feel is alien to me, hard to understand. But I'll do whatever I can to help, in any way I can. It's the least I can do. I don't like to think of you leaving with unpleasantness. Since you're determined to go, I won't fight you."

"Papa. I just want to say . . . to tell you . . . I'm so happy for you. What I want to say is that you and Jeanette . . . I know how much you love each other. I know it doesn't mean you've forgotten mama. But I understand that that's different. Maybe, if you could think of the way you feel about Jeanette and then think about my music, you'd see it's the same for me. I know you can't feel about people the way you do about something that's only *sound*, but it's like love to me. I want you to have your own happiness. You're happy now, having the baby . . . everything. I want to get out and get my own. But I do want to wait, to see the baby."

He smiled, "Believe it or not," he said, "I can understand your wanting that."

"Can you?" Once again, his understanding caught her unprepared. "Why?"

"Because . . . I'm not sure I know how to put it. Do you ever write music, Lee?"

Color rose into her face and she nodded.

"I expect it must be, to you, like completed music. Am I wrong?"

"No," she smiled, delighting him. "You're exactly right. It's something you make that you can see and hear."

"I'm beginning to know you," he said. "It seems a bit of a shame in some ways that it's all happening now when you're on the verge of leaving."

"Isn't it better to know a little, papa, than never know at all?"

"It's better," he agreed.

"Papa?"

"Yes, dear?"

"Thank you."

"It's all right, Lee. It'll all work out. And Lee?"

"Yes, papa?"

"Thank *you*."

Chapter 6

In the weeks before she left, Lisa watched Jeanette with the baby, marveling over how casually and naturally Jeanette handled Aimée. She didn't fuss or coo over her as Lisa had thought she might, but treated her with a kind of sensible loving, carrying the baby on her shoulder as she went about maintaining the household.

The baby had come six weeks early and it was three weeks before Jeanette was able to bring Aimée home from the hospital. The entire time the baby was at the hospital, Jeanette made four daily trips back and forth in order to nurse her.

"So I will not lose my milk," she explained to Lisa. "I have always wished to do this," she laughed. "I think it will never happen. And now, here we are! C'est incroyable!"

Lisa thought so too. Aimée was the first infant Lisa had ever had the opportunity to study at close range. Everything about the baby was fascinating. And Jeanette entrusted Aimée to Lisa, smiling with amusement as Lisa examined the baby's fingers and ears, touching her wispy hair.

"I'd like to have one," Lisa said. "I just knew it'd be like this, having one."

"Time enough," Jeanette said. "For now, you are so busy with driving lessons and everything else, I think baby will have to wait a time, eh?"

Lisa laughed.

It was one of the happiest times she'd ever known. She'd sit upstairs with Jeanette as she nursed the baby, captivated by the oneness of mother and child. Jeanette sat in the armchair by the window with the thin February sunshine picking up gray-blue highlights in her hair, smiling serenely. Lisa watched the baby nurse, falling into a dreamlike, peaceful state, experiencing small shocks of pleasure every time she thought about where she'd be in just a few more weeks. Everything was working out so well. New York, in her mind, was like a picture of the Emerald City in the Wizard of Oz. She could remember exactly the day—she'd been very little—when Jeanette had taken her to see the movie. And the Emerald City twinkling in the distance had taken her breath away. Now she was on her way there. Papa had insisted on giving her luggage as a going-away gift. And Jeanette had given her a makeup case, completely fitted with small bottles and jars and traveling aids—small packets of shampoo and soap. She was all ready to go.

All the way to New York she kept seeing them standing waving goodbye. Hugh, surprisingly, in tears; and Jeanette, smiling, the baby on her hip. She'd quickly kissed them goodbye, slid into the car and driven away without looking back. By the time she was on the entrance ramp to the Shore Expressway, her head was full of pictures of New York and anticipation for the life she was about to begin.

But from the first, New York frightened her. The pot-holed drive into the city, the confusing one-way streets, pedestrians disregarding traffic signals all made her tense and nervous. She lost her way several times before finding an indoor parking garage near Nick's office. Walking from the garage to his office on Park Avenue, she looked up, feeling curiously reduced in size by the towering buildings.

86

Nick, though, was just the same. He didn't give her a chance to sit down, but grabbed his coat and hustled her back out through the reception area, into an elevator and down the street to a Chinese restaurant.

"We'll eat, then I'll take you over, show you the apartment. Where'd you park?"

"Near here," she answered, finding everything otherworldly, like a bizarre night-dream.

He talked and she tried to listen but heard only parts of sentences, random phrases. She agreed to everything he said, wearied by the idea of his having to repeat everything.

The gist of it was that she'd have a week before starting her first gig in a club in Akron. They didn't use lounge acts and he wanted to see if she couldn't play the date up front, without the piano. She kept saying yes, yes, not knowing or realizing what she was consenting to. And, finally, the meal ended and they went to get her car to go to her new apartment.

"It was the best I could do on such short notice, dear," he said, as they rode up in the elevator with her bags. "A little on the overpriced side, but you need a good building with a doorman and a working super. I rented some stuff for you to use until you buy your own."

She walked with him through the one-bedroom apartment, as he pointed out the dishwasher, the built-in clothes hamper in the bathroom. The rented furniture was cheap imitation Swedish modern.

"Probably," he said, "first thing you should do is put the car in the garage, then hop on the subway and go to Macy's or one of the big stores and order yourself a decent bed and a few things." He wrote down the address of the garage where he'd arranged for her to keep the car. "Much cheaper than midtown," he said. "You don't need wheels in town. It's just a hassle. There's nowhere to park and the indoor places overcharge and bang the hell out of your car. Better to leave it uptown till you're set to go. I've got to get back to the office. My private number's on the back of this." He gave her a card. "Are you all right, Lisa?"

"Fine," she said, dry-mouthed. "I'll take you back, if you like, on my way to this garage."

She pushed through a revolving door into the living insanity of Macy's where small, angry-looking women were fighting over counters-full of bargain items, muttering to themselves. She wanted to go right back out again but thought of that rented bed and the numberless bodies that had slept in it and found her way to the proper department.

She ordered a bed then escaped, only to find she'd come out a different door than the one she'd used going in and had no idea where she was. She looked up and down the street, ready to cry, and finally saw a cruising cab and waved it down.

Back at the apartment, sitting in the living room, she considered turning around and going back home. But then she remembered the bank draft she had to deposit and the fact that there was no food beyond the breakfast things Nick had thoughtfully provided and got up and went out again.

The bank manager gave her coffee while he went about opening an account for her, arranging the transfer of her funds. He went away to make a phone call and returned to say, "I've been advised you have an attorney downtown. He and I will work out the trust details, so there's no need for you to wait this out. I'll give you some complementary checks until yours come through and then you can be on your way." He was so polite and soft-spoken, she felt mildly reassured by the time she left. Papa had seen to everything, even a lawyer.

The supermarket looked dirty and when she saw a cockroach crawling casually over the heads of lettuce, she hurried away to buy sandwiches at the delicatessen next door to her apartment building. She never set foot in another supermarket the entire time she lived in New York. She kept only milk, cream, orange juice and butter in her refrigerator and ate all her meals out or went to take-out restaurants.

Her first night in the apartment, she slept on the floor. The next morning, she went to see Nick to give him a check for the money he'd laid out and asked him to call the rental place and have all the furniture taken away.

"You know," he laughed, lighting a cigar, "for a kid, you're some kind of eccentric. What d'you mean you slept on the floor? Are you kidding?"

"I couldn't sleep in a bed when I don't know who else has slept in it. I'll wait until my own comes."

"It's your floor and your body," he shrugged, smiling.

She walked a great deal, slowly gathering the sense of the streets; establishing East Side and West Side, uptown, downtown, midtown. She found some stores she liked, began buying things. On the second night, she telephoned home. Jeanette answered and Hugh listened on the bedroom extension as Lisa restructured her enthusiasm for how good it all was. And, after talking to them, it didn't seem as bad as it had initially. Just because it was different didn't mean she wouldn't get used to it, like the city in time. But even pep-talking herself, something at the back of her head told her she'd never like New York. It was too big, too noisy, too dirty.

The following Sunday at seven A.M. she left for Akron. All the way there, she speculated on how it would feel working six nights a week, seeing a new city. But from the outset, Akron went wrong. Her room at the Sheraton was over-furnished, over-heated and dustily ugly. The city itself made her think New York wasn't so bad after all. Akron looked and smelled dreadful. The downtown area was like a ghost town.

The club itself was attractive, but the owner talked too quickly and Lisa couldn't follow half of what he said. The house trio was good but unimaginative and when they rehearsed on Monday afternoon, Lisa knew it wasn't going to work. She felt gawky and awkward standing alone in the middle of the stage trying to sing the arrangements she'd written out for the trio. The house pianoman faked most of the changes, throwing her off and she returned to the Sheraton to have dinner knowing the night would be a disaster.

No one had ever announced her before. She listened to the mincing M.C., embarrassed for him, and went onstage with the handmike, staring into the spotlight, singing tonelessly through the whole set. The audience applauded disinterestedly and only perked up when the second act, a very pretty belly-dancer, came on stage tinkling, finger-cymbals clinking.

Lisa ran downstairs to her dressing room to find some money then back upstairs to the public telephone to call Nick in New York.

"That man's going to fire me," she told him. "You've got to call him right away, here at the club and ask him to put the piano downstage in the spot and let me play my own charts. I can't *just sing*! They thought I was awful and I was."

"Okay, dear. Take it easy," Nick said. "I'll call Charlie and get him to fix it for the second show. Everything all right, otherwise?"

"Oh, I don't know. I guess so. Just call him, please?"

"I will, dear. You go have some coffee and relax. I'll take care of it."

She was right about Charlie. He was just approaching her with a serious-looking face, fat cigar in hand, when the call came in from Nick. He argued loudly for several minutes, then listened for several more, finally saying, "Yeah, yeah, yeah," broke off and went to talk to the trio and then to the waiter who assisted with the stage shows.

"Piano stays put," he told Lisa, flourishing the cigar. "But we'll move the spot. This don't work, you can forget it, huh?"

"It'll work," she promised, rubbing her wet hands together. "You'll see."

There was a larger audience for the second show and she took a deep breath as the M.C. faked another preposterous introduction for her. But seeing the spotlit piano, she was able to make her way onstage, even managing a smile; enjoying the flow of her chiffon dress as she made her way to the piano.

It worked. From the minute she slid into the spot, she had them. The bassist and drummer followed the changes more smoothly when she laid them down and by the second number, she was into her stride. She did two encores, managed to introduce the bassist and drummer and say, "Thank you," before climbing down.

"So, *okay!*" Charlie said, pounding her happily in the center of her bare back. "That's more like it, huh? I'll tell your hotshot agent we'll pick up your option."

She stayed three weeks in Akron and then drove back to New York to find that the bed had been delivered in her absence. The mattress, box springs and frame, still in their packagings, were leaning against the bedroom wall. She unpacked, changed into levis and put the bed together. The next day, she went to Porthault and spent three very pleasurable hours buying linens. New York, after Akron, felt more comfortable. And, somehow, it seemed the worst was over. She was settled, wrote out a rent check on the first of each month, and was already booked solid for the next year.

But it wasn't until her next out-of-town gig that the loneliness hit her. She arrived in Mason City, Iowa, after two straight days of driving. She checked into a Travelodge and collasped on the bed, overcome with fatigue and a hungry need to see and feel something or someone familiar. Her once-a-week calls home were good but once the connection was broken, Jeanette and her papa seemed to have ceased to exist. Nothing was quite the way she'd thought it would be.

Wearily, she got up and found her way to the club to introduce herself to the clubowner and check out the piano, the sound system and the lights. After her experience in Akron, she was careful to warn Nick about ensuring that all her engagements were either as a lounge act single or in performance with a house band. She refused to work out front without the piano for protection.

"I'm not a singer," she told him. "I'm hopeless without the piano. I don't sound right. I don't look right. And the audiences start talking and don't want to listen."

She'd expected an unsophisticated, rural sort of audience in Mason City, but she was met with requests for sophisticated numbers she herself liked tremendously—'When the World Was Young,' and 'Miss Otis Regrets,'—and loud, appreciative applause. At the end of her first show on opening night, she walked outside and stared up and down the length of the deserted street, hurting with her aloneness. "I need something," she whispered to the silent street, "something, someone." Applause was something; it was wonderful. But after it ended, there seemed nothing left for her. As long as she was playing, she was fine. But as soon as she stopped, depression sidled dangerously close.

She got into her car to watch the minutes slowly tick off on the dashboard clock as music from the radio floated randomly around her rememberings (thinking of how good she'd felt that one time with Fennie, craving those feelings again). "I won't think about it," she tried to tell herself. But she couldn't stop thinking about it, feeling a terrible, gaping hunger inside; the need for something. She could put a name to it but didn't dare.

She got out of the car and went inside to dress for the second show. In the back room, the bassist jumped up guiltily when she came through the door, then sat back down saying, "Jesus! Thought it was the boss." He had a hand-rolled cigarette cupped in his hand and held it out, asking, "Wanna drag?"

Curious, she went closer. She took the cigarette from him and drew on it.

"Suck it in 'n hold it down," he said dreamily. "It's pure shit. Good stuff."

She filled her lungs with the acrid smoke, then returned the cigarette to him, watching as he sucked at it, closing his eyes as he passed it back to her again. She did as he did, returned the cigarette and went back into one of the booths to change her clothes. She wasn't aware of anything happening to her. She just no longer felt anything but calmed and went out to do her set, surprised to find that she was smiling. When, at the end of her encores, the waiter came over to whisper to her that the gentleman in the back at the small table wished to buy her a drink, she nodded and made her way to the rear of the club.

She didn't emerge from the ephemeral, smoke-induced lassitude until she was standing inside the door of her room at the Travelodge, being kissed by the man from the club. And she was so eased by his nearness, by the eagerness of his hands on her breasts, she closed her eyes and held him, grateful.

Mid-morning, when she awakened, sprawled sideways, naked on the twisted sheets, her immediate reaction was one of horror. But as she walked into the bathroom, she said aloud, "It doesn't matter. I won't think about it." And she didn't, wouldn't. She felt better, and that was all that mattered.

After that, it happened at least once in every city she played: in Madison, in Omaha, Minneapolis, Indianapolis, Toledo and Detroit, in Cleveland and Buffalo and Toronto, in Montreal, Boston and Hartford, in Memphis, Milwaukee, Lincoln and Columbus.

She came and went, read and rehearsed through the days, came alive and sang in the evenings; got through time.

She liked being on the road, traveling from one city to the next. There was a definite, rare sort of exhilaration to racing down interstate highways at five A.M. without seeing another car for as many as forty or fifty miles. Watching the sun rise at six A.M. was a privileged kind of viewing. Getting across as many as fifteen hundred miles in one weekend, she had some sense of destination. But, upon arrival, it all evaporated, leaving her to face still another square, air-conditioned room in what was rapidly becoming an endless series.

Patterns developed. She stopped to eat only at certain types of fast-food restaurants: McDonald's but never Burger King; Colonel Sanders but never any of the dozens of prototypes; the International House of Pancakes rather than the trolley-car diners set at the apex of an apron of blacktop. She was a connoisseur of junk food, so much so that when she played in Memphis at an elite, top-of-the-bank-building private club where for three weeks she nightly feasted on Steak Diane and fresh avocado, Tournedos Rossini and artichokes vinaigrette, enormous shrimp cocktails all sumptuously presented to her at a corner table by two attending waiters, her first stop upon departure was at McDonald's for a Big Mac and a large order of over-salted, greasy French fries.

She arrived in each city to check into her room at the

Travelodge, Holiday Inn or Howard Johnson's. She hung away her clothes, carefully set her music case and portable keyboard on the desk, checked the drawers for postcards, scanned the bathroom, and then went out to have a look at the club and meet the new club owner.

Club owners were rarely men of words. Almost all of them had a penchant for thick, rancid-smelling cigars and ornate, monogrammed rings. Most of them, at some point during her engagement, drank too much of an evening and proprietarily fondled her in some dim corner, backing off at once when she stated her age. Nick had told her what to say and how to handle them and it worked. At the first brief touch on breast or bottom, she'd say, "I'm only eighteen," or, "I'm only nineteen," or, finally, "I'm only twenty." They removed their hands, chewed thoughtfully on their cigars for a moment, then went away.

There were always preferred customers with whom Lisa was expected to sit and drink. The women usually wore expensive cosmetics applied in out-of-date fashion with heavy, dark eyeliner and blue eyeshadow. The men seemed to suffer perpetually with the fit of their trousers, constantly, surreptitiously reaching down to shift their equipment to a more comfortable position. Lisa paid her duty visits to these preferred people while they and the club owner rattled on about some deal or other or some person or other. She smiled and drank whatever she'd been given to drink before excusing herself to return to the stage.

For the most part, the club owners spent a great deal of money on getting and maintaining a good piano, but next to nothing on the mike and sound system. In most of the clubs, changing room facilities did not exist, and she was obliged to dress in her hotel room and enter the club as if she were that minute going onstage. This lack of changing rooms also meant that there was nowhere for her to go between shows so that, in the states where it was allowed, she sat at the bar near the hatch where the tray of 'garbage' for the drinks made its home, or at an unoccupied table in the lounge if there was one, or, often, she went out to her car and sat, listening to the radio, trying to read in the dim, interior light until her next show or her next set. As a direct result of all her reading in bad light and performing in the bright spots, she developed a form of sun blindness and she needed to wear sunglasses outdoors. If she forgot the glasses her eyes would water, she'd sneeze, blink, and, unable to focus, she'd have to stop somewhere to buy another pair.

Each afternoon, no matter what town or what club, she'd make her way to the (usually closed) club, wrinkling her nose at the stale, night-before smells clinging to the uncirculated air, to set out her music and practice. Two to four hours each afternoon.

When she was satisfied she was on top of all the current tunes that might be requested, she set aside that music and played the classical exercises and scales, concluding with some favored piece from memory. She was very much afraid of allowing her techniques to become slipshod and careless and forced herself to practice and sight-read more and more difficult compositions to keep at the peak of her ability. It was important to maintain whatever routines she could. And since it was impossible for her to keep to any routine other than her practicing, she rehearsed diligently wherever she was. At home, in New York, she rented rehearsal rooms and spent the better part of her days in the city at some yellowed, neglected keyboard. But it proved something, and she felt pleased with herself. She was as completely conditioned to her music as were the ballet students she'd seen in her days at the conservatory; those sweating, determined kids who spent five, six, seven hours every day of their lives forcing their bodies into ever more perfect attitudes.

So she took care, at least, of her music.

But there were the morning hours—she felt deeply guilty if she slept later than nine-thirty in the morning, even if she'd worked until three the night before and hadn't gotten to bed until four or four-thirty—and the late afternoons and early evening hours when she wanted to dig her fingernails into her skin and rip off chunks of herself. She'd read one paperback novel after another, making herself pay attention to what was unraveling in the story. But she read too quickly and was always running out of reading material. Wherever she went, she left behind stacks of spine-bent paperbacks.

95

The worst was early morning, when, awakening with a smile, she'd realize as she went about bathing and brushing her hair that she had nothing to do. Movies weren't open in the morning. There was no one to see or talk to. Fellow performers she ran into now and then rarely, if ever, got up before one or two. She had no interest in historic landmarks or the cultural curiosities of the cities she played. So she'd walk up and down her motel room with her fingers coiled up into the palms of her hands and an ugly, gray feeling clinging to her spine and shoulders like some parasitic animal, using up time until she could go to practice.

Summers, provided there weren't more than two or three other people present, she'd swim at the motel pool, do a slow crawl up and down, back and forth the length of the pool until, her arms and legs trembled with exertion.

And there were the formula men, the ones she could sit and drink with, talk to. They were unusual, knowing types who seemed to sense what it was she needed and, without words, an invitation was made and accepted. She spent, during those years, numberless nights sleeping in the beds of men she saw only once. These men all shared certain characteristics: they were all older, past forty; they all had a way of visually demonstrating their appreciation and desire; they were all very gentle and grateful; and they all left her lonely, and a little more eager to get back to her music. And a little more depressed.

She learned, with time, how to make social conversation, coming to know which remarks satisfied the obligation of her free drink. She talked but her mind was elsewhere, putting notes and chords together, preparing mental music that she longed to try out on unsuspecting audiences. She wasn't bold enough yet to slip a piece of her own between popular, known pieces.

Walking weak-legged out of some man's motel room at five or six in the morning, she'd look at the sky and the parking lot and erase everything that had gone before; hearing early-morning sounds that had a purity and freshness untouched by the things she did away from music. She'd stare at herself in medicine cabinet mirrors, looking at her face, wondering sometimes that none of the things she did showed in her face.

There were instances when, in the middle of some heated sexual activity, her mind would click on and she'd think, "What *is* this?" repelled by her own lusting energies and those of these past-prime men who so rapaciously kissed, caressed and tasted her body. How could she do these things? she asked herself, all the while opening her mouth or thighs to some tumescent male.

Between afternoon practice time and showtime, she'd find herself dressed and made up too soon, too early. She'd slouch into a chair and light a cigarette, staring at the Paris street scene on the motel room wall, thinking, I'm still no one. Nothing. She wanted to smash the pattern, to move somehow in a different direction. But she had no idea of the direction and kept hoping a picture would form for her. She dreamed of some future time when she might know who and what she was. But in the meantime, she was always ready too soon to go to work. So she sat, each evening, for at least an hour, waiting out the minutes until she could get up, check her evening bag for room and car keys, tip money for the waiters and barmaids, and leave, on her way to the evening's high, the evening's applause.

The blackness which had come only occasionally when she'd been at home now seemed to be becoming permanent, broken only by interludes of performance either musical or sexual; deepened especially after her sexual encounters.

She smoked whenever someone offered her grass but didn't go in search of it. She drank if someone bought her drinks, but never ordered them. She made love if invited by a formula man but otherwise, sometimes for months at a stretch, never sought in any way to accommodate herself. She volunteered only music. And within the music, gave everyone everything: all her fears and loneliness, her hopes, and her dreams, her sorrows.

There were two occasions she remembered always. One was in Indianapolis in the early evening, a nearly-empty lounge where she sang sad songs for no particular purpose to a woman alone at a table near the door. Forgetting herself within the boundaries of the lyrics, she looked up to see the woman—an attractive, well-dressed woman in her early thirties—gazing wide-eyed at her with tears streaking her cheeks. Lisa knew, looking across the room, she was looking at her own possible future self and watched, feeling somehow bruised, as the woman placed a bill on the table, picked up her handbag and quietly went away.

The other was in New York, on one of the very rare occasions when she played the city, when a young couple directly in front of the stand sat with glazed eyes, looking as if they were inhaling the sounds she made, all the while, utterly unaware they were being observed by everyone in the place, the young man's hand stroked and fondled the girl's breasts and the girl, breathing jaggedly, kept her hand out of sight beneath the table. When Lisa wound down the final eight of the last number of the set, her eyes frantically raked the room for a formula face, desperate to be held and whispered to. There was no one there. She went home and stayed up most of the night writing a song about the morning streets of New York called "Early Morning People." She tried to blot the image of that young couple from her mind but once she'd completed the song, it came right back at her.

The next day, Sunday, she walked in Central Park and, while leaning over the rail of the footbridge, watching the boats passing underneath, was approached by a young man who looked so much like Fennie she could barely catch her breath. He wasn't so young, on closer inspection, or so clean either but she went with him to his loft downtown and made love with him for three hours. Then she went back to her apartment, put her fingers against the back of her throat and made herself vomit. She'd done something that frightened her and swore she'd never do it again.

She got through her final week at the club in New York only by reminding herself constantly of the good, long drive she'd have the following Sunday morning. It was that image of highway sliding past and her newest car under her control that prevented her from doing any one of the several finalizing acts that kept presenting themselves to her. She was now kept company by the image of herself in a soothingly warm tub of water that was slowly turning pink with the blood from her slit wrists. She could see herself, lazily smiling, her eyelids drooping closed as the tranquility of death lulled her away from the sick nightmare of living.

Oddly enough, the deeper into depression she fell, the easier it was to converse with people. Because it didn't matter. She could talk with an external insouciance while, inside, her brain was busily filling the tub, then setting out the shining single-edged blades from her music case.

She maintained her habit of telephoning home every Sunday but the sounds of Jeanette's or her father's voices served only to drop her a little lower into the blackness. After these weekly conversations she'd lie on her motel bed and smoke one cigarette after another, trembling and perspiring, yearning to get up and go home but taunted by the sheer impossibility of doing it. She was ashamed to have them see what she'd become.

It wasn't until the Sunday afternoon when she phoned home and Jeanette put Amiée on the telephone to talk to her that Lisa realized four years of her life had gone by without her noticing. After hearing Aimée's piping voice asking, "Are you coming to see me, Lisa?" she felt suddenly grounded. Aimée could talk on the telephone. She was no longer an infant lying in the crook of Jeanette's arm, greedily nursing.

And she herself was no longer a kid, trying to fill her life with applause, trying to find some sort of identity. She worked. She was paid progressively more and more money. But she seemed able to come alive only when the spotlight came on and her fingers picked out the opening changes of her first number.

Chapter 7

She preferred playing the lounges because instead of only two shows a night, she could play however much she wanted during the nine-till-two or ten-till-three contracted time.

Her options were always picked up. She never spent less than two weeks in any one place, more often six or eight weeks. All the time knowing no one. She needed something more. She needed it, and her music needed it. The idea of spending the rest of her adult life playing these lounges was becoming daily less attractive. From time to time, there were guys who came on, claiming to know someone in the recording business who'd be really interested in hearing her. But that's all it was, a come-on. And she ignored the lines, smiling her social smile, knowing better. Nick often told her it was up to her to make her own decisions. If she wanted to get out of the lounges, all she had to do was say so. But there was a certain security, a certain regularity to life on the road that she thought she still needed. She thought so. She was no longer sure of anything. Except her music. She was always sure of that.

It all caught up with her when she was booked to play Mr. Friday's in Chicago. Afterward, she was never quite sure of the details. There were bits and pieces of it she could remember but not the play-by-play whole.

After her last set on opening night, one of the waitresses invited her to join a group of them—waiters and staff—who were going somewhere for a party. She agreed, dimly aware of an undercurrent, a sensation of something going on, but not sure what. They followed her in two cars to her hotel so she could leave her car and go with them. She put the car into the slot for her room and got into the back seat with two of the waiters who looked oddly different, smaller, less massive out of their uniforms. They handed her a paper cup of scotch and soda and she drank automatically, reluctant to offend their hospitality. She remembered later that the man who'd given her the cup only stirred the icecubes around before handing it back to her. And then her vision suddenly became warped, distorted and the faces of the two men on each side of her ballooned, then shrank to tiny, microscopic proportions. The interior of the car shivered, shuddered, changing shape. Flowers burst out of the ashtrays, giant blooms whose scent was overpoweringly strong.

There was a time when the car motion ceased and she was being taken into a house somewhere and she recognized the thickness of incense in the air and the sound of a stereo with too much bass. Candles. And one of the waitresses, it was the one who'd had the silicone injections in her breasts, she was showing her breasts to everyone, lifting her arms over head saying, "I can do it now. See that! They don't even move."

Someone took away Lisa's coat and put a drink in her hand. She looked into the glass and saw small elfin faces smiling up at her, floating in the liquid and set the glass down, watching the petite waitress going from one person to another showing them all her new breasts.

And then someone was showing them Lisa's breasts, saying, "This is the real thing," laughing. Hands floated through the air disembodied, touching her, making slow-motion movements over her breasts, turning her around and around. She was on a merry-go-round and couldn't stop, couldn't slow down the ride, threw out her arms to hold on and one of the women said, "Hey, Frankie! What'd you *give* her? And someone laughed and Lisa couldn't understand what the one called Frankie said. She was lying on the carpet watching the vines and flowers snaking over her body, then she was on her hands and knees trying to crawl backward away from them, crying to them to keep the flowers away from her, keep them away. Then the waitress with the naked breasts came up in front of

101

Lisa's face, her eyes bigger than all of her face, looking into Lisa's eyes and Lisa crawled into her arms so close to those white breasts. Everyone laughed. A voice said, "Jesus! Willya look at *this*!" and they all crouched down to watch Lisa with her mouth fastened to one of those big white plastic breasts, whimpering, clinging.

Voices and movement. The warped sounds of music played at the wrong speed. Incense. And so many people. So many arms and legs. Hands. Strange cries that hung in the air, their ends rimmed with oscillating bands of electric color. A fragment of an exchange.

". . . was it anyway?"

"Aw, acoupla dropsa fly and a little acid."

". . . freaking out."

"So *you* fuck her, man! I'm busy."

It was that word. They talked about fucking and her mind recoiled but she'd lost control over everything: her body, her limbs, her sense of reality. Her eyes bulged hard against the front of her face in horror, yet her voice laughed and her hands roved over other bodies, so many other bodies.

Then the present was caught in a frozen frieze and she saw herself greedily receiving the hard, pleasurable length of someone faceless as she cried, "Oh, please! *Please!*"

She couldn't control the craving that made her tear at her hair and kept her open to receive anyone, anything that would take away the yawning, cavernous emptiness between her legs. It went on and on and on, explosions of noisy color, gravelly, nonsensical growlings, voices hanging bodiless in the air around her ears.

She heard her own voice making senseless word formations, trying to say, "Take me home!" but saying, "Orange book dish."

And then, a blurred vision of dawn streets; two discordant neutered voices closing her into a room. And nothing.

She awoke at two-thirty the next afternoon on the bed of her motel room, wearing her evening gown of the night before, her shoes, a bracelet and nothing else. She sat up slowly, only to fall back with her eyes closed and a terrible roaring in her ears. As she lay there, waiting for the roaring to subside, she knew this was the end. She couldn't go any further.

Eventually, she got up and removed the stained dress, pushing it into the wastepaper backet in the bathroom. She showered and washed her hair, then returned to the bedroom. Her handbag and room key were on the dresser. Her underwear was gone. She stood with the bag in her hand looking at the room, at her gowns hanging in the closet and her shoes lined up underneath them on the floor.

"I want to die," she told the dresses and shoes, the room. But she couldn't die without first making arrangements.

She went to the telephone and called Nick at the office in New York.

"You have to replace me here," she said in a broken voice.

"What's happened?" he asked. "Are you all right? You sound bad."

Initially, she fought off his questions but finally she told him what had happened.

"You dope!" he scolded. "You should know better. It's a lucky goddamned thing you're only twenty. You can fight off all that shit when you're young. Your body's got more resources than you do."

"What're you talking about?" she asked stupidly, noticing a large bruise on her thigh.

"Never mind! Just you get yourself a lot of coffee and some Pepto-Bismol or like that and you go to work tonight. You play it very cool, as if nothing happened and you work it through to the end of the week. I'll cancel out your option with a story. But I want to *talk* to you when you get home, Lisa. I warned you from the top about this kind of shit. It'll ruin a good girl faster than anything else going. Stay away from the staff, do your gig and then haul your ass back here."

"But I . . ."

"Look, dear," his voice softened, "don't get suicidal or start thinking like that. It happens all the time. So you got gang-banged. You'll have a hurt box for a few days and then you'll be fine. It's not the end of the world.

Forget it! That's my advice. Just put it out of your mind and, if it does the trick, pretend like it didn't happen. But don't do anything stupid, Lisa. There are worse things in life than getting fucked by half a dozen spaced-out mental dwarfs who happened to lay their grubby little mitts on a little acid. Make like you weren't there, dear. Soak it out in the bath and get yourself together. I'll see you the end of the week."

The waitresses eyed her covertly. The waiters kept their distance. All except for the pretty barmaid whose husband had talked her into having the plastic injected into her breasts. She approached Lisa before her first set, handing her a brown paper bag.

"Your things," she said softly. "I took them home and washed them. Are you all right?"

"I'm fine," Lisa said stiffly.

"I was worried about you all day," she said, putting her small hand on Lisa's arm. "I would've called the hotel, you know. But my old man, it was his day off cause he finished the night shift last night. And if he'd found out where I was at, he'd of really pounded me around. But I'm real sorry. Nobody meant you no harm. I know you're just a kid. Don't be upset, okay?"

"Thank you." Lisa took the bag and moved away.

And the next night, Brad was there. He seemed so big, so settled and sensible and kind. He'd take care of me, she thought, sitting with him. He'd stay longer than one night; he'd take care of me. So, frightened and reluctant to speak for fear of scaring him off, she closed her eyes and burrowed in deep, convinced of the rightness of the timing. He was old and experienced. He'd protect her from dangerous situations.

Brad had just been divorced, was at loose ends and lived in New York. She cast herself on the water and he reeled her in, delighted with his catch. He couldn't believe his luck. He'd been so affected by her singing, so turned on by her looks that he'd have gone to any lengths to meet her. But that wasn't necessary. Their eyes connected and she joined him at the end of her set.

He'd expected her to be cool, self-possessed and was immediately disarmed by her quiet manner and unassuming humility. It occurred to him she had the ways and habits of plain girls who are always grateful for any show of male attention.

After he'd ordered a drink for her, he gazed at her, absorbing the full impact of her beauty. She wore a long, black dress that was so severely simple yet revealing she looked exotic, lush. He wondered if it wasn't some trick of the lighting in the club; something in the muted atmosphere that gave her that aura of ethereal fragility and innocence.

Her eyes, wide-set and iridescently gray, were like twin wells into which he felt he could swim. And her voice, low and throaty, but educated, her enunciation carefully precise as if she'd learned English after starting out in life with some other language as her native tongue. He wanted her like nothing on earth and couldn't believe it when she agreed to meet him for coffee after work.

They went to an all-night restaurant downtown near the Loop and he found himself talking more freely, more openly than he ever had to anyone. It had something to do with the way she listened, the way her eyes followed his mouth, never leaving his face. And it had to do with her long hands and graceful neck, the way she tilted her head slightly to one side as she listened.

She listened. It was terribly important, she knew, to listen carefully. It was part of what you did in return for receiving protection. And he seemed so glad of her. More than the usual formula response. She agreed to return to his hotel room with him, but her mind was present within this decision and for the first time, because of her mind's involvement, she felt frightened. When they got outside in the parking lot and he kissed her, she was surprised by his technique. It seemed he had a well-developed technique—like hers with music. And she reacted to his height and his age, his look of wide-eyed gratification as his mouth left hers and he said, "I should've known."

"What?" she asked, apprehensive.

"How you'd be," he said, hurrying her into the car.

So it was all right, she thought.

She nurtured his delight, blanking her vision to the sight of his raddled flesh, positive he'd seek—out of gratitude or love or whatever he felt—to protect her, save her from the one-night stands and formula men. With someone to come back to, there'd be no need for those others.

Initially, what surprised him most was her silence. She said very little and remained completely silent throughout their lovemaking, not even making sounds beyond those of accelerated breathing when she came. But what did it matter? He loved making love to her, loved her taste, her scent, her response. She seemed eager to please him, anxious to be accommodating.

His age and his physical condition seemed to have nothing whatever to do with his appetites. He made love to her—properly, coming deep inside of her—three times that night. And other ways, other things he did turned her on harder, higher than she'd believed possible.

"You're fantastic!" he told her. "It's like being a kid again, making love to you."

That was true. At fifty-three, three times was like a miracle to him. Everything about her strung his senses alert and alive. He spread her like a map and traveled over her, charting her terrain, navigating the turns and byways of her long, splendid body with a hunger that seemed insatiable. He drank from her mouth, savoring her mystery and sweetness, possessive of this rare gift that had come to him so unexpectedly. He extended his hands over her breasts, catching her nipples between his fingers like blossoming flowers that changed shape before his eyes. He delved along the folds of her flesh, feeling an enormous potency as she quiveringly lifted to the tantalizing attack of his mouth. To him, she was a dream-creature, someone formed in every way for pleasure. And he'd found her.

While they were resting, he lit a cigarette and held it to her mouth, bending to kiss the slope of her breast, then rising up, smiling.

"How tall are you?" he asked, studying her fact.

"Five-ten."

"Marvelous," he murmured, settling back with his arm folded under his head and the cigarette smoke filling his lungs.

"Will we be seeing each other again?" she asked quietly.

"A lot," he stated, and the question in her mind was satisfied. He'd be willing to look out for her in the ways Nick couldn't.

He was in town three days and then flew back to New York.

The night he left, she felt insulated and cared for and she slipped the first of her own compositions into one of her sets.

Actually, it was an accident. Her brain had been working over the changes and when she'd come to the end of one number, she'd simply slid without thinking into "Early Morning People." She played a chorus and a half, deciding as she played on the few changes that needed to be made, one in the bridge and one in the second chorus. But otherwise she was pleased with the way it all came out. The audience applauded loudly at the end of the number. Someone approached the stand to ask, "Who wrote that?" and, blushing, she lied, saying she couldn't remember the composer's name.

After that, she couldn't stop. She reworked "Early Morning People" until it was perfected. Then she left it and went on to another. And another. Until, each evening, at least half a dozen of her own songs were included in the night's work. No one knew. It made her smile to herself, pleased with the success of the deception. People were applauding what they thought were the compositions of other performers, while all the time they were hearing brand new songs that had never been played before. She was beginning to move forward. She could feel it. And part of the reason she was convinced, was Brad. He often showed up on her out-of-town gigs to surprise her. Or telephoned often just to talk to her. And, in return, she was faithful to him. It seemed fair enough, she thought. She got through more time in this way.

But Brad saw other women. Not only when she was away on the road but sometimes when she was right there in town. And she told herself it shouldn't bother her, but it did. When they did get together, he never seemed particularly interested in the things she had to say. It was always a run to the bedroom. There was no time for anything else.

Brad didn't know what to make of her. The fact that she was there, nearby, at least one week out of every month, took some of the edge off his appetite. If he saw her, he wanted her. When he didn't see her, his thoughts played over her as over someone he'd known many years before and still recalled with considerable, but mildly antagonized affection.

After the first year, he began feeling Lisa was always there when he needed her but it wasn't good to need her too much or too often. It became something of a single-entrant contest, trying to temper and defeat his need for her. He didn't know why he felt as he did, nor did he attempt to analyze any of it. He simply accepted her existence and his reluctance. And from time to time, he felt actually embarrassed, thinking of lusting after a girl thirty-three years younger.

She couldn't figure out what was bothering him. She didn't love him but he claimed always to love her. She was faithful but he insisted her mind was always elsewhere.

"What the hell's in your head anyway?" he'd ask, startling her.

"Music," she'd reply, soothing his anger from the outside in.

In the second year, she tried to open up, to talk to him; thinking this was what he wanted, what he needed. He listened with a paternal, indulgent air, unable to make any sense of her.

She had, upon taking possession of the apartment Nick had found for her, gone to several thrift shops on Third Avenue and, at random, picked out this and that, then had everything delivered. She'd set up a haphazard form of housekeeping in and around these mismated pieces, going away and coming back, changing nothing. Her only expenditure of significance—aside from the bed—was for the linens from Porthault. Brad examined the sheets, unable to refrain from commenting on her tastes.

"They are nice, aren't they!" she said, looking down at her bed, misunderstanding. "My mother always had her linens from Porthault."

She'd go off on the road wondering if keeping on with Brad was such a good idea. All he ever seemed willing to give, all he ever seemed to want, was his body for hers. Trying to talk to him made her feel tired, the way she used to feel when she was first learning French—the effort of translating from one language to another was exhausting.

But as soon as she was in the spotlight, her fingers on the keyboard, her throat open to produce the first sounds, she forgot all about him. It was only during the off-hours —before going to work, or upon rising in the early morning—that she gave any thought to him or to her future. The future seemed to be hurrying to meet her all at once and she'd held off readying herself until she felt in danger of being left at the side of the road while her future, like an express train, went screaming on past her. The future with Brad seemed non-existent. And the past and present with him appeared to her like one long wrestling match she always pretended to lose in order to maintain that illusory protection he offered.

It was in the course of one of her weekly calls home that she herself said something that precipitated her move away from Brad. Jeanette, as always, asked about him and Lisa replied, "He's looking after me." It was such a profound and outrageous lie, she couldn't believe she'd said it.

After the call, she sat looking at the walls of her motel room knowing a time had come to make changes. And the first change had to do with breaking off with Brad. She was looking after herself. Whatever had she been thinking? she wondered. Brad was interested in anything but protecting her. She knew suddenly she'd been nothing more in the last seven years than a humanoid jukebox. Shove in some money and out comes some music. God! she thought, that's awful! Awful, but true. It was depressing to think back, remembering her lofty ambitions when she had began her full-time singing career. All she'd accomplished—aside from learning how to handle any conceivable type of situation that could arise within the environs of a bar/lounge/club—was the writing of a dozen or so songs nobody even knew were hers.

Something had to be done. She'd never liked New York but she still lived there. The lounges and clubs were all the same, never varying. What was she doing? Where was she going? It appalled her to think she'd taken so long to go nowhere. She'd done nothing she couldn't have done just as easily, just as well back home. And if that was the case, she'd either have to find some new direction to take or return home. There was always the old Colony and half a dozen other clubs to work.

When Nick called her the night before she was due to close out of town, she listened with a new awareness working for her.

"I've got a great room in the Bahamas," he told her. "I have to fill it a week from Monday. Let me know if you want it."

"I'll call you when I get back," she said. She wanted a few days to think, to see where—if at all—this gig would fit in with her new plans.

Chapter 8

She arrived back Sunday afternoon and after unpacking her bags lay down for a nap. She was deeply asleep when Brad phoned, and when he asked, "Have you eaten?" she automatically said, "No."

"Would you like to?"

Say no! she told herself. You don't want to go.

"All right," she said, too depleted from the long all-night drive to resist. "Where?"

"I'll come for you. I'm at Finney's at the corner. Five minutes."

Thick-headed, she went into the bathroom to brush her hair and apply fresh makeup. Hastily she dabbed eyeshadow on her lids. The sound of the doorbell startled her, and her hand jolted upwards, leaving a smear of shadow on her eyebrow. She wiped shakily at her eyebrow with a tissue, then went to open the door thinking he must have come in as one of the tenants was unlocking the lobby door. Otherwise, he'd have buzzed.

"You're not dressed," he smiled, reaching for her.

"I haven't had time," she said, and a cold knowledge gripped her. She was seeing this man as she'd never seen him before.

His outer clothing was cold as he wrapped his arms around her, swallowing her up in a probing kiss that contained no pleasure for her whatsoever. She broke away, scanning his face.

"I'll get dressed," She turned to go, knowing he'd follow.

He draped his coat over the bathroom door, then came after her into the bedroom to sit on the side of the bed, his attention torn between the television set and the sight of her slipping off her robe. He switched off the set and lit a cigarette as she rummaged about for underwear in the chest of drawers.

"You're turning me on," he said, drawing deeply on the cigarette as he ran his hand up the back of her leg and over her buttocks.

"Please, don't!" she said, not looking at him.

"I'm not so sure this isn't better than watching you get undressed," he went on, stroking the flowing curve at the base of her spine, his eyes delighting in the sight of her slightly sloping naked breasts.

"Please!" she moved away. "Please let me get dressed."

Stung, he withdrew his hand. "Maybe this wasn't such a good idea." He looked suddenly sober.

"Don't be that way," she said, finally meeting his eyes, finding on his face an expression of vexation and almost childish petulance.

He was very tall, she saw, expensively dressed in clothes that pointed up a predeliction for autumnal colors and pleasant-to-touch fabrics. His hair was thinning, grayed at the temples, an indefinite matte brown elsewhere. He had the features of a big man, gave the impression of being big yet, studying the too-narrow breadth of his chest and shoulders, only his height was exceptional. His lower lip had a prominence that wasn't particularly attractive.

Taken separately, his features were unspecial, yet the

111

total effect had a certain panache. Especially when combined with a positive aura of sexuality that was almost blatant. And when he spoke, she saw that his eyetooth was crooked and his teeth had a yellowish smoker's tinge. She had a stunning impulse to ask, "Who are you? What are you doing here?" but tamped it down, submerging her confusion beneath the immediate necessity of dressing, hiding herself from the patent gratification he was deriving from looking at her body.

"What's the matter, Lee?" he asked, his voice taking on that tone he'd used on the telephone, that authoritarian, parental concern.

"Nothing." She turned back while she buttoned her shirt. "I'm not feeling well."

"Maybe we shouldn't go out," He leaned over to deposit his cigarette in the ashtray.

"No, no," she said quickly, "I'm hungry."

"Who are you?" she wondered again.

Apparently, he was an elderly habit she seemed to have had for quite some time, a not-bad-looking, lovemaking habit. Her eyes traveled to his hands. Beautiful, beautiful hands: broad-palmed, with tapering fingers of considerable length. She liked his hands.

"I thought you had somewhere to go this evening," the part of her that knew him said.

"I did. It was boring as hell and I started thinking about you and thought I'd see if you wanted to go out to eat. What *is* the matter?"

"Oh, I don't know," she lied, unable to prevent the confusion from revealing itself on her face.

"Come here." He eased her down on his lap, peering earnestly into her face. "What is it? Your period?"

"Oh, never. You know that never bothers me." She rested her cheek on his shoulder, momentarily comforted by his body warmth. "It's nothing," she murmured, "I'll feel better once I've eaten."

"I've been doing a lot of thinking lately," he said tentatively, relishing the soft cushion of her breasts. "A lot of serious thinking."

"What about?"

"You. Us. You mean a lot to me, Lee."

"Do I?"

"You've been good for me."

"I suppose I have." It was an automatic response.

"You know I love you."

She waited to hear what he'd say next. His neck was quite hot all at once. Being held by him, listening to him was like reading a heavily plotted novel that intrigued her, made her anxious to read it through to know how it turned out.

"Come on," he said, shifting. "You're hungry. I'll buy you a steak."

"Tell me. What were you going to say?"

Their eyes met. Every fresh viewing of his face was more of a mystery and a disappointment. There was a dreamy quality about the startled brownness of his eyes with their exaggerated roundness, their seeming guilelessness.

"I don't want to make any more mistakes." He lowered his eyes.

"I don't understand."

"No," he shook his head. "Come on. We'll go eat."

As he set her down, she hated him; disgusted by her docile obedience as she trailed after him. Had she always been this way? Or was it only with him? He picked his coat off the bathroom door, then walked to the closet to select one of her coats and hold it up for her. Like a robot, she turned, and he eased on the coat.

Stepping out into the motel-like hallway, she wanted to scream, to see all the doors come flying open and the people inside start popping out like jack-in-the-boxes. I've got to get out of here, she thought. Out of this place, away from this man. Yet she let him take her icy hand, let him—smiling, showing his large, discolored teeth—kiss her softly on the mouth before leading her into the elevator and down, out of the building and into a cruising cab he deftly flagged down.

In the back of the cab, he sat with his arm around her, a half-smile playing on his mouth. It seemed to be part of some incomprehensible game he was playing.

"You're so beautiful," he said throatily, kissing her cheek. "Look at me, Lisa."

She looked at him.

"I dream about you," he said, his face young all at once and filled with something she could only think of as nostalgia. "I actually dream about you."

"Do you?" She tried to smile, failed, and sat thinking about a song she'd heard driving home. It wouldn't come back to her.

His hand snaked through the opening of her coat and up onto her thigh. He was speaking, but she was trying to gather together fragments of the song; then she realized what he was doing and closed her eyes, shuddering.

"What!" he broke off mid-sentence. "Something *is* wrong. Tell me."

"It's nothing. Really," she hedged, creating a smile for him, stifling the revulsion she felt at the weight of his hand on her upper thigh. How had she ever survived nearly four years of this man? It didn't seem possible she'd gone along accepting his gestures and caresses for that long.

Gently, she removed his hand, trying to plan how she'd tell him, trying out opening lines, rejecting them.

She ate hungrily. He drank several vodka martinis, letting his own food go cold as he smiled lovingly at her, watching her eat a filet mignon. She glanced over at him and set her fork down abruptly, barely able to swallow the last of the meat.

"What'm I doing here with you?" she asked, jolted by the sound of her own voice.

He kept smiling. There was a little-girl look of bafflement on her face he found very affecting, touching. As her eyes questioned his face, he wanted to take her in his arms and crush her, eat her alive.

"You know I love you." He set down his drink, placing his hand over hers.

"I don't want to hear that," she said, dismayed by the suddenly offensive remains of the steak. *I don't like meat*, she thought swallowing hard. "I can't keep on with you," she said, "we're not going anywhere. We've never been going anywhere. And I hate New York. I can't function here. I've got to get away."

She wanted to leave that very minute and laced her

fingers tightly together as if that act would hold down her desire to run.

"We've been too close," he began.

"Don't say all that! I'm just not going to be seeing you any more, Brad."

She lit a cigarette, noticing that her fingers trembled as she held the cigarette to his lighter.

"I can't talk in here." He signaled to the waiter, rattled. "We'll go somewhere else."

She watched him put on his glasses to scan the Diner's Club charge slip, methodically adding before penning in a healthy tip. He was entirely someone else behind those glasses—someone she'd seen upon occasion in his office; someone brusque, busy and not in the least happy, despite frequent claims to the contrary.

But once the glasses were off, returned to his pocket, he was again the Brad who seemed to answer every question with, "You know I love you," as if the phrase was magical.

She recalled an occasion very early in their affair when he'd come to her apartment for perhaps the second or third time. She'd hugged him impulsively and there'd been a muffled, crunching sound. He'd laughed as he'd poured the broken bits and pieces of glass and frame out onto the kitchen table. "It doesn't matter," he'd said. But she'd felt reduced, graceless and foolish. Even through his laughter and subsequent embraces, she'd suffered the demoralizing effects of her induced ineptness. A voice in her head now reasoned: "Why ever would you stay with this man who makes you feel that way?" And she dropped her head slightly, knowing she had no reasons for staying.

The hatcheck girl eyed Brad, casting one dismissing glance at Lisa before turning the full force of her nebulous charms on him; holding up his coat, helping him on with it, flicking non-existent lint from his lapels with blood-red, daggerish fingernails. Brad scarcely noticed. He was too preoccupied with Lisa's peculiar behavior.

In a gentlemanly, rather old-school manner that contained the barest hint of a flourish, he assisted Lisa into her coat. He touched the fur appreciatively as she struggled

115

with the catch. Watching his hand absently stroking the coat, it occurred to her that he didn't look like the type of man who spent the greater portion of his free time in the beds of hopeful women. Yet he did. As they went out of the restaurant, she found she couldn't remember what kind of lover he actually was. She knew only that she didn't want him.

It was snowing. She felt eased and smiled as she held out her hand, letting the flakes melt in her palm. Brad stepped out into the road, turning this way and that in a search for non-existent cabs.

"Hey!" Brad called and slipped on the icy pavement as he came running after her. "Where are you going?"

She turned and watched him approach, righting himself with a lurching shift of his shoulders as his feet sought clear patches of pavement. His Gucci loafers looked long and wet and laughable.

"I'm going," she said.

"Let's go to my place," he suggested. "We'll never get a cab now."

He tucked her hand inside his own in his coat pocket as she studied his profile. There was an uncanny handsomeness to his face in profile: the rather flat, smooth planes offering an appearance of sweetness and sensitivity that she knew were not real. His pale eyebrows and lashes seemed to afford scant protection to his large eyes. She wondered if his eyes were cold.

"When do you take off again?" he asked, ducking his head against the snow.

"Nick changed my bookings. One of his boys was lined up to do a lounge in the Bahamas but he had a car accident. Nick's asked me to go. I think I will. The idea of sunshine is very appealing."

"That's a hell of a long way," he said. "Are you going to go?"

"Yes," she decided. "I told you I want to go away."

"Not *that* far away." He laughed stiffly.

"There's not much difference between playing Buffalo or the Bahamas. Either way, it gets me away from here."

"Buffalo's within my range. I'm not so sure about the Bahamas. This is a busy time for me."

"It's not as if you come along on my gigs."

"I've never seen you this way." He applied pressure to her trapped fingers. "What's happened, Lee?"

"Nothing. Nothing has happened."

He opened his mouth to take issue with her but saw the rigid set of her jaw and thought better of it.

They arrived at his building and he pulled open the outside door, allowing her to precede him out of the cold. She looked around his apartment noticing dusty areas, fluff hiding in the dimmer corners and the lingering smell of bacon. Everything appeared tidy enough on the surface but there were threads of dust dangling from the ceiling. The place was just like Brad: superficial, like a plant whose leaves were still green but whose roots were slowly rotting.

He took her coat then followed her with his eyes as she wandered into the living room and sat down beside the fireplace.

"Why don't you light a fire?" she asked, studying the remains of a previous one. Fine gray ash and dozens of cigarette stubs. He dumped his ashtrays in the fireplace.

"All right." He took off his jacket and tie, snapped open his cufflinks, then rolled up his sleeves, all with a fake display of heartiness. "What are you drinking?"

"The usual." She pushed off her wet shoes and curled up in the corner of the sofa that had come to him from his third wife. As she touched the scarcely-worn nubby arms, letting her eyes trail over the Eames chair and foot-rest, she wondered why he kept getting married.

"One T and T." He handed her a tall glass with a spiral of lime rind neatly wedged between the ice-cubes. "Cheers!"

His mouth tasted of mint, his tongue cool. She tried to pull away.

"God, your mouth!" He took the glass from her hand, trying to kiss her again. She was so soft, so utterly totally female. He felt he could disappear into her long body and moist mouth.

"I'd like a fire," she said, retrieving her drink. It was gin and tasted like medicine.

Brad sipped his stinger, trying to figure out what she was

up to. But he couldn't think. He was too taken with the sight of her; had always been completely captivated by her looks. He admired the rounded breadth of her shoulders, the tapering of her back, He visualized the flaring lines of her hips, her long shapely legs and slender ankles. Her body was wonderful, her skin pale and smooth, her breasts very round, fuller than they appeared when she was dressed. She seemed like a set study, coiled on the sofa with the firelight lending an orange-pink caste to her pale face.

The sight of her never failed to fill him with need, with a crucial desire to put his hands on her, to ascertain that she was real and accessible to him.

Her face. The opalescent skin and penetrating gray eyes. Her mouth, wide and soft and capable of offering caresses that he'd never received in quite the same way from any other woman. She had abundant, deceivingly heavy-looking, caramel-colored hair that fell so weightlessly into his receptive hands. Sometimes almost gold-red, sometimes almost white from the sun. Her hair. He thought of that first night when he'd let it down and draped it over her, marveling over its length—it fell below her hips—driven into an obsessive desire by the sight of her breasts hidden behind her hair.

She was threatening him now. He didn't know why or what had brought it on but couldn't seem to bypass his eternal lust for her in order to decide precisely what she was trying to do.

He considered her music, thinking of her long-fingered hands languidly gliding over a keyboard and her mouth opening to make sounds so pervadingly, persuasively personal that listening to her sing, seeing her as she sang, was an unforgettably compelling experience. Her singing was fulfilling, satisfying like a perfect October afternoon, or that restful sleep after making love. It was sensual, evocative, stirring. She sang in a voice that was low, resonant, intimate. He remembered his initial surprise, hearing her for the first time. He'd thought she'd have one of those high, clear, rather thin voices that went with the fresh, young look of her. But her voice was old, experienced, muted by time she hadn't yet lived through. A

118

fifty-year-old voice in a body not yet twenty-five. A complete dichotomy. Even her speaking voice was special, unusual, flavored by a slightly localized up-north accent. More than once he'd been turned in his attentions by the sound of her voice on the telephone. He'd never known what to make of her.

"I told you I've been thinking," he said, causing her to turn toward him.

"Yes," she said blankly, lighting a fresh cigarette from the stub of the one she was finishing.

"You smoke too much."

"I'd like to hear about this 'thinking' you've been doing." She disregarded his lifted eyebrows and widened eyes.

"This is no good," he said. "I shouldn't have started in the first place. Do you want to see if I can get you a cab?"

"No," she said patiently, feeling strangely calm and, at the same time, distraught, churning inside. "I want to hear what it is you keep trying to say. This is such a *game*," she sighed. "I've had enough of games, Brad."

"We've been through this before," he said. "This time —I admit it—it's my fault for starting. But you keep insisting it's all games and I can't make you see it's just life, the way things are."

"No," she said quietly, "*This* is a game." Tears welled up in her eyes and spilled over. She felt so tired and addled. Yet she wanted to try to tie all the ends.

"Don't." He moved closer to her. "I hate seeing you cry. But you make it so difficult for both of us."

She threw her cigarette into the fire, shrugging off his hand. "Trying to talk to you is like playing a defective record," she said. "We keep saying the same things at each other over and over again. Always the same. You keep on and on, playing at some game that has rules I don't understand at all. You're always going out and finding women to fall in love with. And when it doesn't work— it *never* works—you come back to me, for me to make it all better. There's a name for that. If only I could think. What is it?"

"All I want is for you to be happy . . ."

"I don't think so. Your interpretation of my happiness is my being at the other end of the line when you phone because you're feeling blue or you're a little drunk and sentimental and you need my body to keep you from going under. I can see it all so plainly now!" She looked very surprised. "All this time, I thought it was the other way around. I thought you were saving me from . . . everything. But that's not how it is. You don't even listen to the things I try to tell you."

"I don't know what's brought all this on, but I'm sure you don't mean it. You're not yourself tonight."

"I do mean it. I really do."

"You're just tired, as you said." He tried to take her into his arms, thinking he could kiss and caress her into seeing reason.

"Don't!" She jerked herself away from him. "It's only more of what I'm talking about. I'm some kind of headless body or something to you. It's terrifying. I can't believe I've let four whole years get by me without even seeing that none of it was the way I thought or wanted it to be. It's my own fault. I wasn't thinking. I don't know what I *was* doing. But whatever it was, it doesn't matter now. You don't understand what I'm saying, do you?" She jumped up and ran to the closet for her coat. "You don't understand *anything*!" she accused as she unlocked the front door. "I could die tomorrow and you'd just have to find somebody else to fuck. It'd be an inconvenience, that's all. You don't *love* me. You never did. At least I never pretended to love you. Not that. At least I was honest. I . . ." She glanced over at him, then flung open the door and ran, clattering down the stairs. He called after her, shouting down the stairwell, but she didn't stop.

A taxi was letting out a fare at the corner and, grateful for this bit of luck, she got into it.

The telephone was ringing when she arrived home. She wanted to ignore it, paused in the living room waiting for —what? It rang four, five times as she dropped her coat on the sofa and went toward the telephone. And then it stopped. Her hand was lifting to it, and it stopped ringing. Inexplicably, she thought of the bloody remains of her unfinished steak and felt sick. She sat down on the kitchen floor with her head resting on her knees, waiting for the sickness to pass.

She took the telephone off the hook, then undressed, taking her time in the bathroom, planning. First thing in the morning, she'd call Nick to tell him she'd take the Bahamas lounge. That would give her a few days to get rid of the apartment.

She walked from room to room thinking there was nothing she'd keep, not even the books and records. She'd start clean, no matter which direction she eventually took.

Nick was pleased she'd take the booking. Eight weeks on Grand Bahama with one-month options for the season, right through to the end of April. She could be in the islands as long as five months.

"Do you want me to come in and sign the contract?" she asked, anxious to be started.

"Might just as well, dear. My other phone's going. Hang on," he said, picking up a second phone. She could hear him talking, telling someone to hold. It amazed her that he could hold two simultaneous conversations. She'd seen him dozens of times with a receiver on each shoulder, turning from side to side to answer appropriately.

"I'll be in in a couple of hours," she told him.

She looked out the bedroom window to see that the snow was gone, having left a filthy mess trickling into the drains, clouds of stinking steam hovering at regular intervals in the road.

"New York." She made a face, drawing the curtains closed.

She made quite a number of telephone calls: notifying her garage she wouldn't require the parking slot after Friday; booking her flight; arranging for a storage garage in Palm Beach; canceling Con Edison and the telephone.

She felt as though someone was chasing after her, telling her to hurry, get everything done. By the time she'd completed the last of the business calls she was out of breath and sweating.

It wasn't until she was in a taxi on her way to sign the contract at Nick's office that the first pangs hit. And it was exactly the way it'd been in Mason City when she'd

121

realized she was completely alone. She'd come full circle. Now, like a cramp in her stomach, the truth bent her double, making her mouth dusty dry and her palms damp. She belonged to no one. No one belonged to her. She'd tried to create the illusion of belonging in claiming Brad was for protective purposes only. But the truth of it was she'd made a shameful, shoddy attempt at buying herself a family. The price had been her body. The house in Remington Park and the people who lived in it belonged to each other, not to her. They never had. She loved them, was glad of their continuing presence in her life; but they weren't *hers*. She hadn't come as the direct result of either a planned or a spontaneous coupling on the parts of those two people but as a person already made, manufactured in the body of some woman whose name she didn't even know. It didn't matter now; none of the reasons mattered—she'd turned into a music machine with a daddy whose fee for playing "family" came in the form of privileged access to whatever parts of her body he chose to use.

This nugget of understanding made her furious with herself. Never again! she swore, looking at the cab driver's greasy ponytail. It doesn't matter if I spend the rest of my whole life all by myself, but I'll never do any of that ever again.

If she could have grabbed herself by the shoulders, she would have shaken and pummeled herself until all the stupid, infantile ideas were shaken clear out of her head.

Nick pointed her into a chair. He was on the telephone. The contracts were ready and he pushed them across the desk to her, smiling. She signed them, smiling to herself at his remarks into the phone. He looked less like an agent, she thought, than she looked like a singer. The idea that she didn't look like what she was had come to her—along with everything else—while she'd been silently berating herself in the back of the cab.

Nick didn't look like an agent. He never had. A diligent, sharp-witted C.P.A. maybe, but not an agent. She crossed her legs and lit a cigarette, waiting for him to finish the call.

"Okay, love of my life," he said, slamming down the phone. "You're all set. The bread's very tasty, six bills. Free room and chow and, from what I've heard, terrific tips. You should come back with a healthy little bankroll, you gorgeous old thing. You're looking good. Different. You know that?"

"No," she said.

"Really." He laughed and lit a cigarillo. "Looking at you, I realize you're not my kid act anymore. All grown up. How the hell long's it been, anyway?"

"Nine years."

"Jesus! I feel like your father or something. Nine years."

"Do you know anyone who'd be interested in my apartment?" she asked.

"Moving?"

"I'm leaving, Nick."

"Oh? Where'll you go?"

"I don't know yet. Somewhere. Home, maybe."

"You want to have lunch?"

"I don't think there's going to be enough time."

He didn't seem to hear. "Why don't you let me do something big for you, Lisa? This is nowhere, this lounge crap. It's never been right for you. What're you afraid of? You're the best act I've got, the best I've ever had. I could get twelve, fifteen hundred a week for you, especially since you're able to score your own charts. We could get you a record contract in fifteen seconds flat. What's the hang-up?" He stopped suddenly. "You're not serious," he said, as if there'd been a time-gap between her words and his hearing them. "You're going to drop the whole thing and split home?"

"It's not money," she said. "I don't need money. And nightclubs are just big lounges with bands. I'm sick of it. All the club owners. All of it."

"You know," he smiled, chewing the end of the cigarillo, "nobody's been forcing you to play those gigs. You're the one, dear. I was beginning to wonder how long it was going to take you to wake up. You're a purist. But it's a bummer, Lisa. You can't be a purist who's static. All these years and you're still playing the old Colony. You're right, dear. It's time to pick up your chips, cash in and go home if it's just going to be the cheap scene. You can't be a purist who isn't going anywhere. It's self-annihilating."

"What'm I supposed to do?"

"There's something I want to try to work for you."

"I don't know . . ." she began as the phone went off.

"Listen, I'll get back to you on this. You be a good girl. I'll be back to you. If you don't hear from me by the end of the week, don't worry. I'll get to you down there."

She opened the door. He held his hand over the mouthpiece saying, "Don't jump into anything! I'll either talk to you myself or see if I can't work something direct."

"Direct?"

"Later," he smiled apologetically.

She blew him a kiss which he caught and slapped against his forehead, making her laugh.

There were two shaggy-looking kids waiting at the reception desk, holding expensive guitar cases, wearing Asian-looking coats with embroidered trim and sheepskin linings. Somebody's new act, she thought, seeing the barely concealed tension and jittery newness about them. *It used to be me*, she thought, stabbing the Down button.

By that night, she'd unloaded the apartment on one of Nick's musicians. It was all too easy, she thought, closing the door after him, folding his check into her pocket.

When the telephone rang, she picked it up without thinking. Her throat closed at the sound of Brad's voice.

"What's going on?" he demanded, his voice wrapped around righteous-sounding outrage. "What's with running out in the middle of the night and taking your phone off the hook?"

"I told you," she said breathlessly. "It's finished. I don't want to see you anymore."

"I'm coming up. I'll be there in ten minutes."

She looked at the buzzing receiver in her hand, wondering how he'd managed to do that. She was immediately fearful and considered going out somewhere that minute but was more fearful of the prospect of being out alone after dark. She walked into the living room and sat down on the sofa.

The doorbell rang. Brad came in looking rumpled and frantic.

"What are you doing, Lisa?" he asked, dropping heavily to the sofa, not even bothering to unbutton his coat. "I don't like what's happening."

"Neither do I," she said truthfully. "Would you like a drink?"

"No." He grasped her forearm, pulling her back down beside him. "I want an explanation."

"I don't have to give you one. You have no claim on me. I'm leaving. I've taken the job in the Bahamas, given up the apartment. It's all done. Everything."

"So fast! How can you do these things so fast?"

"Fast?" she repeated. "You call four years fast? Please Brad. It's anything but fast. I should have done this long ago."

"But I need you. I . . ." he groped for words, his eyes shifting.

"You can't talk me out of it," she said sharply. "You can't give me what I want."

"I don't *know* what you want. You know how I feel about you . . ."

"You answer everything I say with, 'You know I love you.' It's a habit you have. Everything's arranged and I'm going. That's all."

"No, it isn't. I do love you. I want you here."

"What for? So you can call me two or three nights a week when I'm in town and you feel like working out on my body? I don't like the way that makes me feel all of a sudden. Please go away! I've got a lot to do and we're all burnt out. It's over."

"You're not yourself. Flying around like someone I've never seen, not even sounding like yourself. This isn't the way to make decisions. You're not thinking . . ."

"Maybe I am! Maybe I've finally starting thinking and making decisions. Maybe I'm finally starting to grow up! God knows, it's about time! The big thing I've decided is that I don't need you. I hate the way I behave with you, the way you treat me."

"It's impossible to talk to you when you're this way." He got to his feet. "I'll call tomorrow when you've had a

125

chance to think a little more clearly about what you're doing."

"You always talk down to me," she said, even-voiced. "As if you think I'm too stupid to do anything but play the piano and sing. I'm leaving Friday morning and I'm not coming back here."

"Where'll you go?"

"I might go home. Okay? Now will you please go away?"

"Why now, Lisa? Why right now when everything's finally opening up for us?"

"You know something, Brad? For four years I've been going away and coming back. And every time I come back, I get this awful feeling that you've forgotten me while I've been away. For at least an hour when we're back together, it's as if you're trying to remember me and what it is about me you like. And you know something else? The only think you like about me is right here." She held her hand over her crotch. "And that's really zero. I need at least to be remembered, recognized."

"None of that's true." He took her in his arms. "None of it. I love you." He kissed her, then held her at arm's length.

"You're more important to yourself than I am to you. I'm . . . To you, I'm just a walking wind-up toy with a cunt."

Something inside his head went "click," sending a film of red down over his eyes. He hit her hard across the face then started tearing at her clothes.

Stunned by the force of the blow, she didn't realize for a moment what he was doing. Then she began struggling with him, trying to push him away. Neither of them spoke. Her head was filled with colliding thoughts as she tried to use her knee on him but he anticipated and sidestepped, kicking her foot out from under her so that she fell and he came crashing down on top of her. She could taste blood in her mouth and thought, "He'll kill me," so she closed her eyes and stopped fighting. He didn't even seem to notice. He was too busy tearing, ripping her clothes.

"Don't do that!" she said, trying to make him stop. But he wouldn't. He kept on until he'd exposed her, the rough fabric of his overcoat scraping across her skin. She watched him unbutton the coat and unzip his trousers thinking. "How can he be aroused by this? How *can* he?"

He held her hands pinned over her head with one hand while, with the other, he forced her legs apart and fell heavily between them.

"This isn't happening!" she told herself, trying to squirm away from him, fighting again when she hadn't thought she would, when she'd told herself she wouldn't fight.

He hit her again and she lay still as he came thrusting into her. She waited as he moved inside of her, thinking he'd finish quickly and go away. But then he stopped, withdrew and, raising her, forced his way in below. She screamed and his hand came down over her mouth.

He wanted to destroy her without killing her and took her savagely, vindictively, scarcely aware of her attempts to push him away. He let go in one final rending thrust and then quickly withdrew, appalled to see that her thighs and his trousers were smeared with blood. He felt sick then, looking down at her, seeing her eyes closed, face pale as death, her arms tight across her breasts.

"I'm sorry," he whispered, "I'm sorry. My God! I'm sorry."

"GET OUT!" she screamed, not opening her eyes. She lay still, listening to the sounds of his departure, the closing of the door and then, whimpering, got slowly to her feet and staggered into the bathroom to throw up.

She shook uncontrollably as she shed her tattered clothes and climbed into the tub to stand under the shower. Blood ran in watered streams down her legs and she looked at it, sobbing, unable to think; able only to feel the monstrous pain he'd created. She thought of calling the police, of seeing him in court, in jail, ruined. But she knew she wouldn't do any of it. When the water was running clear, she scrubbed herself, shampooed her hair, then got out. She drank some scotch and took three sleeping pills and curled up on the bed, waiting for sleep.

Friday morning, while she waited for the super to come help with her bags, she stood looking at the living room walls, unable to believe she was actually going; actually transient again, for a time. "But you can always come home," papa had told her. "It's no sin to want to come home."

She switched off the lights, locked the door, surrendered the keys to the super and followed him down to the street. When she arrived at the garage on Ninety-first Street and saw her car, freshly washed and waxed, she felt better for the first time since the attack. The car meant really going, really escaping this city and Brad.

Just before emerging from the Holland Tunnel, she experienced a wave of complete terror. "God, what am I doing? What's going to happen?" But then she remembered Nick had said he'd talk to her. Someone would talk to her. And he'd meant talk about changing the direction of her career, her life. Everything would change.

But, oh Jesus! she thought, pressing her foot down hard on the accelerator, what if it doesn't?

PART TWO

Chapter 9

Lisa's room was cheerily decorated and overlooked the beach and, almost directly below, the pool. She assimilated the details of the place without really seeing, moving in trance-like drifts, getting her bags unpacked and her clothes hung away. She thought of the day and a half she'd have before starting work Monday night. Two afternoons in the sun, two nights of sleep.

She'd taken two dramamine tablets and slept through the short flight, awaking muddled and exhausted, thankful the management had had the foresight to send an assistant manager to help her get through customs and see her safely to the hotel. She was still very much under the influence of the pills, so the goings-on around her seemed fuzzy and senseless.

The customs officers went through her luggage, questioning everything: her tape player, hair dryer and personal mike; examining her portable keyboard with an almost primitive fascination that brought to her mind old movies depicting great white hunters in Africa, attempting to induce native guides to allow themselves to be photographed while the guides backed away in horror, fearing their souls might be taken and trapped inside the little black box.

She looked helplessly over at the assistant manager who stepped forward to explain patiently that she was going to be working for the hotel and these were her personal belongings, things she required in order to perform.

For some reason, the officers insisted on retaining half a dozen or so items for further inspection. The assistant manager took her to one side to say, "Let me handle it. I'll see you get everything back by this evening." And she nodded, so fascinated by his bleached-looking, sun-untouched skin that she barely heard him.

Time was a blur. After stowing her suitcases in the closet, she took a long bath to soak out the travel fatigue, trying to avoid thinking of what Brad had done to her but not succeeding. She was filled with murderous hatred, an almost palpable longing to kill him, wipe him clear off the face of the earth. She'd come to her awareness lightly too late. But at least she'd come to it. From now on, she'd be very very careful with her life and the people she invited into it.

She dressed and went down to have a look at the lounge. She felt heavy again as she came out of the elevator. The air was weighted, humid, tropical. It would probably rain in the night. The thick stillness of the air was almost difficult to move through.

The lounge was dim and cool and just like dozens of others she'd seen, except that the bar was done up with a thatched miniroof effect. Otherwise, identical. And the sounds emerging from the heavy-handed pianist's mouth were also ones she'd heard before.

Through the years, she'd seen dozens of acts, good, bad and embarrassingly mediocre. She'd watched as these performers introduced themselves to strangers with admirable self-possession, easily entering into conversation. Once behind the piano, she could sing, even make brief remarks between numbers. But when it came time to step out from behind the piano, she fell into the old embracing muteness and was forced to act out her "social" role, with the special vocabulary that went with the part—words about the weather and other common-places about clubs she'd played and where she lived when she wasn't working.

She disappointed people. She accepted their invitations, sat with them, drank with them. She smiled and answered their questions, all the while aware by their exchanged glances or a certain narrowing of the eyes that she'd let them down, wasn't in the least what they'd hoped for. They wanted glamor and she couldn't manufacture it, couldn't sparkle the way other performers did. None of the glossy, professional extraversion had rubbed off on her.

She couldn't even select her own publicity stills. Every two years, Nick would arrange a sitting. She'd go to the photographer at the appointed time, sit through the session, then escape. And the proofs would go to Nick who'd put rings in Magic Marker around the ones he wanted printed up and a week or two later, back would come several hundred prints, all with the agency's logo inset at the bottom. She'd see those eight-by-ten glossies in the lobbies of places she played and wince at the backlit, shiny creature leaning so nonchalantly over the keyboard with just enough cleavage to suggest something more than mere musical ability. The pictures were small square turn-offs she couldn't get away from. Everywhere she went, there they were, usually prettied up with a bit of silverdust added at the last minute by the local sign-painter who had the club's contract.

She moved her attention to the pianist who played more wrong changes than right ones. He was so bad. The lounge was empty with the exception of herself and a couple in the corner who weren't listening. She felt genuinely sorry for the piano man.

Between numbers she signed her bar bill and went in search of the dining room. The assistant manager had informed her that the hotel was completely filled, including all the marina slips. Eight hundred rooms filled with holidaying people. Mid-December was the beginning of their season. It surprised her to think there were so many people who preferred to spend Christmas away from their homes.

The hotel was very attractive, the lobby furnished with brightly-pillowed rattan furniture and dozens of enormous tropical plants whose fronds scarcely stirred in the black, airless night. The corridors were carpeted, hushed. Most of the guests were already at dinner or dressing for it.

The air was expensive, redolent of Bain de Soleil and Norell perfume. Who'd worn Norell? Someone. She couldn't think who. Jeanette had always worn Bal à Versailles which Lisa loved. She'd never known anyone else who wore it. Only Jeanette.

The idea of entering the vast dining room alone made her tense up. But the maître d' was very English, subtly gay and endearingly kind.

"Call me Charles," he said. "I recognized you straight off from your photograph. Would you care to sit near or far?" he asked, indicating the stage.

"Are they good?" She looked at the West-Indian band.

"Super!" he exclaimed, smiling. "Absolutely super!"

"Near," she decided.

He swept up an oversized, tasselled menu and led her into the noisy room. She felt pale and conspicuous, surrounded by an orchard of ripe, suntanned faces, some of which inspected her openly.

"I hate eating alone," she confided.

"Oh, one *knows*!" He put his hand on her arm. "Life is so tedious at times, don't you think?" He smiled understandingly. "Simply dying to see you come Monday. Word's out you're divine. Certainly look as though you'd sing divinely. Have a drink and enjoy your dinner." He eased the chair under her. "I shouldn't give any thought whatsoever to the masses, love. They're all so keyed up about the pots of money they're spending on this super holiday, I doubt they'd notice an atomic blast." He touched her shoulder, twitched himself into a posture of royalty reduced to servitude, thrust his chin skyward and sauntered away. She liked him.

She ordered another drink and watched the band tune up. The leader was very handsome, creamy-coffee colour, with a lovely, babyish face and a tall, powerfully muscular body he dressed to display. He smiled at her and she looked away.

The food was excellent but she couldn't eat. Her appetite disappeared after only a few bites, so she gave it up and sat back, listening to the band as she studied the features of individual musicians in the group. Their faces struck her as incredibly beautiful, reminding her for a moment of the way the trio had looked under the pink spot that afternoon at the Colony. Daniel. And Lou. And what was the name of the piano man? She couldn't remember.

The waiter removed the dishes and she ordered cognac. She was on the way to being drunk but not minding because the entire universe was assuming a cordial, amber glow.

And then there was a pale yellow, custom-made silk body shirt, tucked into spotless, perfectly-pressed, cream-colored trousers, belted with a woven brown belt. And she looked up to see who belonged to the trim torso.

"Hi," he said, setting his drink down on the table. "I'm Chas Clayton."

He was tanned mahogany with a fresh overburn shining red in his cheeks. His hair was brown and looked as if he'd just wet-combed it.

"That's nice," she said. "I'm just leaving," and walked out, saying goodnight to Charles, trying to keep her shoulders erect as she went down the silent corridor.

Her things had come back from the customs shed she noticed as she walked through the room to step out onto the narrow balcony and look down at the lighted pool. A couple in evening dress were sitting, dangling their feet in the water, their hands entwined. And, almost beyond her viewing range, on a wooden chaise with his ankles crossed and a drink in hand, sat Chas Clayton, gazing off into space.

She shivered as she stepped back inside, pulling the curtains closed and then turning slowly to look at yet another hotel room. Not as plastic as most, but sterile nonetheless. For a moment, she had a craving to see the scratched and scarred odds and ends of furniture she'd lived with for close to seven years. It wasn't good stuff or pretty stuff but she knew it, knew its inclination to lean just-so or to tilt just-here. Folded matchbooks kept the pieces jacked up, wobble-free.

She felt sick, giddy with fatigue and too much drink.

She reached to unpin her hair and shook it down, feeling the still-damp strands hit the base of her spine like small, slimy animals. She was chilled and undressed hastily. She couldn't get sick. Couldn't. She'd never once missed a night's work and had a very real sense of obligation to the people who hired her to perform. Once you started missing nights here and there, other, worse things would soon happen.

In bed, she sat in the darkness watching the lit end of her cigarette as she drew the smoke into her lungs. She wondered if he was still down there and got up and walked across the room to slide open the door and step out onto the balcony in the darkness. He hadn't moved. She stood for several minutes, finishing her cigarette, finding it curious that a man so exceedingly good-looking should be sitting alone down there.

From time to time, his hand raised the glass to his mouth. Otherwise, he didn't move at all. Finally, her cigarette down to the filter, she stepped back inside, closed the door, disposed of the cigarette stub and climbed into bed.

She slept for thirteen hours. Midmorning—surprisingly, she felt no guilt at oversleeping by an hour—she stood looking down at the crowded pool and, beyond, at the sun-glaze on the scintillating waters. Umbrellas sat tilted against the sun. Half a dozen thatched changing huts were strewn along the beach. And, of course, the chaise was now occupied by an oiled, bikinied woman with a wrinkled mid-section.

It was beautiful. Beautiful. She remained gazing out at the water for a long time, holding her hands up to the soft air, filling her eyes with the scarlet and purple bougainvillea defining the pathway. The colors were so vivid, so impossible. The spread below was like something someone had painted in the final stages of a perfect trip with a mind unimpaired by the shackling encumbrances of truth and reality.

She dressed and went to the coffee shop.

"Bonjour," he said, sliding into the booth. "I had

136

hoped to meet you last night, but you left so quickly. I am Johnny. My group plays in the Tortoise Shell."

"Yes. You're very good." She smiled at how effortlessly she was speaking. "I'm Lisa Hamilton. Perhaps Charles told you that."

He smiled boyishly. She liked the look of his squarish face and large, challenging eyes. She'd have preferred to sit without speaking, examining his beauty as she had earlier breathed in the magnificence of the flowers and water. She drank her coffee slowly, managing to eat half a piece of toast and a strip of bacon. She looked at the large breakfast she'd ordered, feeling slightly sickened by the sight of it.

"Where do you live?" he asked ingenuously, helping himself to a piece of her toast.

"New York," she lied. It was easier than explaining.

"I shall be going to New York in the spring. To make a record." He shone with pride, awaiting compliments.

"That's very nice." She watched him wipe his fingertips carefully on a napkin.

"Your French is excellent," he observed, folding the soiled napkin into smaller and smaller squares.

She'd fallen into it so naturally, even after so many years. She hadn't even realized, until he'd pointed it out, that they hadn't been speaking in English.

"Where are you from?" she asked, thinking how easy it was to make oneself understood without the ambiguities of English.

"Haiti." He slid out of the booth. "I'll come for the beginning of your first set tomorrow night. Bon chance, Lisa." He left, white sharkskin trousers hitting smartly against the heels of his white suede loafers.

"What are you smiling about?" Chas asked. "It's very Cheshire cat."

She looked up, thinking, Christ! Why doesn't everybody leave me alone?"

"Nothing."

"May I?" he asked.

"Why not?" She picked up her coffee cup and drank.

"I hate eating alone," he smiled, picking up the menu.

"And you just hate eating. Something wrong with the food?"

"I'm not hungry."

"You're so hostile. Something about me that bothers you?"

"I . . ." she looked up, saw the gently mocking light of his eyes and his smiling mouth and couldn't think what it was she'd been about to say.

"I'm not hostile. You just seem to be everywhere, all at once."

"Well, maybe if you sat still for thirty seconds, you'd find out why."

"That's a very good, very new line," she said, preparing to get up.

"Here's my card," he said, pulling it out of his shirt pocket, sliding it across the table to her.

She picked it up and looked at it.

"So?" she said.

"I'm in the record business," he said. "Your agent caught up with me in Freeport last night and asked me to catch your act before I go back up."

She couldn't say why but she felt incredibly angry. Nick should've been more specific. He should've prepared her.

"Well, fine," she said, this time making good her departure from the booth. "You catch my act Monday night and report back to Nick like a good little boy."

"You're really something!" he said, unable to be angry. He knew he should be but he simply didn't feel it.

"You too!" she snapped. "You're all alike, thinking the clever words and the embossed business cards make you irresistible studs. It's all a big con. I'm not going to fuck you to get a record. So catch as much as you like, just stay out of my way!"

She scribbled her name on the waitress's pad and ran out, leaving him sitting there.

Under any other circumstances, he'd have cleared out without waiting to hear her perform. But there was something about her, about her immediate and unreasonable anger that sparked his curiosity. "I'll just stick around awhile," he told himself. "This'll be interesting."

The little lounge was a pleasure to work. By the end of the first week, the room was packed for every set, the audiences generous with tips, drinks, and applause. And, for the first time, she was keeping up with the drinks as they appeared on the piano and, daily, her tolerance was building until five or six drinks scarcely phased her where once they'd have rendered her blankly numb.

It became something like smoking: she'd tell herself to cut back, ease off, but she couldn't. The pleasure of that first puff or cool swallow was something she wholly savored: gratifyingly intoxicating inhalations that swept her mind to safe, soft places where thought and thinking and coping with men were muzzy abstractions incapable of seriously seducing her back into reality.

Beneath the pastel distortion of this gladly induced amnesia, she sang and played better than she ever had, doing three forty-minute sets nightly. Who knew that she could accomplish this otherwise arduous endeavor only with the tranquilizing effects of her cigarettes and scotch? And what would it have mattered anyway?

Chas sat at the bar night after night, watching her put drinks away, listening to her sing, trying to get a mental fix on her. He was aware of an anxious look to her eyes, a positive delicacy to the lines of her throat and shoulders, the nape of her neck. A dozen different times he started forward to speak to her, then sat back in his seat, knowing he'd simply be lining up for another rejection. But every time he looked at her, he wanted to hold her face between his hands and say, "Everything's all right," because she seemed, at some moments, as if she was on the verge of disintegrating.

For two hours every afternoon, Lisa sat at the piano in the cool, deserted lounge behind the closed door, practising. She repeated the lyrics of new tunes until they were one with the changes and she was free to improvise and personalize what she'd learned.

139

People passing through the lobby stopped to pull chairs up close to the door where they sat with unopened books and silenced transistor radios in their laps and rapt expressions on their faces, listening. They sat, lured into dreams of past or hoped-for happiness, unaware of anything but the undiluted, penetratingly pure intimacy of the statements emanating from behind the door. Newcomers inadvertently intruding into the hushed silence of the lobby grew instantly quiet, wondering what was going on until they, too, heard and looked about for a chair or a free space on the floor near the door. The drummer and guitarist from Johnny's band set up their chessboard each afternoon to the left of the door and played the game with their eyes fastened on the board and their ears filled with Lisa's sounds.

Chas moved about, usually ending up by the pillar adjacent to the lounge door, studying the faces of those assembled as he also listened, trying to pinpoint what it was about Lisa that so magically lifted people—such dissimilar people—out of themselves and into her world.

The management took notice of what was occurring in the main lobby and at once telephoned Nick in New York to pick up her options for the rest of the season. They'd never made so much money from the little lounge and even started posting a waiter in the lobby in the afternoons in order to take advantage of any additional revenue they might secure through these gratuitous concerts. Business boomed. They added another hundred a week to her paycheck. Lisa didn't notice. She came daily out of the lounge to see people nodding and smiling at her as they went about replacing their chairs, still caught up in the afterglow of what they'd heard. And always, every day, there was Chas leaning against the pillar smiling a welcome to her.

If he was what he said he was, why didn't he make a move? Why didn't he either say something or go away altogether?

For the most part, she went unrecognized during the day. Without benefit of a spotlight and long dress, she wasn't easily identifiable as the performer from the lounge. It was reassuring to be able to pass by the pool and through the grounds unaccosted. She was still wary of daytime confrontations, unsure how long this new verbal facility might last; uncertain how long she'd be able to fend off this persistent shadow before giving him what he wanted and being left to wallow in the ensuing loss of self. At any moment, she expected to open her mouth and find herself once more adrift, floundering for words with which to respond to the people who came near to extend their praise.

She considered all this while she floated around in the ocean, lying on her back, letting the tide carry her around for an hour or two until her eyes were stinging from the salt and sun. Her tan progressed, her paper whiteness was gone. But she felt ill. The smell of food revolted her. She was unable to eat anything but bland, colorless things, white food: unbuttered toast, cheese sandwiches, lettuce, black coffee.

Returning from the beach, she'd see Chas lying on a beach towel, reading. She'd run past and go to her room to dress before coming down again to wander through the shops, picking things up, putting them down, chatting with the salesgirls.

It was while she was staring at the windows of the gift shop that it slowly dawned on her what was happening. She'd missed a period. It wasn't unusual. It happened often on the road. But this was something else. She was on her way to missing another one. Oh wow! she thought, holding her hand over her mouth. Oh, Jesus Christ! She started walking down toward the beach, trying to put it together. How could it have happened? When?

She sat down on the sand and lit a cigarette, trying to think. She'd been taking her pills. She hadn't missed any. When had she had the last period? November. The beginning of November. But she'd been away on the road after that. Her only other contact with Brad had been that night he'd gone crazy. But no, wait. She'd been in New York. That's right. She'd had a week between gigs. And she'd started her period the night after she'd got back.

141

She'd slept with Brad that night. He'd said he didn't mind. "It's warm," he'd said. Was it possible? It had to be because that was the only time she'd slept with him. At the beginning of November. That meant she was close to two months pregnant. She took a deep drag on the cigarette and wrapped her arms around her knees.

Pregnant. "I'm pregnant," she whispered, wanting to hear the words. I'm pregnant. What do I do? How do I *feel*?

She remembered Aimée and how she'd felt holding the baby, how she'd told Jeanette, "I'd like to have one."

"I could have it," she whispered again. She'd never really thought about it, having a baby, a child of her own. She'd always thought of children as part of what happened after being married. But of course it didn't have to be that way. It *wasn't* that way. She was already pregnant and she certainly wouldn't marry Brad. God! she thought. It was lucky he hadn't harmed it, doing that to her. How do I feel? she asked herself once more. She thought about it, watching the sun on the water.

I'm glad! she thought, amazed. I'm glad. Her mind went racing ahead like a small child on the beach, skipping this way and that. She had all the money Letty had left her. More than enough to buy a house—if that's what she wanted—and to live on. Money was no problem. But where? She had to live somewhere if she was going to have a child to look after. And what about her career? She'd have to stop working. At least for a while.

It doesn't matter, she thought, burying the cigarette in the sand and covering it over. I'm having a baby. She smiled. I'm going to be a mother. It was fantastic! All that time trying to make Brad into a protector, a family-daddy. And he'd given her the one thing, she now realized, she most wanted. Her own family. I'm a family. She laughed aloud, thrilled.

"Is this another bad time to approach you?" a voice asked from behind her.

She turned and laughed, saying, "You found the perfect time. Come sit down."

It didn't matter about him. Or anyone. She was a family. She could talk to anybody.

"Something amusing?" he asked, sitting down beside her.

"A little," she smiled, wondering what it was about him that had made her so mad. He seemed very pleasant.

"Listen," he said, "it's now or never. I've got to get back to New York, so we have to talk now."

"I'm listening."

"How many of those numbers you play are yours?"

"How do you know any of them are?"

"It's my business to know." He said this without any hint of pride but with a confidence in his own knowledge.

"About fifteen, I guess. Some of them aren't ready yet."

"I want to ask you something," he said, his expression changing, curiosity flickering in his eyes. "Do you like the taffeta act?"

"The what?"

"The big makeup and evening-gown number."

"Is that what you call it?"

"It's what *I* call it. That and piano-bar and four-bills-a-week. Do you?"

"I'd rather just sing," she said honestly.

"Good. Because I've been working the picture out in my mind."

"How does it look?" she asked, smothering her laughter. All she wanted to do was roll around on the sand and laugh and laugh.

"It looks like this: We scrub you off. No more of the pancake and eyeshadow. Let your hair down. Your hair is perfect the way it is right now. Get you some nice young-looking clothes with decent necklines, stuff the kids are wearing. That's for openers. Then we all sit down and start working. I've got a kid who writes great stuff. Plays first-class piano and flute. His only problem is he can't sing. Not even badly. He just can't sing. I think between the two of you, we've got more than enough material for two sides of an album. Nick tells me you can orchestrate. Is that true?"

"Absolutely." She was watching him wide-eyed now.

"Could you do say, sixteen pieces including brass and maybe a couple of violins? How good are you?"

"I don't know. I haven't done more than trios since I was at the conservatory. But I could probably do it." She thought of the work that would be involved and found herself growing excited. "It'd be something fantastic to try."

"Are you interested?"

"Are you serious?" she asked.

"I'm an independent producer. I'm willing to put up the bread if you're willing to sign an exclusive contract with me. I think you're worth the investment. More than worth it. Everybody from grannies to teenies would buy your sound. I've been watching how they turn on to you every day. You're the best thing I've heard in ten years, maybe more."

"I'm not a 'thing,'" she said.

"It's just an expression."

"How exclusive?"

"I produce your albums, manage your career."

"And what do you get?" She wasn't sure she liked the word 'exclusive.'

"Twenty-five percent across the board. It's more than fair."

"I see. And we'd do my music?"

"Yours and Tim's. You'll have to meet him, you'll work together. I figure six weeks or so, between the two of you for the charts. And then roughly four weeks to do the taping. Ever worked with anyone before?"

"Not the way you mean it, no."

"How does it strike you?" he asked, offering her a cigarette.

"Everything strikes me," she laughed, accepting the cigarette. A baby!

"I'm catching the afternoon flight back to Palm Beach. I've got a few things to do but I should be able to get back here in about three weeks with the contracts drawn up. If you're still interested then, we'll talk some more."

"What were you doing in Freeport?" she asked.

"Catching another act. Duds," he shook his head. "But

144

the trip was worthwhile, hearing you. What's the big joke? You keep smiling to yourself. Am I funny to you?"

"Nothing to do with you. I don't think you're at all funny."

"Sometimes I am," he grinned, his eyes teasing her.

"I'll bet you are."

"Well," he said, sitting on his heels, "it's up to you, Lisa. I think you're sensational. Aside from your jump-the-gun attitude back there. Was there any particular reason for all that?"

"I have reasons for everything I do," she said dryly. If she didn't before, she promised herself, she would in the future.

"Way to go!" He laughed, his hand on her shoulder. "You'll be okay. Think it over. You're a beautiful girl with all kinds of great talent. We could really take it one hell of a long way if you want to try. No strings, no snags. Think about it and I'll see you in a few weeks. Okay?"

"Where would we be working?"

"New York."

"Oh no!" she said, instantly tense. "That's impossible."

"Why?" He sat back down again.

"I hate New York. It wouldn't work. And anyway, I don't have a place to stay."

"Supposing I find you a place to stay? Would that help?"

"I don't know." She looked at his face. He seemed to be very open, very honest. "There are some things you'll have to know," she said, meeting his eyes.

"You want to tell me now or will they hold?"

"It might make a difference to your plans if you know," she said, all at once hoping it wouldn't make any difference to him. She wanted to go back and meet Tim and do charts for a hundred pieces if need be. But she wanted to do it all.

"Tell me," he said gently. "Some kind of trouble?"

"Oh no. Not trouble. I'm very happy about it. I'm pretty sure I'm pregnant."

"Is that what all the laughing and smiling's been about?"

"I just now figured it out, you see. Just now."

"I take it you're happy about it?"

"Every time I think about it, I want to laugh and laugh. I've never even *thought* about it before."

"Congratulations," he said, extending his hand. "Kids are the best."

"You think so?" She gave him her hand. "You have children?"

"No, but I was one once."

She laughed, aware of the warmth of his hand and how good he looked when he smiled.

"Are you sure?" he asked, keeping hold of her hand.

"Pretty sure. I'll have to go see the hotel doctor."

"Well, I think it's great. About the city, will you let me take care of that? You don't have to spend the rest of your life there. But it's where I'm set up to do business. I'll make sure you're all right. After all," his smile grew larger, "it's in my best interest, too, to protect my investment."

"You haven't made one yet," she smiled back.

"But we'll do it, right?"

"If I don't do that, I'll go home. I don't want to do any more lounges. I'm tired of them. I hate getting made-up and dressed-up six nights of every week. I don't feel real with all that."

"Who are you?" he asked.

"I'm just starting to find out," she admitted. "Maybe that's part of what you asked about."

"Keep finding out," he said, getting up, squeezing her hand before letting go. "You're going to make it."

Chapter 10

She went to see the hotel doctor who confirmed the pregnancy and gave her some tablets to ease the nausea. It was official and she took the first of the Benadryl tablets thinking, I have to take good care of myself. It's very important now to take care. She felt as if she'd spent all of her life up until then living inside a mechanical room that required only regular, perfunctory attention. All of that was different now, because of the baby. Her body had become something extraordinary, capable of making another human body. It amazed and astounded her.

In her room, she stood naked in front of the mirror looking at herself. Nothing showed yet. She'd lost quite a bit of weight during the last month without really being aware of it. She'd have to pay attention, to eat properly, build herself up. My own child. The very idea of it filled her with euphoria. She wanted it right away, immediately, that minute; so she could see and touch it, hold and feel it.

Nothing that had gone before mattered. None of it. Chas was going to let her sing her music. She wouldn't have to do any more gigs on the road. She'd be able to stay in one place and be a mother. God! She laughed, looking at her face.

"I like you," she told her beaming reflection. "I *like* you."

That night, between sets, she strolled out to the terrace to stand on the fringes of the crowd watching the Trinidadian troupe who came to perform on weekends. With

147

fascinated horror, she watched the fire-eater breathe out orange snakes of flame. She was close enough to smell his singed facial hair and the acrid odor of burnt skin. Nausea rose inside her and she moved to go but at that moment the wind shifted direction, banishing the smell. There was a burst of applause accompanied by another sort of wind, the expulsion of the held breath of the audience. She looked at the faces in the crowd, seeing there the sheepish smiles and sudden laughter of relief. They'd felt it too, she thought, eased.

The dancers came on, shaking pieces of broken glass from ragged cotton bags they threw to one side before embarking on a frenzied, tribalistic dance that seemed to be some form of mating ritual.

The men's faces were painted white, their chests and sinuous legs bared. Their feet looked strong and hard. They seemed not to notice the broken glass. Lisa heard a man behind her say knowingly, "All smooth edges. Nothing sharp there." She nodded to herself, thinking he was probably right. Yet the glass caught the light, glinting menacingly beneath the flying feet and swooping bodies. The women appeared, looking equally sinuous and lithe as they entwined themselves in and around the men with rapt, shining faces. The hands of the drummer smacked against the drumskins, pounding out sounds that seemed like the erratic, desperate beating of hearts on the verge of bursting. She could feel the thumping within herself as her eyes followed the flashing movements of the dancers.

Then, in an unexpected fall of silence, the dancers held motionless for a full five seconds before, with barely perceptible movements, they shifted positions, each dancer facing a member of the audience. The male member of the troupe nearest her had positioned himself directly in front of a fiftyish woman in an enormous muu-muu who, giggling, reached for her husband's hand, saying, "Oh dear! Oh my stars!" The dancer seemed impervious to her discomfort. His eyes were burning into Lisa's, his entire soul, it seemed, focused on her.

She stood, feeling his eyes like fingers traveling through her brain and body. Her arms hung limply by her sides as she felt herself swaying closer to him. His eyes were like black gems in the white-painted face, glowing, gleaming; threatening. She felt terribly afraid and reached out, holding onto a tree for support. Then, the drummers exploded into sound and the troupe whirled members of the audience off into a mock limbo, leaving Lisa with the impression she'd somehow just been made—in the most terrible fashion—to look a fool. She could feel the heat of shame in her face and neck as she backed off, picking her way through the crowd, heading back to the lounge.

She paused in the lobby with her hand on one of the cool pillars, eyes closed, trying to think it through. I'm not a thing for men to appraise with their eyes, she thought. Why did I let that happen? She was angry with herself because she'd played at being the old Lisa, the one with the formula men and the ungovernable needs. From now on, she thought, *I* choose. I don't get *chosen*. I'm me, not merchandise. I'm not a jukebox or a slotted wind-up toy. I'm *me*. All those things that happened, she thought, they happened because I let them. I wasn't thinking. I was just letting things happen. I can't do that anymore. Not for me and not for the baby. You can't just let things happen if you're going to be responsible for someone else as well as your own self.

I like me. I've always taken care of myself. Now I'll do it right, do it properly; take care of all of me. I don't have to put myself on display and hope to be approved by *anyone*. She pulled herself erect and looked at the lounge doors.

I might go home to have the baby, she thought. I'll have to think about that. She'd only been back on flying visits three times in the last seven years. It wasn't enough. Especially if she was going to be a mother. The baby would need the rest of its family, would have to know it had a family. I have to keep thinking, she told herself. Things mustn't be allowed to *just happen*.

The terrace incident hung in the back of her mind for days, and she flushed with anger every time she recalled

149

it. She'd never forget the sight of the man's mouth opening to emit a shrill bark of laughter as his eyes raked the length of her body and his hands reached for the chubby housewife.

Eventually, it diminished, leaving her with a residue of hurt and the echo in her head of a cutting, mid-western voice that drawled, "All smooth edges. Nothing sharp there."

He'd been wrong, of course, the owner of that voice. She knew that because before returning to her room that night, she'd ventured out to the terrace where she'd found an overlooked piece of the glass. She'd picked it up and held it in her hand, running her thumb over the edges. The glass sliced through her skin so that a bright pen-stroke of blood appeared, welling into a brilliant bubble that had burst and trickled down into the palm of her hand. She'd stood, staring at the blood-stained shard for several seconds before flinging it into the shrubbery and fleeing to her room.

By the following Monday she was counting down the days until Chas returned. She was anxious to begin working, to get started on what she was sure would be good, productive hard work resulting in an end product she very much wanted. She was perfecting the newer songs, walking about fixing up the lyrics in her mind, cleaning up the changes, smoothing out the flow of words and music.

Halfway through her second set, she spotted Charles at a small table in the center of the room with an exquisitely beautiful woman. The woman returned Lisa's look, smiling. Unable to smile back as she'd have liked, but unable too to look away—the woman reminded her so strongly of Jeanette—Lisa continued to stare, mesmerized.

It wasn't so much that she actually looked like Jeanette, but rather this woman was a similar type: a lush-bodied redhead with very white, freckled skin, wearing a simple, low-cut, leaf-green dress. Her bare arms looked very soft, as did her throat and shoulders. She continued to smile, seeming to thrive visibly under Lisa's scrutiny and

Lisa looked away at last, frowning slightly at the keyboard.

At the end of that number, the waiter brought up a drink, indicating it had come from the woman with Charles. Lisa picked it up, nodded over at the woman and received, in return, a brilliant smile.

Charles came up as Lisa finished, inviting her to join them. She went along, receiving a warm, firm handclasp from the woman.

"Meet a very dear old friend," Charles said. "Claire Regan."

"Your music is simply glorious," she said, her hand still closed over Lisa's. "Please do join us, have a drink." A slight pressure brought Lisa down into the awaiting chair.

"Must close up the dining room," Charles said. "I'm sure you can manage beautifully without me for a bit."

Claire ordered another round and sat back looking at Lisa, very much at ease, very much in control.

"Where are you from?" Lisa asked.

"London."

"Oh!" Lisa felt as if she was talking from behind a glass door, unable to completely detach her attention from the questions she suddenly wanted to ask. "You knew Charles in England?"

"Quite!" Claire said, as if that one word bespoke volumes. "We're only stopping here the night, going on to Jamaica in the morning."

"We?"

"My daughter and I. Having a wee bit of a fling before she returns to school."

"And your husband?" Lisa asked without thinking.

Claire laughed, touching Lisa's hand with her fingertips. "I'm not married, darling," she picked up her glass. "Never have been actually."

"I'm sorry," Lisa flushed. "That was very rude of me."

"Not at all," she laughed. "It was refreshingly honest. I don't in the least mind."

'How old is your daughter?"

"Seventeen."

"You don't look old enough to have a daughter that age." It was true. She looked very young, very self-possessed.

"Thirty-eight," Claire said, appearing to enjoy the conversation. "And you?"

"Twenty-five. Tomorrow."

"How lovely! Happy birthday!"

"Thank you."

"I'm afraid I make you nervous." Her eyes were very knowing, very kind.

"No. I'm not nervous. My mind's somewhere else."

She examined Lisa's eyes, fingering the rim of her glass. "Are you pregnant, darling?"

"I have another set to do," Lisa said, suddenly unsure of this woman. She seemed to know too much too quickly.

"Don't let me frighten you away." She touched Lisa's hand again. "It's an unfortunate habit of mine, saying what I'm thinking. If you'd like to talk, I'd like to listen."

"Why?"

"It must be frightfully lonely doing what you do, doing it as well as you do. I can't help but feel you're dreadfully isolated. All those lovely, sad sad songs."

"Why did you say that?" Lisa asked, feeling less uncertain.

Claire leaned closer confidentially to say, "It's a look, my darling. When one's had it, one tends to recognize it in others." She stopped for a moment, placing her hand on Lisa's forearm. "You're a heavenly-looking creature," she said in an undertone. "Heavenly. I'd like very much to relax with you, talk."

Lisa listened to her rich, melodic voice, not hearing the words so much as feeling them; thinking how soothing it would be, how peace-makingly soothing to have this woman hold her, talk to her, explain things. "I'll come back," she said.

She returned after her last set and sat down, curious to see what Claire would do; if she'd once again pounce to the heart of matters and begin diagnosing and offering comfort.

152

It didn't happen. They smiled at her from time to time, supplying her with fresh drinks, attempting to include her in their reminiscing and, finally, she excused herself, thanked them and stood to go. She was very disappointed.

She sat down in the dark of her room, looking at the moonlight spill on the carpet by the balcony door. She lit a cigarette as she kicked off her shoes, sinking deep into the chair, her eyes captured by the puddle of moonlight on the floor, riveted to the sight of the wavering edges of the wet-looking splash of non-color. The edges shimmered like something alive.

How did Claire manage it alone? she wondered, attempting to visualize Claire's daughter. How did she feel? What was it like seventeen years ago, being unmarried and pregnant? She'd wanted so much to know. She felt horribly let down by the way things had turned out. There'd been no chance at all to talk.

She got up and went out to the balcony to look down at the empty poolside area. Chas would be coming back in just a few more days. But Chas couldn't answer the questions she wanted to ask Claire. She felt tired. Despite the tablets, her appetite hadn't properly returned. She wasn't gaining back any significant amount of weight.

There was a quiet tapping at the door and she turned, her spirits soaring as she hurried through the room, thinking it was Chas, bumping into the armchair in her haste. Claire was standing there smiling, a bag in her hand. Lisa stepped back and Claire came in, stopping to lock the door behind her.

As she stood watching Claire set down the bag and come toward her. She felt afraid.

"I can't," Lisa whispered as the woman's arms came around her. "Please. I can't." •

"Hush, darling. It's all right. I'll just make you feel good. We'll talk. Nothing will happen that you don't want to happen."

It felt strange, embarrassing to be undressed by another woman. Yet there was something indescribably comforting in the process. Claire accomplished it quickly, then got Lisa to lie down on the bed as she went to fetch the bag.

"Relax, darling," Claire said, sitting on the side of the bed with the bag in her lap. "A thing or two to clear the mind," she smiled coaxingly, her teeth catching the moonlight. "Turn over on your stomach, that's a good girl."

She felt endangered, imperiled but did as she was told, hiding her face in the pillow, her eyes tightly closed. Time passed and then she felt a weight tilting the bed and something cool being applied to her back and shoulders, all the way down to her heels. She turned her head to look.

Naked, her breasts silvery-looking, Claire knelt beside her, massaging something into Lisa's skin.

"Gorgeous, isn't it?" she said softly, her hands working, kneading. "You'll sleep wonderfully well tonight."

"What is it?"

"Oil of wintergreen. You'll smell a bit like a sweetshop but you'll feel marvelousy loose. Turn over now."

"It is good," Lisa murmured, thinking nothing bad would happen after all. She turned.

Claire reached once more into the bag and brought out a small pipe which she lit, drew on, then passed to Lisa.

"Go on, darling. Good, too."

They smoked the pipe out in silence, then Clair set it aside and began applying the oil to Lisa's shoulders and breasts.

"My darling," she whispered, "You're so thin. *Are* you?"

"Yes."

"Glad?"

"Yes. Tell me about you," Lisa whispered, catching hold of Claire's hands, studying her face in the semi-light. "Why did *you* do it? How?"

Claire sat down. "I swing both ways, darling. It's nothing extraordinary. I hate obvious people. Swinging *hard* is obvious. I don't like it. I do what I like to do, what feels right—provided it doesn't harm anyone else. That's important, not harming anyone else. I very much wanted a child. Marriage seemed too confining, too lim-

154

iting. It wasn't a question of fidelity, not in the sense of sticking to one man. None of that. It was more that all the legalities seemed to be directed to depriving me of my right to choose, do you see? And if you're married, with all the terms they make you agree to, then so much of the spontaneity goes out of your life. For me, in any event. It wasn't easy. But then, I had money of my own, and that's a tremendous factor. The money gave me the freedom to walk away from unpleasantness. There certainly was a goodly supply of that. But since I was doing something I wanted to do, what other people said and did wasn't all that important. Oh, some of it hurt. There's always that. But not enough to take away the joy of doing what I wanted to be doing. Suzanne's wonderful. She's my anchor. She keeps me from flying away off the face of the earth when things happen that I sometimes can't handle. It happens to all of us," she said, curving her hand over Lisa's cheek. "You're at the beginning," she smiled. "You're only just starting to find out what you want for yourself, what you need. I don't think you'll be sorry, darling. It's not all lovely and light-hearted having a child on your own, but it's a great great deal in terms of self-fulfillment. Not for every woman, necessarily. For me, yes. I think for you, too. What happened to you, darling? There's such a well of sadness and little-girl hurt in you. Can you talk about it?"

"What do you do? Do you have a career?"

"Oh yes," Claire smiled. "That's a very great part of the why of it all, don't you see? I couldn't bear the idea of being somebody's loving drudge." She laughed. "They don't want to let you be both. It's either the one or the other—mother-wife or career. It made me so bloody mad! I damned well wasn't going to be an either/or just because *they* said that's the way it had to be. I'm a designer," she said. "Rather well known at home. Make heaps of money and laugh to myself every time I think about all the ones who said, 'You can't do that, Claire.' The hell I couldn't! I wasn't born with just organs or just brains. It's all one, my darling. Why not use it all?"

"You remind me of my stepmother," Lisa said, smiling. "I think you'd like her."

"I like *you*, darling. Are you still frightened of me?"

"No." It was a lie. She looked at Claire's body. Not only was she afraid, she was beginning to feel the stirrings of depression.

"I don't think," Claire said quietly, "you need fear for your heterosexuality, darling. Being with me isn't going to turn you gay. It's simply a need you have right now to know, to find out. I'm not a recruiter. You're perfectly lovely as you are. I haven't any desire to change you. I don't expect we'll ever cross paths again. But you're beautifully made in every way and I care very much to know you. I fancy any number of men myself. But every so often, there's someone—a woman—who moves something in me. What happened to your mother? Were your parents divorced? Or did she die?"

"She died. But she wasn't my mother. I was adopted."

"I see!" she said, lifting her head. 'I do see! Then it's all so right for you, isn't it? Having the child. Oh yes," she nodded earnestly. "That's very right. It was an accident, I gather."

"It really was. I'd never even thought about it before, not without somehow being married. That's why, when you said that, I wanted to know. Does it hurt? How was that part of it? Will you tell me?" Keep her talking, she thought. Then nothing can happen.

"Lord!" she laughed. "It was all too easy," she said. "I'm rather built for it. We're all so different. But, yes it hurt. But when it comes to that, it doesn't matter. Because the pain is *for* something, not just pain, do you see? You don't really even think about all that afterward, not really. The baby makes all the difference. All you can think of is: I want to *see* it. I want to know what it looks like, what it'll be like. It's just a lot of jolly hard work and some nasty pains that go away sooner than you expect. And afterward, God! I remember every minute of it. I was so happy, so bloody smug and self-important. Because, after all, darling, if you think about it, it's a miracle in one sense. Bloody marvelous making another person right inside of you. I can't begin to tell you how many times I've been tempted to do it all again. Of course, one tends to forget all the more tedious aspects of caring for a child. You know, the dirty nappies and spitting up, all of that. I don't have the patience now I once did. One child's enough."

"What about her? How has it been for her not having a father?"

"Oh well," Claire sighed. "Of course there's always some fool of a child—or adult, too—who'll say something heartless and stupidly cruel. There is that. But it so depends on you, darling. If you're truthful, it has great value. I've never told Suzanne anything but the truth. It hasn't been all that easy, but it hasn't been all that bad, either. She relates well to her peers, she doesn't feel the need to go about searching the world for a father. I might've been plain lucky in that. I can't honestly say. So much of it is just hoping for the best. You can't make the child turn out the way you want. You just do the best you can and try to be honest. How long have you been traveling about on your own?"

"Close to nine years. It's funny," Lisa said thoughtfully, "up until just a few weeks ago I never thought about me, about being my own person. All I cared about was singing, playing. And all at once, I started realizing that I could control the things I did, the things that happened to me. Not about the baby. That was an accident. But the rest of it. What I did, how I was. And then, when Brad did . . . that . . . it sort of shocked me into the world. I was just trying to feel my way out of everything and that happened and I was out. It was real and the rest of the world was real, and I had to stop and stand still and look at everything and at me, too."

"What did he do to you, darling?" Claire's hand slid down the length of Lisa's arm, then back up again and across her shoulder to her throat.

"He . . . attacked me."

"He raped you?"

"Worse." Lisa closed her eyes, remembering the pain, the water-blood streaming down her legs.

"Christ!" Claire said softly. "I've always had a horror of being abused. Tell me," she said. "Get rid of it. I can see from the look of you it was ghastly."

"He . . . I was with him for four years. I started it thinking I needed someone to protect me. But when I realized he wasn't doing any of that, I decided to break it off. When I told him it was over, he went crazy. He was old, much much older."

"How old?"

"Fifty-seven."

"A wee bit elderly," Claire smiled encouragingly. "Go on."

"He started hitting me, tearing my clothes off. I stopped fighting. I thought he'd just do that and go away. He started to and I fought when I hadn't planned to. Then he went out of me and I wondered what was happening. I knew he hadn't finished. Then he . . . it was . . . I screamed and he held his hand over my mouth."

"He sodomized you."

Lisa nodded, "All at once. Just . . . forced himself into me. And afterward, he started saying he was sorry and I screamed at him to get out. I was bleeding. He had blood all over his trousers. It hurt. It hurt so badly." She started trembling, reliving the incident again, tears spilling over.

"Bastard!" Claire said fiercely, gathering Lisa into her arms, holding her as Lisa sobbed. "Poor darling," she crooned, her hands stroking, gliding up and down the length of Lisa's spine. "The things they do! Men with their bloody cocks thinking they can do the things they do. There are so damned few of them who don't used their cocks to think with. Walking about being told what to do by their penises! It's all so bloody stupid. I'm so sorry that happened to you, darling. You'll learn to know, though. As you find yourself, you'll find out about others."

She was right, Lisa thought. She did feel better. Telling about it made it less, took away the numbing terror she'd been carrying around without even realizing it.

"I feel better," she whispered, only to become aware

now of a number of other things: the scent of Claire's body, the feel of another woman's bared breasts pressing against her own, the incredible softness of Claire's skin, the intensity of Claire's body. And she was frightened, filled with reluctance. Why couldn't it be just the talking? Why did this have to happen? I don't want this. Oh, please! she thought, I don't *want* this.

"I . . . I've never done any of this," she whispered, her mouth dry, fear pulsing in her throat.

"No matter," Claire murmured, her mouth on Lisa's neck. "Don't be frightened. You're so sweet."

Oh God, I can't! Please, I can't! But there was no way out. And she wanted to hate this woman, despise her for being just like Brad but in different ways. Making her pay for a few minutes of kindness, not allowing her to decide for herself. Extracting payment. And Lisa was going to have to pay.

"Don't think about it," Claire said, using small signals to indicate to Lisa that she should lie back. And Lisa, paralyzed by her reluctance, took her mind back to the night when she'd watched Jeanette standing naked in her room; back to the feelings she'd had that night, the longing she'd felt for being held, loved, reassured. Closing her eyes, transforming this woman into Jeanette, convincing herself this was an act of love, an act of need. Something to get through and never think of. Ever again.

But Claire wasn't going to allow her to pretend. Claire wanted her to know, to see. Lisa tried to close down her mind, unable to say, "I don't feel this way. You're forcing me into something I don't want. Couldn't you be kind and leave me just with the understanding? That was good for me, that helped. But this isn't helping."

"You're lovely," Claire whispered, her hands laying claim to Lisa's breasts. Her mouth following her hands, bestowing pleasure where it wasn't wanted. But pleasure. Claire's hands, her fingers proprietarily stroking, investigating, insisting on pleasure. And Lisa responded, unable not to. Responding because, at the very least, no pain came with this encounter; no force physically.

For one instant, Lisa thought, "My God! This is insane! How can this be happening? I don't want *this*." But then she felt Claire's mouth on her and closed her eyes, flying off to other places, other times; unable to face the reality; unable to open her eyes to look, to see another woman—not a man, but a *woman*—between her legs.

And yet the feeling was good, the pleasure was there. My God! she shuddered under the onslaught of this pleasure. "Oh, *God!*" You come here and help me so much with my thoughts and then you open me up and do all this, make me scared again. But of new things, different things. But the feeling. My God! The *feeling*. And small, strange gratification knowing this woman cannot do one thing, that one thing, cannot be a formula man, is not a man.

But what am I, who? To lie here, all open, while you're doing that to me and I can't even pretend you're someone I love because you're not anyone I love. You might have been. If you hadn't had to do this. I wish you didn't have to do this but oh my God I can't—I am.

Claire's hands reached up to cover Lisa's breasts. And Lisa, her eyes locked shut, telling herself no, no, thinking, but this doesn't matter. It'll be like all the other times it doesn't matter. I'm me now I have a child inside it doesn't matter even your mouth is different feels different not like a man's, knowing, making me come I'm going to come how can this happen to me I'm coming I'll live alone for the rest of my life never need anyone want anyone no one's ever going to use me again never I'm not a machine you can turn on this way making me come but you're the end the last one never again making me come.

Chapter 11

Next morning, as she was passing the front desk, the assistant manager called to her. "There's something for you, Miss Hamilton."

Puzzled, she stood by the desk, watching him pull a small package out of the mail-slot for her room.

"Lady left this for you this morning when she was checking out."

The box contained a tiny, enamelled scarab pin and a note which said, "Happy Birthday. Think of today as the start of the first year of your life. Perhaps it is. Bless you. Claire."

She couldn't take it in. Her mouth was filled with water, her face bathed in perspiration and she turned, flying to the ladies' room adjacent to the coffee shop. It was unoccupied. She sank to the floor by the sinks, bending her head forward, letting her forehead rest against her knees, breathing slowly, deeply; praying no one would come in. Fool! I forgot to take my pill.

Ten minutes later, she was able to get to her feet. She splashed cold water on the back of her neck and over her face, then made her way out to the lobby.

She stood for a moment. A plane must have arrived. People were pouring out of the hotel hospitality vans, straggling in through the front doors, approaching the desk. And, looking through the doors, she saw a black rental car pull up and Chas climbed out.

She felt a surprised leaping inside her chest but was suspicious of it and walked out through the doors to meet him, fighting down the temptation to be glad to see him. No more invitations. She wasn't going to be inviting any more invasions. I have to be very careful from now on. This is business.

"Hi!" he smiled. "I told you I'd be back."

She stood, watching the driver lift Chas's bags out of the trunk of the car, allowing a small smile to form on her mouth.

"Come on," he said, reaching to take hold of her hand. "We've got a lot of talking to do."

She withdrew her hand casually.

"What's been going on the past couple of weeks?" he asked, as the driver moved the car on out of the driveway so that they were left standing in the middle of the incoming traffic.

"More finding out," she said. "We're blocking traffic."

"You want some coffee?" he asked. "I'm starved. Had breakfast? You look a lot better."

"I'm hungry," she said, falling into step with him, watching as he accepted the ignition key from the hotel driver. It was interesting, she thought, that he didn't seem to waste any time in the things he did.

"Tell me what you've been up to," he said as they seated themselves in a booth. The same one she'd had the morning that he'd tried to explain to her who he was.

"Nothing really," she said, thinking, yes, he was just as good-looking as she'd remembered. She'd have to be very careful. "A lot of thinking. Things."

"And junior?" he smiled. "How's the family?"

She took a tablet with a sip of water. "I forgot you knew about that." She smiled automatically. "It's almost three months already. Who are you? All I know is your name."

"Who are *you*? Every time I see you, you're different. Better but different."

"I am," she said slowly, looking him straight in the eye, "Lisa Hamilton. I play piano. And I sing and compose music. I'm your new star. We're going to do business together. That's who I am."

"D'you know I stayed down here ten days because you're someone I've always wanted to know? That's the

162

God's honest truth. I couldn't wait to get back here, to find out if you'd changed your mind."

"What would you've done if I had?"

"I'd've been damned disappointed, I'll tell you. But you haven't and that's great! You look so good!"

"Are you going to tell me?" she asked, swayed toward more than liking him.

"I'm me, too. Thirty-six. Divorced. I don't live anywhere at the moment but I have to think about that. And I'm glad as hell to see you. Business aside. Scare you?"

"Maybe. I don't know yet."

"What *have* you been up to? I can't believe you're the same hostile lady who a month ago was telling me to fuck off."

"I'm *not* the same hostile lady. I don't want you to fuck off. We have business to do together."

"You don't eh? I like that. I like that a lot."

The waitress came and they ordered.

"I'd better give you the rundown," he said, then stopped, his head slightly to one side as he looked at her. "God, it's the best feeling to see you. You're so positive, so sure. You haven't fallen in love with some guy down here, have you?"

"Would it matter?"

"Sure, it'd matter."

"For you, yourself, or for business?"

"Both," he said openly. "I thought about you the whole time I was gone. Is it what you want to hear?"

"It might be. I don't know."

"That's fair. Okay, down to business for a few minutes. I've cleared it with Nick, so you're out of your options. In fact, your replacement was on my flight. You can leave any time you're ready."

"So soon?" she said. "I didn't know it would be so soon."

"Hey," he laughed. "We've got to get to work. We can't have you delivering junior in the middle of a session. I want to get this show on the road as soon as possible."

"I wish people would tell me these things. I'm not ready."

"I'll help you pack," he said lightly. "How'd you get over? Fly or come across on the hotel yacht?"

"I flew. My car's in Palm Beach."

"Fine. We can fly over, pick up the car and drive back."

"And spend a few cozy nights together on the road. No way."

"Ah! The old suspicious Lisa just came steaming to the surface. Did I say one word about anything like that? No, I did not. You're going to do whatever you want to do. I knew that the first time I tried to talk to you. You're jumping the gun again."

"Well, I'm still not used to everything. It takes time."

"Tell me about this guy, the one, you know."

"Brad," she made a face. "I'm not going to tell you all about me unless you're going to tell me all about you. I'm not signing my life over to you, Chas."

"I should hope not. I don't want that kind of responsibility."

"What does that mean?"

"It means I've been over that route already, having a dependent. It's no good. If I'm going to be involved with someone, a woman, it's going to be mutual, equal. I'm not going to play he-man and do all the work while my 'appendage' lies on a chaise longue and eats bon-bons. That stinks! I'm no idealistic kid, Lisa. I'm a grown man with a good life and I don't have any suicidal impulses to hand myself away with vows and promises, saying I'll do things I don't want to do."

"I don't understand."

"It means, if I'm going to get involved, I'll get involved for the right reasons and not because it's the way my mother and father did it forty years ago. You follow that? Shit! I sound ridiculous. I'm very turned on by you. I like everything I've seen of you so far, even the defensiveness. I'm willing and a whole lot interested but I'm way past the stage of playing house. Games of any kind. It's one of the reasons I haven't made up my mind about stay-

164

ing in New York. That whole scene. The girls all out looking, cruising the East Side bars. The guys all making out. I get too goddamned tired of all that. One of the things I've liked about you from the word go is your honesty. You're a very straight lady. It's a very nice change. Believe it! If you're happy because you're finding out about yourself and you're into a growth process, terrific. You should be happy. You've got a whole lot going for you. So much, I'm willing to put me and my money on the line."

"About the money," she began. "I've been thinking about that, about what you said. The exclusive contract and the twenty-five per cent. All of that."

"And?"

"I don't like it. I'm not paper you can sign and take over. I'll make a deal with you, but we'll talk terms."

"You have my complete attention."

"It's like my arrangement with Nick. I'm the only act Amalgamated doesn't have signed to a standard five-year contract. I wouldn't do it, and Nick's never asked me to. And it's all part of what I've been finding out in the last weeks and months. You shouldn't make people . . . shouldn't treat them like documents. I don't like the idea of that. I know it's fair if you put up your money that you should have some kind of guarantee. But I have some other ideas. I'd like to try to work them out."

"Tell me," he said. "You're making good sense so far."

"Okay. What I think is this: I think we should each put up an equal amount of money, however much it costs to get the whole record done."

"Hold on a minute!" he interrupted. "Have you any idea how much we're talking about?"

"It doesn't matter. I have a lot of money. A lot. However much it costs, I can handle it."

"Now, wait a minute, Lisa. What you think of as a lot and what I *know* is a lot might be two vastly different things."

"I have *a lot*," she said.

"Like how much?"

"Like more than half a million. Maybe more. I haven't

checked with my trustees in a couple of years. The only time I've ever gone into the money was to buy my first car nine years ago. Is that enough?"

"It's enough," he laughed. "Give me the rest of your idea."

"Okay. We split everything right down the middle, including the profits if we make any. No exclusive contracts. No contracts at all. If we can't trust each other, we shouldn't do business, period. That's the deal."

He sat back in the booth and looked at her thinking he wanted to see her every day for the rest of his life; to talk to her and argue with her, to touch her and love her and hear her laugh.

"You've got a deal," he said, finally, coming forward again. "A joint venture."

"You agree?" She looked surprised.

"Sure." He smiled. She liked the way his eyetooth slightly overlapped the front tooth. It was a nice, slightly imperfect, slightly teasing smile.

"Okay," she said. "Now what do we do?"

"First we have breakfast. Then we get your stuff together and book space on the afternoon flight back to Palm Beach. We pick up your car and work out the fine print on our way north."

"What was your wife like?"

"A nice girl. Traditional. Boring."

"Why'd you marry her then?"

"Because everybody was doing it."

"Really?"

"Really." He wasn't smiling. "We all, one time or another, do things because we think we're supposed to do them. I'm not a nine-to-fiver and I'm not a 'husband.' Not the way she wanted it, anyway. It was a mistake, no one to blame especially. What about you?" he asked.

"I was scared. I used to go to bed at night and when I closed my eyes, I'd see miles and miles of highway sliding past underneath me—like being in a car with a glass bottom. Brad made that stop, in a way. He held me down with his body and I was grateful. I believed him because I convinced myself I wanted to believe him:

166

because I thought I wanted someone to look after me but I was really still looking after myself. And if I was doing all the hard work, what did I need him for? I didn't. Not at all. When I told him I wanted out, he got very . . . violent. He hurt me, physically hurt me. I didn't know how much until I met someone who helped me get it out, to talk about it and understand it. It's over now and I can forget about it. I'm alive and I feel okay and that's all."

"Where are you from?" he asked. "You have family?"

She told him where she was from, about the family. "I'm starting my own family," she said. "You can laugh at me, it doesn't matter."

"Why the hell would I laugh at you? It isn't funny."

"You don't think so?" she asked.

"No, I don't think so." He looked angry. "There's not one goddamned funny thing about trying to find yourself, your life. The point is, you're trying. I don't find you funny, Lisa. Anything but. *Anything* but funny."

She looked down at his hand firmly closed over hers, then back at his face, feeling certainty spreading through her like a positive interior warmth.

"You didn't get angry when I was so rude," she said, thinking aloud. "You stayed. You were always there. And I couldn't make sense of you, couldn't figure you out. I thought you were just out to score, dangling the record as bait. But you weren't, were you?"

"No."

"And it wasn't just the record, either, was it?"

"No, it wasn't."

"How did you know?" she asked softly.

"I just knew."

"But how?"

"You're the one," he said soberly. "I don't know how I knew but I did. What is it for you?"

"The same," she said, her voice barely audible. "I've never felt this way before. You won't push me, will you?"

"You wouldn't let me," he smiled.

"No," she smiled back. "I wouldn't."

"Does it feel right?"

167

"I can't believe it's all going right all of a sudden. All of it. Everything. For the first time in my whole life, I'm happy. You know?"

"I could see it, right away."

"You were only part of it."

"We're all only ever 'part of it.'"

"You think so?" Her eyes widened slightly.

"Listen," he leaned very close to her. "I'm in love with you. Let's work it out."

"If I tell you something, will you try to understand?"

"Of course I will. I want to know you."

"I met a woman last night. She told me things I needed to know, made other things better. But then, I had to pay for finding out. People shouldn't make other people pay that way. Are you going to make me pay, Chas? Are you going to start making demands, expecting that sort of thing? Can you be straight with me? Can you?"

"I don't know, Lisa. It's never gone that far with me."

"But would you try?"

"I'd have to, I think. This is new for me, too, you know."

"Is it?"

"I had a nice, ordinary background, too. I am what I am because I'm still trying to grow, to know more. What I'd like to do, to try to do, is fill the gaps somehow. Is that what you want to hear?"

"I don't know if I'm sure what I want to hear. I want to find out about you. And more about me, as well. I feel so easy with you. I was only hostile at first because of what Brad did. I was very scared, very hurt. But you're not like all the others. And you do the things you say you're going to do. And you seem to be willing to listen, to play fair."

"I am willing. What can I give you that you want and need?"

"I don't know," she said, thinking about it. "I'll have to find out. Maybe I don't have anything *you* want or need."

"You're you. That's enough."

"Enough for what?"

168

"For openers. You can't plan all the moves in advance, Lisa. Maybe just some of my experience, some of my extra years of living might help make the difference."

"Are you," she asked slowly, "to be trusted?"

"For you, yes. Not necessarily for everybody."

"Why just for me?"

"A lot of reasons. I think we could move together, progress. I might be wrong, but it's better than going it alone. And I like the idea of waking up in the morning, maybe watching you sleep."

She shivered and his hand tightened over hers.

"That scared you?" he asked.

"I don't know. We're talking about being in the same bed. It makes me nervous."

"Why?"

"Because I don't know that part of you yet and I'm not sure I'm ready. I want to but I'm not sure."

"Whenever you're ready," he said quietly. "There's no hurry."

"Do you mean it? Don't say it if you don't mean it because I'll believe you if you say you do."

"I mean it."

"Okay," she exhaled slowly. "Then we'll see if we can work it out."

Once they were on the highway heading north, she let her head fall back against the seat, turning slightly to look at Chas.

"I like your choice of car," he said. "You have good taste, Lisa Hamilton. I like your non-taffeta clothes, too. That's the the kind of thing you should always wear."

The hum of the wheels on the road made her drowsy.

"Are you all right?" he glanced over.

"Fine. Your driving doesn't make me nervous."

"Thank you. I thought we'd stop for dinner once we get into Georgia."

"I'm so sleepy," she yawned. "I can't seem to stay awake."

"Sleep then. Close your eyes. Go on."

She looked at the bulky diver's watch on his wrist,

thought of his bag back there in the trunk with hers and wondered what would happen when they stopped for the night. He'd probably make his move then.

He pulled into the first decent-looking restaurant he saw over the state line and switched off the ignition. He sat looking at her. Her hair had fallen across her face when the pins loosened, and he pushed the hair back, reluctant to awaken her, although her head was on his arm and her body at an uncomfortable angle. He shifted her so that she lay squarely against his chest. She slept on, her face flushed, her breathing soundless.

'I love you," he whispered, settling back with his arm around her.

He lit a cigarette and smoked, holding it in his left hand, lazily watching the cars pass on the Interstate, relishing the weight of her. He thought of things he'd do once they arrived, purchases he wanted to make, time allocations. He opened the side vent and flicked out the cigarette as her hand opened and slid down to fold inside his like a nesting bird.

"Are we here?" she asked, eyes still closed.

"We're here."

"I'm still sleeping."

"Sleep," he said simply. "There's no rush."

He watched as her eyes flickered closed and she sank back down into her sleep. His mind wandered over random thoughts. He pictured the way he'd like her to look on the album cover; the way she'd look without her clothes. He thought about how she'd react to the apartment. He thought about how much he wanted to make love to her and tried to imagine how it might have been for her making love—being naked, she'd called it—with another woman. There was something about her, about her way of explaining her actions and feelings that contained an untainted innocence, a newness to the world. He loved that quality in her. She had the potential to find every experience a new, conceivably beneficial one. He wished he still had that kind of openness. Perhaps she might restore that to him. He thought about her baby

170

and the baby became his own, somehow. Perhaps she'd share that with him, too.

Before leaving the restaurant, he spoke to the manager, then came back to take her to the car.

"There's a decent inn about forty miles from here," he told her, opening the car door. "I think that'll be about enough mileage for today."

She sat in the car while he went inside to arrange the accommodations and while he was gone she speculated on whether he'd come back with one room key or two. He came across the blacktop and slid in behind the wheel.

"All set," he said, putting the Mercedes in gear and backing out.

A suite. Two bedrooms separated by a sitting room. She told him which bag she'd need and he brought it and his own inside.

"We'll start early," he said, setting her bag down in her bedroom. "I'll wake you. Have a good sleep."

"Chas?"

"Yes?" he turned.

"Can we leave the connecting doors open? So I can hear you."

"Get yourself ready for bed. I'll be back to say goodnight."

All the time she was showering, she kept expecting the shower curtain to come flying open and there he'd be. But nothing happened. She dried and powdered herself, brushed her hair, then went into the bedroom. He wasn't sitting in or on the bed. He was in his own room down there, moving about. She got into bed and turned out the light. When she heard his footsteps approaching, she thought, *This is it. Here it comes.* He walked in and came around the side of the bed, still fully dressed.

"Everything all right?" He sat down beside her.

"Fine."

"I've got some work to do. You sleep now. Did you take your Benadryl?"

"Yes."

"Good. Then I'll say goodnight and see you in the morning."

"Goodnight, Chas."

"Goodnight." He got up and stood for a moment looking down at her.

"You're all right?" he asked.

"I'm fine."

"Good. He kissed her forehead and went away.

She pulled the blankets up around her and lay staring at the light from the sitting room. And, finally, comforted by the sounds of slowly-turned pages and an occasional quiet cough, she slept.

He awakened her at eight, touching her arm, saying, "Here's some coffee. I have to make a few calls, then we can have breakfast."

He was dressed, freshly shaven.

"You smell nice," she murmured, sitting up to drink the coffee.

"You have beautiful breasts." He smiled and kissed her bare shoulder before going into the sitting room where she could hear him starting on the first of his calls.

He was finishing a call when she appeared in the doorway, her bag packed to go. He motioned her to sit down and she listened as he made several strong remarks into the telephone.

Every time they stopped, he went off to make another telephone call. By the time they'd arranged for their rooms that second night, his demeanor seemed to indicate he'd solved whatever problems he'd been having. His eyes paid full attention to her over dinner and when the coffee came, he smiled at her and said, "You're very patient. You don't intrude. You don't ask obvious questions. It's a nice change."

"It's none of my business," she said, accepting one of his cigarettes.

"Everything I do is your business. You just don't know it yet, that's all."

"Does that mean that everything I do is *your* business?"

"Not if you don't want it to be. It simply means there's nothing I do that you can't know about. If you choose to include me in the things you do, fine. If not, fine."

He'd booked another suite. And as he'd done the night

before, he left her to get herself into bed before coming in to wish her a good night's sleep. He kissed her forehead and then left to make more telephone calls.

Sometime in the night, she heard the telephone ring in his room and his voice, dulled by the distance between their rooms, low and insistent speaking for a long time. She fell asleep before he completed the call.

Chapter 12

The next afternoon as they approached the outskirts of the city, Lisa grew visibly agitated.

"What's the matter?" he asked, reaching over to take her hand.

"Brad lives here. I'm scared, all of a sudden, of running into him."

"Don't be. I'm around for that."

She turned very slowly and looked at him.

"I think," she said, "this is going to work."

"Do you? Good. I hope so."

"Where are we going?" she asked, relaxing.

"Friend of mine is lending me his apartment. He's out of town for a few months. Is that okay?"

"I guess so. Where?"

"Fifth and Ninety-second."

"What about the car?"

"I'll take care of it. Is that okay, too?"

"Yes."

The apartment was enormous. He carried the bags inside and dumped them in the huge foyer saying, "Come on. We'll look over the layout."

There were two children's rooms and she stopped to look at them. "Your friend has children?"

"That's right. Three boys."

"Where are they?"

"Away on their boat, down south."

"Oh," she nodded, following him along the corridor.

"Take whichever room you like," he said, throwing open two doors. "I'll take the other."

After they'd decided on the rooms, he said, "I think an early dinner and an early night, so we can get a good start tomorrow. What d'you think?"

"Fine," she said. "I'm tired."

"I know it. Driving's a hassle."

"Chas, where have you been living?"

"The Harvard Club."

"Did you go to Harvard?"

"Nope. I went to McGill."

"Are you Canadian?" she asked.

"It's a good university. And I like skiing."

"I quit the conservatory when I was sixteen. I don't have any education."

"You have all you need, and you're getting more every day. Let's go eat. I'm tired, too."

"Chas?"

"Hmm?"

"Does it matter to you it's somebody else's baby?"

"It's a baby. I guess what matters is who's there when it's born, when it's hungry or thirsty or scared."

"So you'd think of this as my baby and not Brad's?"

"Maybe," he said, putting his hand on her arm, "I might like to think of it as mine."

"Would you?"

"Would *you*?" he asked.

"It needs discussing."

"I love kids," he said. "I'd especially love yours. That's the way I feel."

"Okay," she said. "I wanted to know."

"Now you know. May I buy you dinner? Or will you want to go Dutch?"

She laughed and touched his face.

"You're beautiful," she smiled up at him. "I'm getting used to you."

"Oh, before I forget. I rented a piano for you. I thought it'd be helpful. It's in the den."

"That's great."

"We'll sit down later, way later and go over the bills together. Okay?"

"How'd you know that's what I was going to say?"

"I'm getting used to *you*." He kissed the tip of her nose and they went out.

Tim was thin and nervous-looking with long brown hair and the worst singing voice Lisa had ever heard.

Chas was very brotherly with him, clapping Tim on the back after he'd played the first of the numbers, saying, "Was I joking? Did you ever hear anything so bad in your life?"

Tim laughed and at once the nervousness evaporated.

"Chas called me when he got back," Tim said to Lisa. "You've got to be dynamite. He never likes anybody."

"I like the song," she said. "What's it called?"

" 'Night Flight.' "

"Isn't that funny?" she said. "I've got one called 'Early Morning People.' "

"Let's hear it," Chas said eagerly as Tim slid over on the piano bench.

She played it and Tim said, "That's a very heavy song."

Chas said, "If we put 'Night Flight' on top and 'Early Morning People' on the flip side, we've got a hell of a single. Let's concentrate on getting those two ready first. Tim has some good ideas for it. Maybe the two of you can work up the charts for all the numbers."

"Where did you study music?" Lisa asked Tim, liking both him and his music.

"The Eastman School. You?"

"The conservatory in my hometown. This is going to be good."

"Let's hear some of your other ones," Tim suggested.

Chas backed off and left them to get on with it. He knew they'd work fine together.

175

It was the most pleasurable work she'd ever done. She and Tim played all of their songs for each other, then went back over them, eliminating this one and that one, narrowing it all down until they had six of hers and seven of his they thought would be good for the album.

Chas approved their selections, supplied them with boxes of score paper and they set to work on scoring "Night Flight."

At the end of the first day's work, Tim packed his music case and went along home and Lisa stood up, stretching, saying, "I've never worked so hard in my life. But he's great and he's got great ideas. He plays beautiful flute. We're going to use it over the voice on 'Night Flight,' a counterpoint. It should be beautiful."

"I'm leaving it up to the two of you," he said, coming around behind her, massaging her shoulders. She swayed back against him with her eyes closed, enjoying the strong pull away from the tension that had built up during the day.

"That's wonderful," she sighed, letting her head hang forward. "It feels so good."

"When you make up your mind, I give good all-over massages."

"I'm getting there," she said softly. "I'm getting there."

It took them eight days to prepare the orchestrations for the first two numbers. After that, they were into their stride, into each other's tempo and the work went more quickly. Lisa was developing great fondness and respect for Tim and the days were punctuated with laughter and a camaraderie she'd never known.

"You're my first friend," she told him near the end of their second week closeted in the den. "I'm glad."

"This is going to be the best album ever to hit the streets," Tim said, shoving his glasses back up his nose. "When they hear you, they'll go bananas. You're the best."

"Let's just stay in here forever," she laughed. "We'll just keep it all to ourselves."

"Sure. And starve to death."

"I've never seen anyone eat so much in my entire life,"

she laughed at him. "Where the hell do you put it? You're the skinniest thing ever."

"What are you?" he countered. "In training to be a Jewish mother?"

"I don't know what that is but I might be."

Tim folded over, howling. "She doesn't know what that is. Too much!" he laughed, removing his glasses. "Too much!"

A routine had evolved. Each morning, Chas and Lisa met in the kitchen for breakfast. They exchanged their plans for the day. Then Chas went off to arrange for the studio and the musicians, the engineer, all the technical aspects of the session, and Lisa got ready for her day's work with Tim. At six-thirty or seven, Tim would depart for the loft downtown he shared with his girlfriend and Chas would be back, waiting to take Lisa out to eat.

In the middle of the third week, at breakfast, Lisa said, "I've got to think about things for the baby. And a place. I have to think about that."

"I guess you do. Anything in mind?"

"I should get myself a regular doctor, for one thing. And then there are clothes and all the stuff a baby needs. And where we'll live. It seems like such a lot."

"You don't want to stay in New York?"

"Chas, I really don't like it here. And the idea of trying to raise a child here absolutely petrifies me. I read the newspapers. I watch TV, see things about eight-year-old girls being raped and then tossed off the roofs of buildings. I get so scared here."

"I have a place," he said tentatively.

"You do? Where?"

"In Connecticut. It was my parents' place. I rent it out. But the lease'll be up in a couple of months."

"Where in Connecticut?"

"On the Westport/Wilton line."

She was listening and suddenly she wasn't listening because something was happening. At first she thought, *It's just gas*, because the motion was so subtle, so barely there. But then it happened again and she knew what it was and couldn't believe how real it all was all at once.

"Chas!" her eyes were huge.

"What is it?"

"It's *moving*! I'm so knocked out. It's moving!"

"How does it feel? What's it like?"

He looked excited too. She could hardly believe how excited he seemed to be.

"Give me your hand, you can feel it."

She held his hand down over her belly and they both waited, lookilng at each other. Then it moved again and he felt it and they laughed aloud.

"That's great!" he laughed, keeping his hand on her belly, seeing the readyness on her face as he bent his head and kissed her. She sighed and put her arm around him as his hand moved up from her belly to her breast.

"I want you," she whispered.

"Come on." He took her hand and gently pulled her up.

They went into his bedroom. "I love you," he said. "I've wanted to do this since the first time I saw you." He placed his hands on either side of her face, saying, "It's all right," before kissing her sweet-soft, slowly not like any other kiss she'd ever received. When he drew away, she brought him back. His kisses sent darting spasms of response all through her. He seemed so strong, so solid and positive and whole. He'd have no need to cause her pain in order to show himself to be male. When they separated, she found herself taking in air in small gasping draughts, taut with expectation as his hands unzipped her dress and cool air touched the skin of her back.

Her hands moved out to unfasten the snap at his waist before sliding the zipper down. She pulled at the tail of his shirt so she could undo the buttons, parting the shirt to put her mouth on his collarbone, the side of his neck, the base of his throat. His skin was as smooth as it had always looked to her to be, warm and fresh-smelling, good against her lips.

They undressed each other unhurriedly, stopping to kiss and touch each other, finally lying down together on the bed.

He painted circles around her nipples with his tongue, making her suck in her breath with pleasure, her hand falling lightly on the back of his head to keep him there.

"I've never made love before with someone I love," she said, opening under him, drawing him down to her.

"I love you so much." His fingers slid down her thigh.

"I love you. I wanted to be sure. Oh!" she quivered as his fingers dipped into her. '*Chas*!"

She put her hand between them guiding him forward, lifting, all open as she removed her hand, no longer needing to direct him. He was there, easing forward, parting her, entering, his hands over her breasts as he knelt between her thighs and immersed himself fully in her then stopped, resting there. She lifted her arms and brought him down on her breasts, anxious to give to him, to love him. Her hips shifted, beginning a counterpoint, playing a melody that was perfectly timed to his slow-thrusting theme. All the music of her life had come to center in him. And of the best and most beautiful of all the songs she'd ever heard inside the hollows of her skull, of all the music that had ever played in her ears and behind her eyes, of all the music woven in and out of every day of every year of her life, his was sweeter than any she'd ever heard. He held her, filled her more completely, more perfectly than anything or anyone and it all made sense. She could open her mouth and whisper, "I love you," and he could answer, "Yes," and make all this happen for her, make her soul sing.

He'd guessed at how she'd be, had believed that when she ultimately sought to declare herself, she'd place all of herself, every part of her at the giving point, timing herself to him, seeking nothing. And never, not ever, had anyone purely given to him without seeking something *from* him somehow, somewhere along the line. No one but Lisa. And this he would give her. This. And all of this. Until she reached up to bring him down again on her breasts, holding her mouth to his, giving still more to him. I give you this, he thought, and this. I give you everything.

She whispered, "Go on. It's right. Go on." And he

stopped for a moment to look at her and she said, "It's right. Don't hold back," and he thought, yes it is right and stopped holding back. He moved inside of her, stirring something deep, something profound so that when she hadn't thought she'd be able to, she found herself at the coda and held still as that soft, dying cry came from her mouth and she shuddered going; clung to him moaning softly, her eyes closing finally as she rose up then fell, gasping. And a minute later, as the last of the spasms were passing, she felt him come spurting into her. He was aware of her lifting even closer to meet him and came into her, finally, in great love and gladness, his own hopes reaffirmed.

"I'm so happy," she said after several minutes.

"That's all I want," he caressed her arm, "for you to be happy."

"And that makes you happy?"

"Yes it does. It really does. Everything else was there, working for us. This confirms it all."

"I'm what you want?"

"Hey listen," he pulled her over on top of him. "I'm not the mythical man who's like an old Jimmy Cagney movie, all tough and singleminded, ready to push the grapefruit into some broad's face if she opens her mouth once too often. That's not me. I'm not the stud, either. Or a crazy. At least I don't *think* I'm a crazy. If you feel happy with me, maybe it's because you find something in me that *lets* you be happy. And that's the good part for me. I've been around a few times, just the way you have. I know all about that part where you try to change people, thinking your influence can make someone over, reshape her more closely to the ideal you had in mind when you started. It doesn't work. That never works. I want to be with you because when I am, I don't feel all hyper and defensive. I feel alive. I feel we're going somewhere together."

"What was your family like?"

"Ordinary, I told you. My dad had a small store. He sold carpets, interior furnishings. My mother did the bridge-club number and the PTA."

"You're an only child?"

"I am."

"Is that why you like children?"

"Who knows? I just like them. Don't get too analytical on me, honey. I'm not that good at it. Jesus, I'm thirsty. Want something to drink?"

"I'll come with you. I want to keep looking at you."

He slipped on a blue terrycloth robe as she picked up his shirt and put it on, holding her arm up to her nose, sniffing at the sleeve.

"What are you *doing?*" he laughed.

"Smelling you. It's like putting you on, wearing you around."

"Beautiful!" he took her arm, and steered her toward the kitchen.

"What'll you have?" he asked, peering into the refrigerator.

"Juice. Any kind of juice."

He poured out two glasses of apple juice and handed one to her.

"Come on into the den," she said. "I want to play a song for you."

"Jesus!" he exclaimed, following her into the small room. "We'd better start getting this stuff to a copyist. It's beginning to stack up."

"Have him do an extra copy of the violin, okay? Tim and I can't decide on three or four, so we'll do the extra just in case."

"You're really into it," he said, sitting down in the armchair. "This is going to be so fantastic! I can't wait to hear what the two of you have done."

"We'll be ready to start rehearsals next week," she said, setting her glass atop a newspaper on the floor before settling herself on the bench.

"You're ahead of schedule," he observed, lifting one of the scores. "That means you'll have a few extra days for rehearsal."

"I've always wanted to have someone who fit this song," she said, laying out the opening changes.

181

He listened, feeling a shiver of pleasure at the sight and sound of her as she sang:

"There are places I'll remember all my life,
Though some have changed, some forever, not for better,
Some have gone and some remain.
All these places had their moments,
With lovers and friends I still can recall,
Some are dead and some are living,
In my life I've loved them all.
But of all these friends and lovers,
There is no one compared with you,
And these mem'ries lose their meaning
When I think of love as something new.
Though I know I'll never lose affection
For people and things that went before,
I know I'll often stop and think about them,
In my life I'll love you more.
Though I know I'll never lose affection
For people and things that went before,
I know I'll often stop and think about them
In my life I'll love you more.
In my life I'll love you more."

She turned around on the bench, saying, "Do you think I'm corny and dumb?"

"Corny and dumb. Come on over here. Do I think you're corny and dumb?" She sat down on his lap and he slid his arms around her. "If that's corny and dumb then I'm just as dumb and just as corny because it's a beautiful song and you're the best thing that ever happened to me. I know, I know," he held his hand up between them. "You're not a 'thing.' It's just another one of those expressions."

"Do you . . . would you like to know how long it's been since I . . . never mind. I . . ." She dropped her hand and laughed, pleased. "And I was trying to think how to say it," she kissed him. "We'd better get out of here. Tim'll be coming."

He looked past her at the clock on the wall and said,

"Not for a while and I don't feel like waiting. Do you feel like waiting?"

"No," she said breathlessly, unbuttoning the shirt. "I've never been in such a hurry."

He shrugged out of the robe, saying, "Down here," sliding onto the floor. She stood over him for a moment, feeling herself already contracting in anticipation and came down over him, holding her breath as she fitted herself on top of him; shivering as he seemed to expand inside of her.

"I get so excited," she whispered, "and then when we start, I'm afraid I won't come. I'm afraid to care too much."

"So am I. Not about coming. But caring too much. It feels as if it might be dangerous."

"You feel that way, too?"

"Oh, Jesus!" his hands curved over her breasts. "It's like it's too good to be true and if I believe too much, I'll wake up and find there's something I didn't notice. About you, about me, about everything. I need you, Lisa. I didn't think I was into needing. But this. This is so deep, so big. I want it all with you. I'd like to see your baby born."

"Would you?"

"All of it."

"It shouldn't be scary, Chas. I don't know why but I know it shouldn't be. I feel a little crazy doing this. I can't concentrate on what I'm thinking, what I'm trying to say."

"Does it feel good to you?"

"Does it to you?"

"It all feels good to me. We fit so well. All the girls the women I've known. They've been too small somehow. But not you."

"No," she smiled, "I'm not small. Would you go shopping for baby things with me?"

"Oh, Lisa! Don't hate me, but I'm not into that store scene. If it's something you have to have me for, okay. But if it isn't, will you promise me you won't get brought down if I don't?"

"I guess," she said, "if I'm going to expect you to play certain things my way, I'm going to have to play certain others your way. It's all finding out."

"It doesn't mean I don't love you and that I'm not very high on the baby. It just means stores are a bummer."

"It's okay. Really. I'm starting to go," she said softly, holding him hard. "So fast, when I thought I wouldn't at all."

"I want you to care that much. It's in me for you. All of it. Go, honey! God! How that feels! My *God*, how that feels! I love you, *love* you."

The following Tuesday, they had their first rehearsal session. Lisa and Chas arrived at the studio first. Lisa stood looking at the huge, empty room feeling everything seize up inside.

"Come on, we'll look in the control room," he said, leading her up three stairs and into the booth. She looked at the tape spools and control panels, the big speakers and felt for a moment as if she knew nothing and being there was a big con, a put-on.

"I'm so nervous," she said, looking at all the switches and buttons on the panel. "What if it's all no good?"

"I know it'll be good. Here's Tim." He leaned over and flipped a switch on the control panel, then spoke into the mike. "We're in here, Tim." Tim looked over and waved and came up the stairs and into the booth.

"You nervous?" he asked Lisa. "I'm scared shitless. What the hell are we doing here?"

"You two," Chas laughed. "Genius at work and you've got the jitters. Get yourselves out there and lay out the parts. Who's conducting?"

"We both are," Lisa said.

"You both are?" Chas looked from her to Tim. "That's half-assed. One of you has to be in the booth. You want to flip for it or what?"

"I'll do the booth," Tim said quickly, setting down his case on one of the seats in front of the panel. "You're going to be out front anyway, Lee."

"Okay. But if I bomb, you have to save me."

"Don't worry. Anyway, I'll get a cleaner overall sound in here on the playback. I'll keep track of the tapes."

"Well, help me lay out the parts," she said, looking like a kid about to take final exams.

Chas sat down in the booth to watch the two of them discussing who should sit where, positioning the pieces by sight, regrouping the chairs. Lisa looked about sixteen in faded jeans and an Indian overblouse she'd found in Azuma in the Village, her hair pulled back into a long braid that fell below her waist. Without makeup, in that outfit, with her hair that way, he thought she was the most beautiful human being he'd ever seen or known. Even claiming nerves and uncertainty, there was a vibrant positivity to her moves and gestures as she and Tim discussed the seating arrangements.

The engineers arrived, bearing paper cups of coffee and went about checking the panel, flicking switches, rolling fresh tape onto the deck.

"That's your girl?" one of them asked Chas.

"She's the one. Wait till you hear what these kids have done. It'll blow your mind."

"Sure is a nice-looking girl," the other one said. "Y'always pick 'em, Chas. Got an eye for all kinds of talent."

"Don't come on that way in front of her," Chas said quietly. "That's a very special woman."

The musicians began drifting in, looking tired and already bored, with cigarettes between their lips and paper bags containing coffee.

They began seating themselves at random and Lisa looked at Tim, saw he looked paralyzed, and stood up on the conductor's block to get their attention.

"Please, don't sit down until we know who you are, okay? We've got the sections laid out. So, if you'll tell me which instrument you are, I'll tell you where we've put you."

The men looked up in surprise, making no effort to move.

Tim finally decided to wake up and approached the brass man who'd taken the right front seat.

"You're brass," Tim said. "Trumpet?"

"Right."

"Trumpet," he told Lisa.

"Put him on the side in the center."

"What the hell's this?" the trumpet man said. "Kid show?"

Chas, who'd been listening, flicked on the mike switch and said, "Haul your ass, Earle. You might learn a thing or two."

Lisa's head jerked up and she saw Chas leaning over the console looking angry as he talked into the mike.

"The rest of you smart-ass union types, just pay attention to what you're told. You're not doing this for charity and it's not another routine session. Half you jokers probably can't even read a properly scored chart. Just do it!"

Lisa felt she was way out of her depth and Tim turned scarlet and took flight, leaving her there to cope with placing the men already there and the ones arriving. She finally stopped, finding herself winded from rushing around and said to the ones coming through the door, "Just stay there, please, until I get these guys taken care of."

Finally, everyone was seated properly and unpacking their instruments, tuning up. She stepped up onto the block and started looking over the score. Tim returned with a cup of coffee and she thanked him, running quickly through to the end of 'Night Flight.'

"We'll start out with 'Night Flight,'" she said, "if we're all together here."

The air in the room was so full of suppressed humor and skepticism, she felt she could scarcely breathe. She'd never been in such close contact to so many people she was convinced disliked her. Her heart pounding, her hands soaking wet, she clapped her hands together to get their attention.

"We're going to do this in a nice, even four-four. I want the drums nice and hard but not too rocky. Just lay them in strong and steady. And take the pause at the end of the first four, then come in low and together on the first

186

bar of the eight. It has to build to the bridge. At the bridge, we'll break it out. Think airplane," she smiled stiffly, knowing she sounded like a fool. "Think motion, going. Let's take it on the four count and fly."

She let them run it through one chorus and then stopped them. Lowering her head to the mike she said, "Tim, what d'you think? Too much brass?"

He came back on the PA, saying, "Cut back on the second trumpet. Don't lay out, just lay back."

The second trumpet smiled and nodded and for the first time, Lisa drew a breath that didn't seem to hurt.

"Okay," she said. "Now on the bridge, something's wrong. A little too much bass on your guitar. Can you cut that a bit?"

The guitarist ran a riff, asking, "Better?"

"Better," she smiled, gaining strength minute by minute. "Everybody else feel all right?"

The bassist lifted his bow, saying, "You want me to back down with the guitar? It'll be too heavy if I'm playing full and he's down."

"Try it full. I think it's what I want."

They all looked up at her waiting and she nodded, then counted out the four again. This time she let them get through the entire chorus and a half. At the end, the musicians all reached for their containers of coffee. She took a sip of her own, then said, "I think that's about perfect. Mark your charts, okay? So you remember what we decided. Let's break for five minutes and then we'll go into the next one."

Stiff-legged, she got down off the block and made her way past the seventeen musicians and up the three stairs into the sound booth where she collapsed into an available chair.

"That's murder!" she said. "They think I'm an idiot."

"They think you're a professional," Chas said. "And don't worry about what they think. It sounds so good, it's too damned much!"

Tim smiled eagerly and the two engineers grinned over at her encouragingly.

"You look so cool, doing it," Tim said. "Seiji Ozawa would freak!"

She laughed and reached for one of the cigarettes in Chas's package.

"What'd you think?" she asked Chas. "Is it good?"

"Dynamic. I can't wait to hear the rest of them. This is going to be even better than I'd hoped."

During the lunch break, Lisa said, "I'm going over to Bloomingdale's to buy some baby stuff. I know you don't want to come so I won't ask you. I need some fresh air anyway."

"Go ahead," he said. "I've got a couple of things to do. What time did you tell them to be back?"

"Two-thirty."

"Okay."

She gathered up her handbag and sunglasses, pulled on her coat and left the building.

I'm an orchestra conductor, she thought, smiling to herself at the idea of it. That's really funny. I'll have to phone home and tell them about it. She'd have to do that. With a pang of guilt, she realized she hadn't called home in two weeks. They were probably worried to death. She ducked into a phone booth and made a collect call home, quickly explaining what was happening and why she hadn't called. She didn't mention Chas or the baby. She was waiting before she did that, but not sure why. After the call, eased, she flagged a cab and continued on her way to Bloomingdale's.

The children's department knocked her out. She stopped to look at the 3–6X girls' and boys' clothes before going on to the section where all the baby things were. She looked at the tiny outfits on the racks thinking, I'm going to have a baby who's going to wear these things. It's going to sleep and eat and need changing and holding and bathing. She saw herself walking in Remington Park with a small child clinging to her hand; saw herself laughing, bending to press her face into the soft baby hair, the soft baby skin. God! It was so real. She let her hand trail over baby bonnets and receiving blankets and fancy embroidered crib quilts with matching carry-alls, trying to think of the most immediate needs.

Her attention was torn between the events of the past weeks and the events of the weeks to come. She moved about, fingering vari-colored baby garments, thinking about how Chas had taken her and Tim and joined them up to BMI. She'd always thought of ASCAP because all the old songwriters had been ASCAP. But BMI gave them an advance against royalties on Chas's say-so-ing peptalk and now she and Tim were legitimate with their songs copyrighted and published by the company Chas had set up years ago in order to keep all the profits centered around his groups and himself. So, all and any sheet music that emerged from their joint venture would read Lisa Hamilton BMI and Timothy John Jenkins BMI copyrighted Clayton Music Corporation 1975. She could see exactly how it would look at the bottom of the page of music.

And Chas had told her he'd started it all because he'd heard a girl sing one night in a bar in Montreal—all this while he was attending McGill—and thought about all the singers he'd seen in lounges and how they never seemed to go anywhere, eventually disappearing from clubs altogether. He used to wonder where all the talented ones got to. It bothered him. So he approached the girl and was truthful, saying he didn't know the hows and whys or ins and outs but was willing to try if she was willing to try. And they made every conceivable mistake but the girl and her first single had hit the Canadian top forty and after that never stopped. Now she lived in California and designed her own album covers and clung fiercely, defiantly to her Canadian passport and Canadian origins.

Lisa had often sung her songs. And now, knowing Chas had been responsible for lifting that girl out of lounges and into the public ear where her natural gifts and showmanship were properly aired, Lisa wondered if he hadn't loved her, too; if he hadn't played it out as part of a subtle master scheme in order to accomplish his own ends. But what would he get from that? she wondered, picking up a fine yellow terry jumpsuit shorter than the length of her forearm.

Aside from the monetary gains and a sort of second-hand glory—not to mention being permanently hounded by hopefuls until he'd given up proper offices altogether and worked out of his head and public telephone booths —what did he gain? Reflected success? Personal success? He was a success. When she'd stopped in to see Nick to tell him what was happening and the deal they'd made, Nick said, "You're lucky, dear. You can trust him and he'll lay on the best of everything. He doesn't skimp on production and he won't take one penny that doesn't rightly belong to him." But reassuring as all that was, and professionally it was highly reassuring, she felt a small, persistent doubt about him. Maybe because he seemed so perennially delighted with her. The only criticisms he'd made were at the beginning because she'd been so rude. But now . . . they never seemed to disagree. Nothing that couldn't be settled by talking quietly or lying in bed in the morning, caressing each other into a state of frictive amnesia. She felt addicted to Chas's body, his lovemaking ways, his laughter and his low, resonant voice.

Did he have something, know something she didn't know? Maybe that was it, she thought. Maybe, in the course of the successes and disappointments, he'd learned something she had yet to discover. It had to do with conflict—internal and external conflict. And it had to do with a positive knowledge of his own limitations and needs. But if he knew all this, what was he doing with her? Was he just on some sort of crusade to save as many lounge acts from anonymity as he could? Was that his thing? He couldn't stop referring to her as the "best thing that had ever happened to him," or the "greatest thing they'll ever hear," or this kind of "thing" or that kind of "thing," and she wanted to pound him on the head or open up his brain and take that part of him that thought "thing" out entirely and shove in a new set of sensors that beeped out "person" every time he went to say "thing." Of course, he laughed and said it was

190

only an expression. But that didn't stop her from wanting to yank the word from his vocabulary altogether. And that, she thought, is what's bothering me.

She couldn't relieve herself of the nagging idea that he thought of her as a thing. A variation on a theme of Brad. He didn't hit or abuse her, did everything imaginable to anticipate her needs—sexually, emotionally, physically—but he still let those "thing" references slide out of his mouth. They'd have to talk about that. They would, she decided, selecting a white pajama set and laying that down on top of the yellow jumpsuit. Because until that was clear, until it was firmly established for her that he thought of her as Lisa and not a "thing"—not in any way—she couldn't feel completely free to hold back from caring too much.

She wasn't wrong about what she'd told him that morning in the den. The doubt interfered with the sexual fulfillment she knew was attainable with him. But every time she approached the wavering perimeters of the ultimate, blindingly perfect orgasm, something in her mind triggered something deep in her body that said, "Not yet, don't give yourself too completely. Not yet." And so it was not the soul-satisfyingly free-spirited merging and release it should have been. She couldn't be sure that he didn't intend for her to wind up in California somewhere in a house with redwood decks and panoramic vistas of Big Sur displayed for her private viewing, while he went back lounge-haunting, searching out more lost little-girl-singers to promote into the solar system.

The saleswoman said, "Can I help you with something?" and Lisa looked at her blankly for a minute before saying, "I guess I have to have a layette."

And the woman—it had never happened to her before in any store in New York—smiled happily, asking, "For you, dear?"

"For me," she answered, thinking, This woman likes me just because I'm pregnant.

It seemed to be true, too. Mrs. Shuster, her name was. She asked Lisa about when and what she thought she needed and talked happily about her own two children and their children and, all the while, laid out undershirts and sleepers and receiving blankets and a carryall and half a dozen diapers—"Even if you use the disposables," she said, "you always need diapers. For spitting up or burping. You'll see. Take my advice and get them." —booties no longer than Lisa's little finger and a baby pillow—"Even if you use it and the baby doesn't, it's such a sweet thing to have."—and a tiny hairbrush-and-comb set. The counter was piled high with just the necessary things.

"A toy," Lisa said, smiling because this was the one of the pleasantest hours she'd ever spent with another human being on a purely personal level. "One of those little pink pigs that winds up and plays music."

Mrs. Shuster laughed and added the pig to the rest of the things. Lisa wrote out a check, gave the delivery address, then stood waiting while Mrs. Shuster scurried off to have the check okayed by her supervisor. While she was gone, Lisa looked at an enormously pregnant girl studying the racks of clothes just as she'd done herself and thought, For nine months, we're very special. Knowing you were pregnant, everyone automatically assumed a deferential stance toward you, trying to be accommodating, trying to share, even fractionally, in the mystery of what you were doing. The girl looked over and they smiled at each other. We could be from anywhere, good at any number of different things, she thought, but for this time, right now, we're exactly the same. The idea nearly moved her toward the girl to talk, to find out about her baby, about how it moved and when and if it did the funny things this baby seemed to do inside Lisa. But Mrs. Shuster came back and Lisa glanced at her watch to see she only had ten minutes to get back to the studio. Mrs. Shuster held out her hand saying, "Good luck to you, dear. The best of luck to you," and Lisa gripped her hand then hurried away, her mind already racing over the last numbers to get the orchestra through.

Chapter 13

On the last day of rehearsals, she and Tim sat in the empty studio, discussing the start of the taping sessions the following Monday.

"You'll have to have the piano up front," Tim said, looking around at the grouped chairs. "We can have three mikes. One for you, one for the piano. One for the flute. And we'll just have to hope like hell they're going to have the sense to follow what's happening up front."

"One thing that bothers me," she said, holding her hand low on her right side where the baby seemed to be tapdancing. "I can't hear well up front. I've been trying to throw in a few bars here and there to feel it out and I can't hear myself. It's like trying to sing in the shower. All distorted."

"We could mike the sound back into here."

"No good," she said. "It's so damned distracting. Every time that PA comes on, everybody gets thrown. I don't know. We'll have to run a track on 'Night Flight,' and see what comes back. I'm still bothered by the bridge. Something's not quite right with it."

"What?"

She looked at his narrow, round-eyed face and his steel-rimmed glasses, his rather concave chest and over-long arms and legs thinking, You're a dear soul. You're one of the dearest souls I know.

"You're scared again," Tim said, cleaning his glasses, holding them up to the light to check for spots. "I thought you'd got past that."

"*You* don't have to sing. These guys think we're

clowns. They know Chas but they think he's flipped out letting us run this whole thing. I can tell by the way they look at us. They think I'm just an expensive lay that Chas is indulging. So, okay, they can tell I've got some training, that we both know musically what we're doing. But I can feel it, the way they look at me. I half wish I was out to here already. Maybe they'd stop looking at me that way."

"I think you're wrong," Tim said, settling his glasses back on his nose. "You wait. You'll see. I did the charts for the last session he did with Melinda. You should've *seen* the treatment they gave that chick. And she did her numbers in the sound booth. None of them would *talk* to her."

"But why?"

"Who knows? Well, I know part of it. Union scale stinks in New York. For a start. And most of them are first-class men. You know the drummer is the tympanist with the Symphony?"

"No kidding!"

"The second trumpet, Earle. He's been around and back half a dozen times with Kenton, Getz. But there's not enough happening, unless they go on the road—and even then there's not all that much anymore—to keep them in the bread with just one gig. So they farm out for the sessions and for some reason, a lot of them get very hostile. I don't know. Maybe it's because it's somebody else's gig, you know, and they never made it all the way up to where they probably should've gone. But it isn't you, Lee. It's them. You shouldn't feel that way."

"Maybe. But they wouldn't give you half as much flak as they give me because I'm a woman."

"Maybe. I still think you're wrong. They could give a shit if you're Barbara Stanwyck or that gravel-voiced dude who played on 'Highway Patrol' or some such thing. What's his name? Broderick Crawford. You could come in here weighing two-eighty, standing seven-four in your bare feet, with balls and the whole thing and they'd still slip you the raspberry every time you went to the john. It's not you. Believe *me!* You'll see."

194

"How'd you meet Chas?" she asked, rubbing her side. She was positive she could feel a small baby foot pressing against her hand.

"I was playing piano and flute for one of Melinda's Town Hall gigs.

"Oh?"

"An accident," he said, lighting up a cigarette, passing it to her. "Their man O.D.'d on something and he called the union in a flap. They sent me at the old eleventh hour. He liked the way I played and we started talking, one thing and another; he asked me about this and that and the next thing, he asked me to sign. So I did. He's been paying me for seven months, keeping me working on the songs. Course when I had a gig, I'd cool it on his bread. He's something else. Really. He's got two kids in the Bronx that he signed a year ago. He's waiting for them to finish their senior year at college before he starts working it out for them. He does a lot of that stuff."

"I didn't know that," she said, handing back the cigarette. "He has a lot of kids under contract?"

"Not a lot. I know about those two and there's another guy he's been thinking about who's playing piano-bar in town. He's got them on recording contracts. He lets the rest of it slide once they're started. Melinda's got some wavy-haired dude managing her act now. And what's-her-face in California bought herself out two years ago and set up her own company. She's gonna bomb out, too. Her last two singles were duds, sloppy compared to the stuff Chas produced for her. He likes to get them started and then go looking for new faces."

"What does he get out of it?"

He looked at her curiously, scratching the side of his nose.

"That's kind of a funny thing for you to ask," he said, drawing on the cigarette. "I mean, we're *doing* this, right?"

"I don't mean it that way. I mean what does *he* get out of all of it?"

"Ask him, babe. That's a very personal trip. I don't

know what kind of a turn-on it is for him, spreading out a lot of bread on possibles. All I know is he does what he says he'll do which is about ninety-nine percent more than anybody else I know does."

"Why," she asked slowly, "do you do that, look at me that way? I'm not property, Tim. I don't belong to Chas."

"It's a thing, right?"

"What the hell's a "thing?" she said angrily. "I'm getting so goddamned sick of this 'thing' business!"

"You have a relationship," Tim said patiently, unperturbed. "It's a euphemism."

"I don't think so!" she said, more calmly. "I think the whole lot of you think of women and anything to do with women as 'things.' It bothers the hell out of me. Am I a 'thing' to you?"

"You're you to me. Just because somebody uses euphemisms doesn't mean he doesn't have all the coins in the right slots in his head. Nobody here thinks you're a 'thing.' Least of all Chas. You think this is a trip he's taking, Lee? That you're just another gig to him? Cause you're way off if that's the way you read it. Why the hell should I have to explain him to you, anyway?" he said quietly. "Don't you know where you're at?"

"Maybe I don't," she admitted. "I didn't mean to shriek at you."

"You're just uptight about Monday. That's all. But dig it," he said, tossing the cigarette stub into a half-empty coffee container. "I can see where he's at with you. If you can't, that's for you to work out with him. From where I sit, I see a very motivated guy. You know? I've been around a year now. He's done three other sessions. Two with girls. It's been all business, all professional, all hands-off. So when I see the way he jumps up every time you come within a mile of him, I can tell he's into what the two of you are doing in a very heavy way. This is weird, my sitting here laying it out for you. You need that?"

"Is that so terrible? I'm just a provincial type. Sometimes I get a little frightened that I'm into a lot of stuff that's too far over my head. And when was the last time you did anything like this? You're just as spooked as I am. Chickenshit liar."

He laughed and laid his arms across her shoulders.

"Trouble with you, you idiot Brunhilde, is you're too insecure. Now if I could sing, babe. You'd be in all kinds of trouble."

"I love you," she laughed, kissing his cheek. "Are you my friend?"

"I am your friend, your true friend, your myopic, over-eating all-time friend. And if Mandy walks in here and gloms onto this action, I'll be without a girlfriend. And Chas is in the booth."

"You're not a chickenshit liar," she whispered. "You're a chickenshit coward. Go home to Mandy." She straightened up and smiled at him. "Is *she* a Jewish mother?"

"God forbid!" Tim laughed. "Irish mothers are bad enough and I've got four-in-one of those."

Chas flipped the switch on the PA and said, "Come on in for a second, Lee," as Tim made his way out.

She sat a moment longer looking at Chas in the sound booth, annoyed at being ordered around that way. What did it take for him to poke his head out the door and ask her, like someone he recognized, to come over?

She got up and walked across the room and up the stairs into the control room.

"What's wrong?" he asked, studying her face. "Is something wrong?"

"Why did you have to do that?"

"What? Do what?"

"Come over the PA that way. Why didn't you just come out and talk to me?"

"I'm sorry," he said, nonplussed. "I didn't think about it. That bothers you?"

She didn't answer. She sat down in one of the chairs, fishing in her dress pocket for her cigarettes and lighter.

"That's not what's wrong," he said, sitting down opposite her. "Come on, Lisa. What's got the wind up your sails?"

"I'm a thing to you," she said, dropping the cigarettes and lighter back into her pocket, furiously exhaling a thick cloud of smoke. "All of you. Even Tim. You all think I'm a 'thing.' I don't like it."

"Hey!" he said softly. "I've told you before, it's just a manner of speaking. You're no kind of 'thing' to me, honey. I don't think of someone I love and respect and like as much as I do you a 'thing.' You don't really believe that."

"I don't know about you, Chas." She looked at him puzzlingly, studying his eyes and mouth. "I'm not at all sure this whole business, sleeping with me, pandering to me isn't part of something you do a lot, with a lot of girls."

He didn't say anything, just looked at her for a long time before reaching for a pack of cigarettes lying on the panel, taking his time lighting one.

"You think it's a con, right?" he said, the line of his jaw assuming a rigid set. "You think I'm so fucking stupid and underhanded that I set up 'all my girls' in Fifth Avenue apartments and diddle them around so they'll be all happy and meek while I get them to make their records. Right? Is that the picture? I've got nothing better to do with my time or my brain but placate a lot of little girls by keeping them so nicely fucked they can't say boo to a goose or answer back. You're too much!" His eyes were shooting sparks of anger. She was a little frightened by how instantly angry he'd become.

"You . . . shit!" he said, jumping to his feet. "Jesus! That makes me so fucking mad! What the hell do you want, Lisa? What? I . . . Oh, Jesus Christ! I can't even talk, I'm so goddamned mad. What's this about? What the hell's it all about?"

"Why are you so mad?" she asked quietly.

"Why'm I *mad*? Because you're so goddamned suspicious! Because we're doing this whole number the way *you* wanted, the way you insisted. And you think it's some kind of half-assed number I do to make records. That makes me mad. I think you think of *me* as a thing! That's what I think. I think you're so used to all your goddamned formula men performing to order you don't know how to tell your ass from your elbow anymore. That's what I think. And I'll tell you what else I think. I think you're scared, just plain scared. Of the session, of me, of yourself, of every goddamned thing you'd like to name. So, cause you're scared, you want a scapegoat to take it all out on. I shouldn't be this mad," he said to himself. "I shouldn't be rising this high up the pole. I'm nuts getting this worked up. Did you need an argument? Is that it? You need a little verbal fireworks to take the edge off your jitters?"

"I hate fighting," she said, drawing nervously on the cigarette. "It frightens me."

"It frightens you." His tone softened and he sat down again. 'Come on!" he said. 'Out with it. Spill it out. What's in there working at you?"

"I'm not sure about you," she said softly.

"What the hell makes you so positive I'm sure about myself? Or you for that matter? Nobody's *that* sure. I'm sure I love you. I'm working at all the rest of it. What do you need for proof, Lisa? What's missing here that would satisfy you?"

"I don't know."

"You don't know," he repeated, the anger ebbing rapidly. "I'll tell you what," he said more quietly. "I think I know. How does that grab you? You went shopping today and bought yourself a whole gang of baby goodies and you did yourself some thinking. About how maybe Chas is on some kind of zany ego trip and how maybe Chas is just using you and how maybe what you'd really like is some out front reassurances. Stop me anywhere if I'm wrong," he paused. She said nothing, so he went on. "Maybe Chas needs some reassurances too. Or hasn't that occurred to you? Maybe all of us are just as insecure underneath as you are. I'd like to know you're glad of me, of all this. If you don't hear it often enough from me, I'm sorry. I'll try to do better. I love you. And when the hell are you going to get yourself to a goddamned obstetrician and stop procrastinating? You're five months pregnant. D'you plan to wait until the kid's halfway out before you do anything as sensible as getting a doctor to look after you? I'm not your mother, Lisa. I didn't think you needed that kind of looking-after, that kind of constant prodding. If it's what you're expecting from me, forget it. I see you as all grown up, as a big girl with a pretty goddamned good set of brains. Stand up and act like a big girl and start taking care of the things that need taking care of. I'm not going to babysit with you. I just assume people—even a woman I love—can handle the simpler aspects of life. Show some positive initiative about yourself and maybe all the rest'll come along with it. I'll be glad to match you action for action. But don't come charging at me with accusations that I think you're some kind of 'thing.' When I see you taking proper care of yourself because *you* don't think you're a 'thing' then I'll be out there leading the band up Main Street celebrating your own realization of that fact. The 'thing' business is in your head, not mine. I've never known any woman more talented, more creative and less oriented to herself. So, okay, for a hundred years you thought you were a jukebox. Get past that in your own head! Because I think of you as a fully-functioning woman. I think of you as my woman. I love you. I do not think of you as a goddamned fucking *'thing!'* "

"I've already got an appointment to see a doctor," she said, feeling dizzied by the buzz of his words filling the room. "I've been a little busy. Or haven't you noticed?"

"I'm sorry." He reached for her hand. "I'm not sorry I said all that. I'm sorry you're so suspicious of me. We're none of us the ideal beings we'd like to be, Lisa. I'm trying to do the best I can. For myself and for you. What do you want? You want to be married? Is that what's bothering you? I'll marry you. If it's what you want, what you need, then I need that for you. Whatever you want. I'll go it with you. But don't accuse me of things that aren't true. I'll be with you whatever way I can. But I can't make myself over to be some kind of plastic person you can mold to yourself. Tell me!"

"I want to live someplace," she said. "I don't know about marriage. I don't know about that. But I want someplace that's mine, ours. I hate camping out in somebody else's home, having to stop and think about their things, their stuff. I want something settled that's ours together, not somebody else's. It doesn't *feel* real this way. I can never feel properly relaxed, always surrounded by things that don't belong to me. And I don't want a whole lot of things, Chas. But I want to feel that wherever I am, it's the place where I am with you, where we do our living together and not a pitched tent at a campsite until we move somewhere else. I can't do any more of that. Even when I had my apartment, it was still camping out. I'd come back from being on the road and look at all the stuff there and not recognize any of it because it wasn't any more mine than all those damned motel rooms with the chenille spreads and infra-red lamps in the bathrooms. I want a *home*."

"Okay!" he said resolutely. "Okay. That's what you want, what you need, you've got it. You want to buy a house or do you want to look at the one I've already got?"

"I want something we start ourselves."

"Any particular place?"

"Anywhere but here."

"Is that everything? Have we covered it all or is there more?"

"There's going to be more. You *know* that."

"Sure I know that. But I mean right now. Have we taken care of right now? Can we go out and have a good dinner and be at peace together or is there anything else you want to thrash out?"

"*Do* you love me?"

"Do you love *me*?"

"I do, yes. I'm afraid too much."

"Well, that's just how much I love you. So much it makes me a little afraid, too."

"I keep thinking you'll go out and find another girl singing in some lounge and fall for her, too."

"Nobody else is you, Lisa. A singer's just a singer for the most part. You're not just a singer. You're *you*. I'm not, four years from now, going to start whacking you around and then shove my cock up your ass because it's not what I thought it was going to be. That's not a turn-on, Lisa. I'd like to cream that fucker. I'd like to wipe him out. I'm never going to be Brad. I've never hit a woman in my life. I've never raped anyone, either. You're what I want, what I need, what I love. I'm not that stupid or emotionally fucked-up that I'd start working at destroying you *because* of loving and wanting and needing you. Okay? Are you okay?"

"I'm okay. Don't get so angry, Chas. It really frightens me."

"Anger's healthy, Lisa. You might try swearing in the john or something, to get it all out. But know where you're going with it, that's all. If you don't know where to direct it, we'll talk it out. I'm not that sure all the time myself. I need you for that just the same way you needed me for this. Let's get out of here now. I'll treat you to dinner."

"Kiss me," she said, leaning closer. "So much is happening, I can't help having doubts, getting scared."

He kissed her, then held her face between his hands. "Just *tell* me when you feel that way! Don't fight me, tell me! It's what I'm here for. Really! It's what you do for me being there in the night when I can turn over and hold on. Okay?"

"Okay."

Monday morning she was suddenly—at seven-ten—wide awake and petrified. She got up carefully in order not to disturb Chas and went into the bathroom to light a cigarette and sit on the john trying to fight down her terror. Today was the day and she knew something would go wrong. Or she'd make a complete ass of herself in front of those musicians. She thought of everything Tim had said, everything Chas had said and none of it did one bit of good so far as removing her doubts.

She heard Chas get up and go into the bathroom down the hall, heard the toilet flush and water running, then the door opened and she knew he'd gone back to the bedroom.

202

She extinguished the cigarette, brushed her teeth and returned to the bedroom.

"What's up?" he asked as she slid back into bed beside him.

"I'm terrified."

"Everybody is first day of taping. Go with it. Nerves make for a good sound."

"You think so?"

"I know so. Past experience and all that. What's Bojangles up to this morning?"

"Still sleeping," she smiled, somewhat calmed. After all, he knew what he was talking about. He'd done all this a lot of times before.

"With your clothes on you don't even look pregnant," he murmured, his hand moving over the slight swelling of her belly. She pushed the blankets away and watched him stroking her, trying to put herself inside his head, to know what he felt when he did that.

"What do you think when you're doing that?" she asked, touching the soft secret place behind his ear.

"I try to imagine what it's going to look like," he said, leaning beside her on his elbow, his arm across her middle. "I wonder if it's going to have big gray eyes like yours or little squinty mean ones."

"Dope!" she laughed, pinching his ear.

"I also think about how much I like waking up this way."

"You always wake up ready," she said, turning on her side to face him. "I've never slept with anyone all night through except for you. I like it. I don't think I'd ever again like sleeping alone."

"You won't have to."

He leaned closer and covered her mouth with his own, delivering one of those gentle, lingering kisses that erased any need she felt for preliminaries. When he kissed her that way, she felt everything inside of her going loose and eager. He pulled her closer and she aligned herself against his body experiencing an overwhelming sense of departing self, something that had never happened to her before. She was aware only of his warmth and his actual presence. Her thoughts and fears seemed suddenly unimportant because whatever happened, he really was going to be there. She simply knew it all at once, believed it absolutely: he was going to always be there. She disengaged herself and knelt over him, lost to the need to speechlessly communicate this new understanding to him.

She loved the shape and feel of him, the tightened muscular responses to the caresses she was giving and she kept on a very long time knowing he wouldn't let it finish this way. He liked to go slowly, drawing it out as long as possible. When he began stroking her back, the arm with which she supported herself, she stopped and lay over on top of him kissing his mouth, moving slowly from side to side against him, her hips rotating in satisfying circles that heightened her anticipation.

"God, you're good," he whispered, rolling over with her, holding her breasts, kissing her throat.

She closed her eyes and felt him moving down, his hands parting her and the always-overpowering, sudden attack of his mouth as he buried his face between her thighs, making her arch closer; urging herself harder into him.

She lunged closer and closer to the edges of something huge and ferocious; something nameless she'd never before understood and wanted forever to stay inside the feeling, torn wide open and glad about the feeling. He eased away and she frantically grabbed for him, pulling him in one desperate drive as far into her as it was possible for him to be. Everything inside her was melting, drowning, giving way and she wound herself around him, locking him tight, racing headlong through glass walls that shattered one after the other; layers of sense and sensitivity that flew open revealing a final, awesome, breathtaking splendor as she came flying back through one after the other of those opened expanses to meet him and draw him back with her into that perfect center; the glorious glowing stillness at her very core.

"I love you, Chas. I love you." Her voice was a dazed whisper emerging from the depths of tranquility.

". . . love *you*," she heard him say as she closed her eyes and with him still joined to her, fell into a pure white silence.

In the taxi on the way to the studio, he checked his pocket diary, saying, "We've got a session with the photographer tomorrow morning at eight in Central Park."

"Why Central Park?" she asked, her nerves tightening as they got nearer to the studio.

"Because that's the way I want you to look on the album. Tall and beautiful and natural. No studio lights, no makeup, no nothing but you. If it was a nude shot, it'd be perfect."

"Are you joking?"

"Half," he said, returning the diary to his breast pocket. "Nude in the morning light would be so incredible. Anyway, it's been done."

"You're nuts if you think I'd do it. I've never been able to understand how those girls can do the spreads in *Playboy*. I always look at them and wonder what they're thinking while the guy with the camera is stuck between their legs."

"I didn't know you read *Playboy*," he laughed, tucking her arm through his.

"I'm not going to tell you I bought it to read the articles either," she laughed. "I was checking out the rest of the girls. I used to wonder how they could find so many girls with perfectly straight legs. None of them have any thighs. D'you ever notice that?"

"I've noticed."

"And if the girl's got small breasts, they always do lots of bottom shots and leg shots. If she's got big breasts, they always seem to shoot from the waist up. Just once I'd like to see someone who looked like a real person. Somebody maybe with thighs and pubic hair the same color as the hair on her head. Maybe that's why they don't seem real."

"This is one of your bigger concerns, right?" he grinned.

205

"It keeps my mind off other things, like: what I'll do if those guys start giving me another rough day."

"You'll handle it," he said sensibly. "Just stand your ground and do what you have to do."

She and Tim ran through the bridge on 'Night Flight' a couple of times before the musicians started arriving with their brown bags of coffee and doughnuts.

"It's still not right," she said. "These four bars before we go into the second chorus. They're off, somehow."

"Let's hear how it sounds after the first run-through. "Nobody says you can't change it."

"I know that. I'm just not sure what to put there. The sound's too full."

Chas went out for cigarettes and came back with coffee and Danish for her and Tim and himself. They sat together in the engineer's booth watching the musicians laying out their charts, tuning up, sipping their coffee, lighting cigarettes.

"Everybody looks set," Chas said.

"I want to test the three front mikes," Lisa said, dropping her cigarette into the remains of her coffee. "Let's run a rehearsal to make sure all the mikes are positioned properly."

Floyd, the first engineer said, "Everything's on. Just give me the go when you want to roll the tape."

"C'mon, friend," Lisa clutched Tim's hand. "Jesus!" she smiled into his face. "You're as cold as I am."

"Worse. I think I have to go to the john."

"You've already been three times," she laughed. "You'll have to wait. Something about your mother's toilet training," she said as they went out of the booth.

Tim positioned himself on her left side in front of the stand-up mike and Lisa flexed her fingers, looking around at the somehow disinterested faces of the musicians.

"We'll run it through once from the top to check the mikes," she told them. "I'll count it out and we'll do a full chorus and a half."

She looked at Tim who appeared to be as terrified as

she, and then across to Chas in the booth who smiled and made an 'Okay' signal to her.

She counted down and it was on. She started the first chorus, straining to separate the whispery sound of her own voice from the tremendous surge of the other instruments. She could feel herself straining and knew the playback would be bad. She simply could not hear. If she couldn't hear herself, she couldn't sing true. And the bridge didn't sound right. It was too big, too lumbering. But she didn't stop them. They went right through the entire chorus and a half, then she stood up, said, "Take five," and walked over to the control booth.

"Can I hear it back?" she asked Floyd, slumping into the chair by the door.

Chas said, "It's very strong."

She shook her head. "It's not good enough. I'm going to wreck my vocal chords. I'm straining because I can't hear and the bridge sounds like a dive-bomber instead of a 707. You'll see what I mean."

She listened to the blurble of the rewinding tape and hunched forward with her elbows on her knees and her chin in her hands as Floyd set the tape for replay.

"Don't let them hear it!" she said. "Just play it back on the speakers in here."

Chas leaned over to pull the door closed and they all sat smoking, listening to the tape.

"Sounds good to me," Floyd said, swiveling in his seat at the end. "All the mikes are right."

"It's wrong," she said. "First it doesn't sound like me. And second, the bridge is worse than I thought."

"How about earphones?" Junior suggested.

Lisa glanced up at Junior, the second sound man, positive it was the first time she'd ever heard him speak.

"Earphones how?" she asked.

"Wear a dead set to blank out the volume. It puts your own sound back into your head. I've got a set here in the drawer somewhere." He opened a drawer under the console and came up with a cushioned headset. "Try it. I think it'll work."

"Okay," she accepted the set, "thank you."

"What about the bridge?" Chas asked her, his eyes watching the tape rewind.

"I'll just have to run it again and hear it as we go. I don't know."

The earphones worked. Her skull became something of a microphone so that she worked easier, felt less forced and as they rolled into the bridge she suddenly said, "Stop the tape. I think I've got it," and pulled off the headphones. "Listen," she told the group, "I'm going to try a change for the bridge. I want everybody to lay out except the bassist. Floyd, can you up the mike on the bass?"

"You got it!" Floyd came back over the PA.

"Okay. Now Tim'll play over the voice. I'll lay back completely on the piano. And what I want you to do," she told the bassist, "is to just build up to the biggest climax you ever had on that thing. Just finger it to death."

The entire room erupted into laughter and the bassist slapped the bass so that it pirouetted under his fingers and came to a halt front-face once again.

"Take it easy on the poor bastard," Chas's voice laughed over the PA. "Sixteen other guys and you are watching."

"You shut the hell up!" she laughed, finally feeling at one with the musicians. "He knows what I mean. We'll run the bridge and you'll see."

Tim said, "You want me to play it the same?"

"Play above everything I do, like an echo. You'll see what I mean. Okay," she looked over at the bassist. "Are we set?"

"Set!" Floyd said.

She counted them into the bridge and they took it through. She sang it without the headset, in order to hear exactly what the bassist would do. And he did just what she'd wanted.

"One minute." She jumped up. "Don't anybody go to the john or light up. I want to hear that bit and then we'll go right into it and do the whole thing again."

In the booth, Floyd had the tape already rewound

and pressed it to play as soon as she came in. They all stared at the speakers, listening. "See!" she exclaimed. "Didn't I tell you? It's an engine taking off."

"Get out there and *do* it!" Chas smiled, squeezing her hand. "You know what you're doing."

She ran back and put on the headphones, leaving one ear uncovered as she said, "Let's make this a clean one. I think we've got this perfect now."

She readjusted the headset, counted them in and they played from the top, through the full chorus and a half down to the close. She was soaking wet at the end as she pushed the headset off her ears and said into the mike, "Let's play it back in here, Floyd."

Tim dropped down beside her on the piano bench wiping his mouth with a handkerchief and they listened to the Donald Duck sounds of the tape being rewound.

"This is it!" she said, hanging onto Tim's hand as the opening came out over the speakers. She looked up at the out-sized speakers on the wall and listened to the playback.

"It's fantastic!" Tim whispered.

She squeezed his hand, listening for impurities. She couldn't hear any. The tape ran to the end and there was a moment of complete silence in the room. Then the musicians all started applauding and she turned, amazed, to see them all grinning, smiling, clapping like hell.

"I'm going to cry," she whispered to Tim.

"Didn't I tell you? They respect what's good. And *that's* good. *You're* good."

Chas was clapping inside the booth and she felt as if she'd just been given the prize of all time. Her mouth opened and closed and she wanted to go from one to the other of each of those smiling men and hold them and kiss them and thank them because it was all going to work out well after all. And they accepted her.

"Wow!" she said, taking a big gulp of air. "Thank you. Really. You think it's good, guys?"

They all shouted things at her and, happily, she said, "That one's *done*! Let's break for fifteen minutes and see if we can't get the rest of them to come out as beautifully."

They completed 'Early Morning People' that day, as well. Chas said, "It's about the best session I've ever done. They're working their asses off for you, Lee. I told you the nerves make it better."

"Hey Floyd?" she called to him as he was about to leave.

"Yeah?"

"Can I get you to stay for an extra hour? I want to lay on two tracks of singing on top of the last eight of 'Early Morning People.' "

"Oh yeah? Sure, I guess so."

"How come?" Chas asked.

"Because it's a little thin at the end. And I think if I lay a couple more voices on top, it'll flesh it out. Okay?"

"It's your show, honey. Do it."

"I love you for letting me do this."

"I love you for being so incredibly good at it. Go on. I'll hang in here."

He sat back and watched her run one tape, hear it back, then run a second. She did it quickly, neatly, with a perfect sense of what was needed, then came up to join him in the booth while Floyd reran all three tapes for the playback.

"I'll mix 'em later," Floyd said.

"Fine." She was anxious to hear how it sounded. "Just a rough run will be all I want to hear right now."

It took him several minutes to get it all synched, then he got the tapes rolling and they listened. She'd done it. Three perfectly harmonized voices emerged from the speakers, lending an altogether different perspective to the final eight.

"Right?" she smiled at Chas.

"Right."

He couldn't believe how professional, how knowing and sensitive she was to something she'd never done before. It was as if she'd been making albums for ten years and this was just another in a series. When he told her that on their way home, she said, "All I've ever heard inside my head, from the time I was a little kid, is my own voice. I've always had an idea of how I wanted it all to sound with the music."

"Believe me, you *know*. I'm going to get that single out on the streets so fast the first million'll be sold before we've finished the album."

She looked at him in surprise. "Really?"

"Faster than that if I can get it done. Early tonight, okay? We've got to be up to get to the park to meet the photographer."

"I'm wiped," she said, leaning on him. The taxi was hitting every pothole in the road. "I'm starving, too. I just want to eat and go to bed."

"As Floyd would say, You've got it!"

Chapter 14

In the breaks between sessions, she went for her first visit to Dr. Riley, prepared for someone like old Dr. McKenzie who'd cared for her mother; finding instead a young, debonair Irishman with a delightfully musical, lilting accent, a marvelous whimsical sense of humor and a habit of saying, "I'm sorry if you find this a wee bit uncomfortable," at the start of each internal examination. He checked her out, weighed her himself, saying, "You're healthy as can be, darlin', but you could stand a mite more meat on your bones." His nurses were silent, featureless shadows who glided into the room only when the appearance of a second person was ordained by state law (or some personal preference of Riley's—she wasn't sure which), never intruding, never reducing the quality of the visit to anything less than ultimately rewarding.

When she was dressed again and seated in his office in front of his desk, he asked her a number of questions, wrote out prescriptions for multiple-vitamin tablets and a mild diuretic, then leaned way back in his chair and lit his pipe.

"A singer, are you?" he asked, between puffs. "Isn't that grand? And you're making a record. I'll have to buy it." He pushed the prescription pad across the desk saying, "There's a good lass, write down the name of the thing for me now. I'll buy it."

"You really like this, don't you?" she smiled, writing 'Night Flight,' and 'Early Morning People' on the pad.

"Shouldn't anyone be doing things they're not liking. Nothing nicer first thing in the morning than the grand sight of some lovely young thing with a great round belly," he laughed. "I'm laying it on a bit thick for you. Seriously," the accent toned itself down from Barry Fitzgerald to a close Olivier, "you could do with a bit of building up. More protein. I'll have the nurse give you the salt-free diet. I know it's near impossible to follow, but try. At the rate you're going, given another month, you'll be so swollen in the legs you'll have to start wearing support stockings. You don't want any varicose veins, not at your age. So stretch out often as you can, get the weight up off your legs and take care of yourself. Everything looks just fine. Probably going to be a smallish baby. But nothing to be getting fearful about. Any questions?"

"What about . . . making love?"

"Oh now, you've got months before you've got to think about stopping any of that. It's perfectly safe to continue on until a couple of weeks before baby's due. I'll let you know when. Will you be wanting me to make arrangements for the hospital?"

"I hadn't thought about that. I mean, I don't think we'll be staying in the city."

"I see. Well, look now. Come back in a month. You'll

have decided by then and we'll see what we can work out for you."

"We might be going to Connecticut," she said. She liked the sound of it from what Chas had told her.

"Where in Connecticut?"

"Westport possibly."

"Well, you'll certainly be close enough to get yourself into Greenwich Hospital. That's a fine hospital. I've a couple of O.B. friends in Greenwich. I'll be more than happy to pass you along. You let me know next visit what you've decided on. When'd you say I'll be able to buy this record, then?"

"Soon. I don't know when. But don't buy it," she said, on impulse. "Let me send it to you."

"Good girl!" He smiled at her, setting his pipe down in the ashtray. "I'll see you next month."

He shook her hand warmly, his eyes fixed on hers and she left the office with the feeling that he'd definitely remember her the next time they met. It wasn't a feeling she'd often derived from her encounters with doctors. Or anyone, for that matter.

Chas sat on the photographer, pressing for a rush job and came in two days after the session with the contact sheets, dropping them into Lisa's lap in one of the breaks.

"Have a look at some truly beautiful photographs," he said, watching her open the envelope and lift out the two pages.

"The light's so bad in here. I can't see." She got up and carried them over to Floyd's reading lamp where she carefully studied each of the small proof prints, shaking her head.

"You don't like them?" Chas asked.

"They're incredible!" she said softly. "I can't believe that's how I look. I mean, if I thought I looked like that, I'd be very happy."

"Honey, you *look* like that." He leaned over her shoulder, pointing. "This is the one we'll use for the album cover. What d'you think?"

"They're so small, it's hard to tell."

The shot showed her at a three-quarter angle, full-length, her eyes fixed on something off to her left. He'd undone her hair and asked her to wear a long white gauzy dress. She'd felt foolish posing but Chas had kept distracting her and all the while the photographer had kept saying, "That's lovely. Hold that. Don't move. Eyes a little that way. Smile a bit." On and on until she felt stiff and tight-mouthed from all the smiling. And, after all of that, the picture he'd chosen was the one where she'd finally insisted, "I'm *not* going to smile." And she hadn't. Her expression was serene, but alert. The background was slightly blurred, sending her into sharply contrasting focus. The dress, surprisingly, made her look somewhat smaller, more fragile than she thought she really was.

"It's the best one," she agreed finally, once more reviewing the rest of the shots. "They're certainly not black and white glossies, are they?"

"That's lounge crap. This is going to be big and beautiful, full-color. You'll see."

He replaced the contact sheets in the envelope and she watched him—his movements accurate and tidy as always—saying, "I keep thinking any second now somebody's going to tap me on the shoulder and say, 'It's all off, kid.'"

"Won't happen," he said, his arm around her shoulders. "What'd the doctor say?"

"Bojangles is a perfectly fine-looking, somewhat small-sized tapdancer who's going to arrive on schedule and I have to get a couple of prescriptions filled. No salt. Lots of protein. And—big laugh here for the audience—stay off my feet."

"Really?"

"Of course, really."

"Don't get uptight. If he said it, you'll have to do it."

"Of course! I can always take brief naps on the piano. It'll have to wait until we finish the session."

"I'm not going to push it. Good news," he said.

"What?"

"I swung a rush deal on the pressing. We'll have the first 45's ready for distribution by the end of next week."

"You're kidding!"

"Of course," he mimicked her gently. "I'm kidding. Right. Meanwhile, I'm going crazy trying to find enough dimes for all the calls to get the promotion moving. You're going to met a D.J. tonight."

"I am? Who?"

"A nut. But a good friend. He'll give us a free run for our money if he likes the side. I'm going to take the tape along and play it for him tonight."

"This is a movie," she said slowly. "A science fiction movie."

"You keep telling yourself and while you're doing that, keep the rest of the tunes rolling. We're halfway to that album. By the time we're finished, I'm willing to bet 'Night Flight' will be hitting the Top Forty."

"It's so scary when you start prophesying this way."

"You'll get used to it. And you know what else?"

"I can't take any more. What else?"

"If it all works the way I think it will, by next fall, we'll have you do a concert. Town Hall or maybe Carnegie Hall. Can you see it? The kids'll snap out! Lisa Hamilton conducting from behind the big Steinway grand while she sings them into orbit."

"That's enough, Chas. You're getting a little crazy."

"Hey!" he said seriously. "No joke. This is for real. A big first-time concert. And then some colleges, some TV and you're a superstar, honey. While the first album's climbing like crazy up the charts, you and Tim'll be working on the new tunes for the next one. On and on."

She backed away from him, trying to absorb the images.

"You're going too fast, Chas. I wasn't prepared for any of that. When are we going to have a life? What about my child? I can't just sit down and write songs because somebody tells me to. I have to feel them. They have to grow inside my head. I can't just turn them out that way."

"Better yet," he said, looking as if he was having inter-planetary visions. "We'll do an oldies-but-goodies album, with you singing all those great old things the clubbers liked so much. 'My Buddy,' and 'Miss Otis Regrets' and all those old chestnuts."

"Stop, Chas!" she said softly. "You're running off without me."

For an instant, his eyes were still out there somewhere, seeing those visions. And then, her words seemed to reach him and drag him back so that he looked at her and his expression changed, lost that driven imagination and became recognizable to her.

"I'm tripping out," he said apologetically. "I'm sorry, Lee. It's just that I'm so high on you. I want everybody in the world to know what you do."

"Not that fast, Chas. Really. I need some kind of private life once we finish this. I want to be at home somewhere, have the baby, enjoy being with you without any of this day-afer-day pushing. I've never had a vacation. Not ever. When I was little, nobody thought about it. My mother was dying. No one was thinking about vacations. I'd like to have one. I'd like to go somewhere, anywhere, where nobody expects me to have my drink and then jump onstage and sing. Please, don't make it all happen all at once. I don't think I can handle it. I'm *tired*, Chas."

"I know you are." He hugged her to his chest. "I wasn't thinking. We'll wrap up the tapes and take off, go househunting if you like."

"I'd like to do that. It'd be nice to be even part-way settled before Bojangles comes."

"End of the week after next. My promise. We'll pack up and take off."

"But you said the single's being released. How can we?"

"Week after that. I'll write it down in my book right now. In fact," he pulled the diary out of his pocket and handed it to her, "you write it in. In big letters with asterisks. You have my word on it."

They completed the taping three days ahead of schedule. Lisa listened to the last of the tapes, then she and Chas went back to the apartment.

"It's been the hardest few months of my life," she said, folding up on the sofa. "Never again like that. Please. I feel as if I just ran the race of all time."

"'Night Flight' gets its first airing tomorrow morning on Donn Quincy's morning show. We'll have to tune in to hear it."

"You tune it in. I'm not going to wait through six hours to hear it. I've heard it so many times it plays in my head as if I'd never heard anything else but that one damned song."

"If he gets good response, we're launched, Lisa. I know you're tired but believe me, it's important. I also —much as I hate to mention it—am about to present you with a bill for your half."

"Just tell me how much. I'll get my checkbook."

She didn't blink, didn't argue, simply sat down with the checkbook balanced on her knee and wrote him a check for an even twenty-two thousand dollars.

"You've got some style!" he said admiringly. "I've never yet known a woman who didn't haggle over pennies. You're the first one."

"I honestly don't care. And that's the truth. It's worth every penny of it. Even if nobody buys the record, Chas, the fact that you believed enough in me to want to do it is my success. Honestly! That you were willing to put your money and your reputation in it for my sake means more to me than anything else. I've always wanted to make a record, to do something that sounded the way I wanted it to. You've done that for me and nothing else matters. Even if it bombs. If it bombs, at least we did it."

She was dimly aware of the radio and surfaced for a second or two to see Chas smoking, fiddling with the volume control on the portable AM/FM on the bedside table. She turned over and returned into her sleep. She had no idea how long after that it was when she heard Chas saying, "Son of a bitch! What the hell's coming off" and she was awake again, listening.

"What's wrong?" she asked thickly.

"The idiot's playing the flip side. Listen to this."

The announcer was saying, ". . . and here it is. This is beautiful, people. Drink your coffee and fill yourself up on this one. A groovy newie by a lady named Lisa Hamilton. Dig it! 'Early Morning People.' " and the opening bars came out of the radio speaker.

She sat up asking, "How did that happen?"

"Going to call that asshole." Chas was raging, reaching for the telephone, knocking the radio off the table accidentally.

She'd never seen him so angry. She lit a cigarette and listened as he dialed, shouted at a network operator, shouted again at someone else and, finally, shouted at the announcer. There was a long silence as he listened. Lisa climbed over him to pick up the radio and set it down on the table on her side of the bed. She tried to listen to Chas but her attention was caught by how different the song sounded coming over the radio. Radios always gave you all the highs, never any of the lows. And 'Early Morning People,' full of radio highs and slightly buzzy the way all but the best stereo radios sound, came across to her as sounding just exactly the way she'd wanted it to. She shivered with pleasure.

Chas was talking more quietly now. He listened again and then hung up looking absolutely dumbstruck.

"What did he say?" she asked.

"Turn up the volume," he said blankly. "He'll tell you himself."

"Hey, hey Lisa Hamilton!" the announcer barked. "We just had a call that you're listening. The switchboard's lit up like neon, baby. You're on your way to being a golden oldie. Love ya, sweetheart! And now, for. . . ."

She switched off the radio, blushing.

"That's weird," she giggled, feeling giddy. "What does it mean?"

"He liked the flip side better. All the rest of the D.J.'s will follow suit. That's the side that's going to make it. You heard. They're all calling in."

"I loved it," she laughed, trying to pull him out of the semi-comatose state he seemed to be in. "I've never heard myself on the radio before, Chas. It's like the Emerald City."

"Jesus!" he said, running his hand over his hair. "I was so tuned in on 'Night Flight,' I completely forgot about the flip side. What was that?" He laughed suddenly, his eyes connecting with hers. "What was that about the Emerald City? Are you Dorothy?"

"Don't be nutty! It has to do with how I felt when I first left home and was on my way here. All I could think of was that New York would be all green and glowy like the Emerald City!"

"You must've been retarded," he teased.

"Chas! I was only seventeen."

"Don't make faces at me, honey! It was another one of those jokes you never seem to get. Bojangles dancing?"

"Not yet. Can we leave sooner?"

"I need one more week in town."

"So can we go a week early?"

"We'll go."

"Chas?"

"Hmm?"

"Would we really do a concert?" She could actually *see* it.

He laughed and tumbled her down. "I knew you wouldn't be able to resist the idea of that! I knew it! You've got the fever. The Emerald City. Jesus! That's pathetic!"

"It is not! It happened to be a very nice little picture in my head."

"I'll buy you red satin slippers. You know," his eyes started moving toward the distances, "it might be kind of an interesting thing to do."

"Oh wow! What?"

"Something," he shook his head as if to clear it. "I'll think about it. Nothing important."

"May I go back to sleep now?"

"You're going to sleep? You think you're going to sleep?"

"I'd like to try, if that's all right with you."

"Be my guest." He plumped up her pillow and urged

her head down. "If you can sleep, I'll take you to Tiffany's this afternoon and buy you a solid gold whatever."

"Whatever what?"

"Whatever you like?"

"I'm going to sleep."

He returned to his side of the bed, positive she wouldn't be able to sleep. He got up and went into the bathroom and when he returned he could tell by the soft flush of color high in her cheeks she was really sleeping, not faking. Asleep.

"I'll be," he whispered, climbing in beside her. "A woman who can sleep knowing she's going to Tiffany's."

Just as Chas promised, they packed up the bags at the end of the following week. Chas took the car keys and went off to pick up the car and Lisa sat down to wait. The telephone rang and she picked it up to hear Jeanette excitedly saying, "Chérie! Do you *hear* this!" Lisa could hear very faintly what sounded like 'Early Morning People.' Jeanette came back on the line saying, "We are so very happy and excited, chérie. It is playing on the radio all morning. Aimée has gone completely mad. Are you very well and happy, chérie?"

"It feels like a dream," Lisa laughed. "We're leaving this morning. We're going to try to find a house. Chas has promised we'll drive in to see you. In about a week, okay?"

"It will be so wonderful to see you. We will celebrate, eh? And baby?"

"We're all great. I'll call you from wherever we are, to let you know when we're coming."

Shortly after she finished the call, Chas came in waving *Variety* and *Billboard*.

"You can read these in the car. Let's get going!"

"My family called. They're all so excited. We're getting heavy air play."

"Good, good." He tucked a bag under each arm and carried two more in his hands. "You do the switching off and the locking up, okay, honey?"

"I told them we'd come to see the ι."

"Great!"

"Anything wrong?" She asked as the elevator door opened.

"Not a thing."

"You're sure? You look a little peculiar."

"You try carrying four bags this way. You'll look more than peculiar."

"No, tell me! Did something happen?"

"Wait till we get in the car."

She glanced across at the elevator operator, then shifted her eyes to Chas's profile as they descended.

"I can carry the small one," she offered as he struggled out of the elevator.

"I'm balanced. It's okay."

Finally, with the bags stowed in the trunk, safetybelts fastened and the engine running, Chas turned slightly and smiled at her.

"What?" she asked.

"We made the Top Forty. Take a look at *Billboard*."

"No!"

"Number thirty-three and moving up. Didn't I *tell* you?"

She flipped through the pages, scanning the titles until she saw it.

"I'll bet you any amount you like that I can, within the next two hours—between here and Hartford, say— keep switching stations and pick up 'Early Morning People' at least five times."

"Hartford? But I thought we'd stop in Westport, do our house hunting."

"Wouldn't you rather go home first?" he said, still smiling, putting the car in gear.

She flung her arms around his neck, kissing him.

"You *knew*!" she said, so pleased by his understanding. "I want them to see you, to have them know you."

"That's the way it'll be."

She sat back, twisting her new bracelet round and round on her wrist. Everything she saw seemed so clean and fresh. Chas switched on the radio as they were heading crosstown, aiming for the F.D.R. Drive. The announcer finished speaking and 'Early Morning People' came on.

Every time she heard it now, tingles of mingled disbelief and excitement shot through her.

"That's one!" he said with a grin. "Four more to go."

"You win," she laughed. "You knew you were going to win or you wouldn't have bet me. The light's changed, Chas."

"I know. I just wanted to look at you. Just looking at you is so nice."

"Thank you. But they're honking."

"Let them! You're all the way out now, Lee. Can you feel it? I can feel it in you."

"I feel it. Please, let's go. I hate it the way they all lean on their horns."

He touched his forefinger to the tip of her nose, laughed, and went through the light just as it turned red.

KING ST.

Set Three
BOOK 2

Send for the Doctor

Send for the Doctor
King Street: Readers Set Three - Book 2
Copyright © Iris Nunn 2014

Text: Iris Nunn
Editor: June Lewis

Published in 2014 by Gatehouse Media Limited

ISBN: 978-1-84231-127-1

British Library Cataloguing-in-Publication Data:
A catalogue record for this book is available from the British Library

Gwen is watching the late film
on TV.

Harry is asleep.

When the film ends,
Gwen goes up to bed.

She looks in on Harry,
sleeping in his cot.

He looks hot.
His face is very red.
His hair is wet.
His hands are damp.

Gwen picks him up.

She gets him a drink,
but he will not wake up.

She shakes him,
but she cannot wake him.

She thinks of going next door
to get help.

She will take Harry with her.
She cannot leave him.

She gets a big blanket
to keep Harry snug.

She runs with him to bang on the door
of number nine.

Neeta is at home.
She looks at Harry.
He is not very well at all.

He still feels much too hot
and will not wake up,
so she rings for the doctor.

Neeta tells Gwen to stay
until he comes,
so that she is not alone.

"Cup of tea?" says Neeta.
"He will be here soon."

The door bell rings at number nine.
Neeta lets the doctor in.

"Mrs Smith is here with Harry,"
she says. "Come on in!"

The doctor sees Harry
sleeping on Gwen's lap.

Now there are red spots on his face,
red spots on his neck,
red spots on his hands.

And when the doctor looks
under his vest,
there are red spots on his chest too.

Harry still feels much too hot.

"Chicken pox, I think,"
says the doctor.
"Take the blanket off
and cool him down a bit.
He has a temperature,
but he will be fine."

"When you take him back home, keep him in bed with lots to drink. He needs to rest and then he will begin to feel better.
I will look in on him tomorrow."

The doctor gets back in his car.

Neeta makes up a bed for Gwen.

She stays the night with Harry
so that Neeta can help
if she needs her.

"Both mine had chicken pox,"
says Neeta.